The Hunt for Elsewhere

A Novel By Beatrice Vine

WITHDRAWN
MILNE LIBRARY
S.U.N.Y GENESEO

D1711042

2

The *Hunt for Elsewhere* is a work of fiction. Names, characters, places, and incidents are either a product of the author's imagination or are used fictitiously. Any resemblance to actual persons, living or dead, or events is entirely coincidental.

Copyright © 2013 by Bettina Selsor / "Beatrice Vine"
Cover art copyright © 2012 by Jen Philpot

Public domain images used in this book were obtained from
http://www.clkr.com.

Printed in the U.S.A.

PROJECT LINE-UP

As Beatrice Vine
(Young Adult – Fantasy – Sci-Fi – Action-Adventure)
Athena Academy of Mind and War

As Betty Vine
(Adult – Romance – Comedy – Drama)
And God Laughed

To my friends, who support me.
To my family, who loves me.
And to my husband,
Who makes every day a beautiful journey.

Acknowledgments

Special thanks and accolades to artist, Jen Philpot, who designed the lovely cover of this book, hair by hair and grass by grass. Though the saying goes that one should not judge a book by its cover, I must say that Jen Philpot's artwork has brought more life to my characters than I thought possible. I also owe many thanks to my editor, Crystal Schall, who went through my manuscript and its revisions multiple times with a fine-tooth comb, and allowed me to poke her brain when mine felt fried. Without her, there would be grammar and continuity errors everywhere.

Further gratitude goes to my dear friend, Jenny Gibbons, also known as the author 'Jayden Woods.' If not for her friendship and guidance, this book probably never would have been. Thank you to my friends Natalie and Andy Holmes, who have been and continue to be harbors of great joy and creativity.

Thank you to my family: my dad, who sacrificed so much for my dreams; my mom, who taught me to never lose faith; and my brother, whose gentle heart and sense of humor are an inspiration. And last, but certainly not least, thank you to my husband, and dedicated second editor, Andy Selsor, whose love and serenity anchors me while gently pushing me forward.

PROLOGUE

SPRING

Vulpes vulpes. The fox's fox, the Great Trickster of the wood, is a lonely and cunning creature whose fur burns brightly in the pitch black night, hot as copper. His courage is fueled by the unflinching desire to live, and his cleverness grows with every brush with death. He walks between man and wild on a tightrope made of gossamer. One misstep and he is no more. Ever wary, there is no room for such luxuries as love and loyalty, honesty and faith. There is only selfishness and unforgiving necessity.

He is a *Lonely Thief*, a creature of habit, and nothing more.

It was late December when a fox and a vixen came upon one another in a forest, and quickly became mates. By early spring, the vixen became a proud mother and had given birth to a litter of six kits. One died immediately after birth, while another two fell ill and lived only two weeks.

The other three, fortunate as they were, fought one another for mother's milk. They were small, blind, and covered in downy gray fur. Despite looking very much the same, their mother could tell them apart easily, and gave them each a special name.

She named the first Russell, for he was big and spirited, bright and hot, like a newly born flame. But for all his vigor, he was also of an ornery sort, prone to announcing his displeasure with an angry nip or a high-pitched bark.

The second kit was female. Unlike her older brother, she was quiet and sweet, and she favored burying her little face into her mother's tail for warmth. Mother named her Flynn, believing the name meant a softer shade of red.

Then there was the youngest. He was neither aggressive nor demure, neither foolhardy nor overly cautious, and his mother and father could not yet tell what kind of fox he would one day become.

Mother waited fourteen days for her kits' eyes to open. By then, the last of the frost had disappeared and flowers of every color bloomed across the forest floor. When her still nameless kit gazed upon her for the first time, she realized his eyes pierced more sharply than the tip of a man's blade.

And so she named him Saxton, a name she thought would cut through stone.

The kits' world was no more than a tiny den with walls made of thick soil, dead leaves, and overhanging roots. When the seasons changed, and the air grew thick and hot, the kits shed their gray natal fur and in its place grew sandy brown hair.

One morning, Father gathered the kits and led them out of their home. In that moment, the world suddenly grew bright and large, and it dawned on the little foxes just how small and insignificant they were.

"There are only three kinds of creatures in the world," their father said, "the killers, the survivors, and the dead. All of us here, you kits, your mother and I: we are survivors. We're too small to kill wolves and bears, but we're also too smart to die without a fight. You want to live? You think about yourself and yourself alone. Anything less, and you can count on shaving two to four years off your life, and we foxes don't live all that long to begin with."

Father was a cold and practical fox, but he dutifully brought his family food and observed their territory for any sign of danger. Every morning, just before he served breakfast, he would offer blunt words of wisdom.

"Don't talk to strangers."

"Never stray too far from your territory."

"Answer to no one."

The last advice he would give his kits before everything would change was this:

12

"The world is unkind. Everyone lives and dies alone."

PART I

Chapter One
AUTUMN

Gunfire, dogs, and men. The fox family awoke in the middle of an afternoon nap to the sound of paws clawing at soil and to the scent of human sweat. The hounds were digging at the den's entryway, determined to flush the entire family out into the open, where two loaded shotguns were held at the ready. Luckily, Mother and Father had the foresight to dig an escape exit. At Father's urging, they crawled toward the back of the den and through a narrow tunnel.

"Go ahead," Father said in a low voice. "I'll guard the rear."

The tunnel eventually curved upward, and Mother cautiously poked her head out of the hole.

"They don't know we're here," she whispered. "Come out and keep your heads and tails low to the ground. We cannot let them see us."

One by one, each of the kits clambered out and scurried with their stomachs close to the earth. They had grown too big to carry, so Mother had to patiently push them along with her muzzle.

"Hurry!" she hissed. "Keep moving!"

"What's happening?" Flynn sobbed. "Where're we going?"

"Stop asking questions!" Russell snapped. "We're being hunted! Don't you know what that means?"

"Leave her alone!" Saxton growled, ignoring the long brush that whipped across his face as he stumbled forward. "Can't you see she's scared?"

Bang! Bang!

Two shots fired. Father sprinted up from behind them, leaving a trail of fallen leaves and tall grasses shivering in his wake.

"Go! Go!" he urged. "We've been spotted! Go!"

Two dogs emerged after Father, running at full speed. Russell ran ahead, bolting for safety in the thick forest. Flynn, however, lagged behind. She was shaking and had difficulty moving her legs.

"Be brave!" Saxton said, trotting at a slower pace to remain at his sister's side. "You're gonna be all right."

But the dogs were drawing closer, and Father would have none of it. "Don't be foolish, Saxton!" he scolded. "We don't have time for coddling!"

Saxton glanced behind them and could see the pair of hunters approaching. He then gazed at his sister and, upon seeing her big, golden eyes full of fear, felt a sharp twist in his chest.

And with that he took off in the direction of the dogs.

"Saxton!" his mother cried. "What are you *doing?*"

In truth, he wasn't quite sure, but he knew if he could distract the dogs into running in the wrong direction, he could buy enough time for his family to make it to safety.

His heart raced, pounding against his ribcage. Jumping high in the air, the dogs caught sight of him and swerved left, away from his family. Saxton rushed through the open field, dodging rocks and broken tree branches. With his legs not fully grown, it did not take long for the dogs to catch up with him, and Saxton felt their hot breath blowing across his hind legs. One of the dogs nipped at his tail, but he pulled ahead just far enough to remain uncaught.

Bang! Bang!

Shotgun pellets hit the soil, narrowly missing Saxton's head, and dirt burst into the air like fireworks. Wind caught the dust and blew it into his eyes, blinding him. In pain and disoriented, he realized too late that he did not know where to hide.

Mother stayed at the edge of the forest, watching her son dart left and right across the field, aimless. She turned to her mate.

"We have to go back."

He shook his head. "Leave him."

"But—"

"You want to risk the lives of our other young? We must cut our losses! Leave him!"

Father turned and led the kits through the forest. Mother hesitated, cast one last look at Saxton, and silently wished him a sorrowful goodbye.

As he ran, Saxton caught sight of an overturned tree trunk in the distance. With no other plan, he dashed for it, praying with every footstep that the trunk was hollowed out. Reaching one end of it, he almost cried with joy. It was hollow. Crawling inside, he remained still and hoped the dogs would not be able to reach him.

The dogs slowed to a halt before circling the log with their snouts lowered to the ground. Saxton trembled as he watched their nostrils flare and their big, clumsy tongues lick their oversized noses and yellow teeth. His ears perked up when he heard a different sort of footsteps approach. They were heavy and graceless. They plodded around without any regard. Suddenly, a pair of boots appeared before the end of the log.

"Well, what do we got here?" one of the hunters asked.

"Looks like we got him cornered," the other hunter replied. He lowered his hand to ruffle the ears of one of the hounds. "Good boy!"

Saxton backed away from the opening in the trunk until his tail bumped into something hard. He turned and what he saw made his insides turn over. The other end of the log was still solid from within. He was trapped.

Thinking fast, Saxton tore away at the bark beneath his feet with his teeth.

Click, click, click.

Saxton had never heard that sound before, but it immediately made the hairs on his back stand on end. He pried away the last bit of bark and began digging the uncovered soil for his very life.

As he worked furiously, one of the hunters crouched down and pointed his gun. The gun barrel met his eyes, a dark tunnel with no light at the end of it.

The hunter's finger rested calmly on the trigger.

The finger squeezed.

BOOM!

Saxton leaped into the small ditch he made, deafened by the sound of the shotgun. Pellets zipped over his ears, and splinters sprayed everywhere as they made contact with the timber. Saxton squeezed his eyes shut to protect them from the falling debris.

His ears rang. His heart pounded. Yet, he could still discern the muffled sound of humans talking.

"That got him. Hey, Mitch, you got a flashlight? I'm gonna drag him out if I can reach him."

A beam of light flew through the log and danced within. Saxton curled into a ball and lowered his ears to keep from being seen.

"Holy … I can't believe this!"

"What's wrong?"

"The fox isn't in here!"

"Must've dug a hole from inside. Let's roll the trunk."

The trunk shifted around him. Saxton couldn't believe their tenacity. Run ragged, he gathered the last of his strength and dug as deep as he could. Moving the log was not easy for the men, and this bought Saxton the precious time he needed to turn the hole he was making into a tunnel. When the log was finally moved away, Saxton heard one of the men whistle in delight.

"Wow," the hunter, Mitch, laughed. "Gotta give the little guy credit."

Saxton heard Mitch reload his gun, but the other hunter gently lowered the shotgun with his hand.

"This one's got spunk. We'll get him next time."

"You sure? Might not be a next time."

The man shrugged. "Like you said, gotta give credit where credit's due. Besides, a critter this small ain't that much to be proud of. It'd be a shame to kill him before he can get bigger and come up with more tricks to cram up his sleeve. Heck, he might even have kits with brains like his."

"You gotta be kidding me. All this nonsense wasn't enough?"

The other man said nothing. Saxton sensed Mitch hesitating, then, to his great relief, relenting.

"Oh, all right," he said. "The hunt's only as good as its story. Don't want to end it prematurely, I s'pose." He whistled and the dogs came panting and barking at his beckoning. "Come on, boys. Home's a waiting."

Saxton shook his head, but failed to rid his ears of the incessant ringing. He peered out of the log, and though the men were indeed gone, Saxton dared not move. He couldn't have raised a paw even if he'd tried, for he was so tired that he instantly fell into a deep, troubled sleep.

Saxton awoke not one, but two days later. His empty stomach roused him soundly from his slumber, all but begging him to step outside and look for much needed food. Still cautious, however, he lifted his nose and examined the air. He found no trace of man, gun powder, or dog. Nor did he smell the pungent odor of bear or wolf. Slowly crawling out, he squinted as the sun's rays beat upon him and released a shuddering breath he hadn't known he had been holding for so long.

But while he could not smell danger, he could not smell his family either.

Hungry, Saxton scoured the field, chasing, pouncing, and catching a number of insects. Though such modest fare temporarily placated his stomach, it did not satisfy the deeper, sharper hunger that lingered beneath.

Remembering the hunters had mentioned one day returning, Saxton gulped the remains of his grasshopper and traversed the field until he entered the forest into which his family had disappeared. He had only been in the thick of the forest a couple of times, and both were for lessons from his father. Saxton sniffed desperately for any sign of Mother, but her trail had become cold from the air and the scent of other animals moving across her older path.

The clouds rolled and thunder clapped, and every now and then a few droplets of cold water would splash Saxton on the head. He looked up at the darkening sky and realized that a storm was imminent. Sighing, he hastened his steps in search of new shelter.

He considered digging a new den for himself, but his paws and nails were still too sore. Settling beneath a tree wouldn't do as the wind was picking up and he did not want to risk getting sick with no one to care for him. His best option, he concluded, was to find an abandoned den.

From above, birds and squirrels eyed him warily, some of them ducking into their nests in the hopes of not being seen. As he continued onward, he came across a snake's nest, which was too small, and a porcupine's burrow, which was laden with quills.

At last, when the rain began pelting down relentlessly, Saxton stumbled upon a burrow of just the right size and comfort. There was a musty, almost dreadful stench within, but it was not too bad given his other choices. Relieved that he was once again met with good luck, the fox didn't waste any time crawling down the burrow.

But just as Saxton thought all would be well, an angry face covered with black and white fur poked through the hole and bared a set of jagged teeth.

"What are you doing in my home?" The skunk growled.

Saxton sat up quickly, tripping over words. "I— I'm sorry … I needed a place to stay."

"If you need a place to stay, stay with your mother and father, kit!"

"I don't know where they are," he replied quietly.

"Well, then, that's just tough, isn't? Get out of my burrow!"

"But—"

"I said get out!" The skunk snarled, turning around and raising his tail, threatening to spray him. Saxton coughed and gasped.

"Okay!" He gave in, feeling as though he might choke on the skunk's horrible odor. "Okay! I'm leaving!"

Saxton scrambled outside, tumbling forward and sliding across the mud. Shaking off the loose soil from his fur, he ambled away with his tail between his legs. He curled beneath a large tree and covered his nose with his own tail to fight the blustery wind and rain.

When the rain ceased and the sun reappeared, the fox lay sluggish with cold and fever. His head felt unbearably tight, and his ears felt as though they were stuffed full of cotton. Aching all over, he tried drinking from a puddle of rain water, but found that swallowing was not only difficult, but painful as well.

He forced himself up, despite feeling so weak, and searched for a flat rock to sun on. Eventually, he found a suitable stone with a large lizard already lying upon it. With a half-hearted bark, Saxton chased away the reptile and took the sunning area for himself.

Though the pounding in his head eased, he was still bleary-eyed and could no longer breathe through his nose. He could not hunt, not even the tiniest beetle, for he would miss with each calculated pounce, and the fortunate little bug would scuttle off to safety.

After three days of fighting a cold and not eating anything but berries and nuts, Saxton noticed that the rodents and birds began boldly flitting about him without fear. Their haughtiness soured his already foul mood, and in his most angry thoughts he imagined eating them all in one bite. But thinking of such things only reminded him that his stomach was clawing for real food: rabbit legs, robin wings, and perhaps even a snake egg or two. That he could not provide any for himself scared him to numbness.

The search for his family was proving futile. Saxton could only guess that they had left the forest and gone in search of a new field in which to build a new home. He had no choice, but to accept the fact that his father was right: he was alone.

And, in all likelihood, he would *die* alone.

As he lapped from a stream, the shadow of an eagle flew across the running water. He frowned and looked about him, but saw nothing.

He shrugged off his concern and continued drinking, occasionally attempting to catch a minnow with little success. But as he peered at the water's surface again, he noticed the eagle's silhouette had grown larger.

Now alarmed, Saxton stepped away from the stream's edge. He looked up, seeking the eagle, but still could not locate it.

The air shifted behind him. He turned.

The eagle swooped down, talons outstretched. He dodged out of the way, and the eagle cawed in frustration as she grabbed nothing but a foot full of brush. She spiraled in midair, diving toward him for a second try. Again, Saxton jumped away from the eagle's reach.

"Hold still!" The eagle screeched.

Saxton ran back to the forest, hoping the trees would protect him. But the eagle flew lower, maneuvering around the branches.

The fox tripped and fell hard on his chest. A moment later, sharp talons wrapped around his body and whisked him away.

"Let me go! Let me go, you stupid bird!" He wriggled with all his might, but did nothing except inspire the eagle to grip him tighter.

"Of course, I'll let you go," said the eagle. "I can't serve my chicks live meat!"

With that, she beat her wings harder and flew them over a valley of sharp rocks. She intended to crush him!

There was a shriek and a sudden flutter of black feathers. Without warning, the eagle dived and began fleeing the valley. Saxton twisted his head around, wondering what had spooked her. Once again, a flash of black appeared before them.

"Get back here at once, you miserable bird!"

It was a crow, and a rather irate one at that.

"If my talons weren't full, you'd eat those words!" The eagle returned. Yet despite her obvious advantage in size and speed, the crow persisted, pecking and clawing her face.

"Stop it!" she demanded. "Stop it!"

"You stole my kill!" the crow shouted. "You stole my kill after three long days of hunting and scavenging! Why shouldn't I return you the favor by stealing this fox?"

While the eagle was distracted, Saxton searched for a safe place to land. At this height, his only hope was the lake several yards away.

"Hey, crow!" the fox challenged. "If you're so mad, why don't you pluck her pretty tail feathers?"

A spark of mischief lighted the crow's eyes. He darted behind the eagle, and proceeded to harass her by doing just that.

With every pluck of her tail feathers, the eagle flew forward, drawing closer and closer to the lake. When he felt it was now or never, Saxton strained his neck and bit the eagle's leg.

The eagle squawked and released him. He plummeted so fast that he thought he would faint. But he held strong and turned his fall into a dive. Saxton twisted in the air, pointing his face downward. If he dove into the shallow end, he would hit rock and die. If he dove closer to the deep, perhaps he might make it.

He held his breath and closed his eyes.

He didn't know water could be so hard.

Submerged, the fox continued to plummet and his left ankle caught against the corner of a stone, twisting it. As the water slowed Saxton's fall, it also began lifting him toward the surface. Breaching, he watched as the crow and eagle continued their fray above.

He swam for shore and dragged himself across the soft sand. He coughed out water and collapsed beneath a thorny shrub that matched the color of his fur. Camouflaged, Saxton hoped that for the time being he would be safe.

Before he shut his eyes and allowed hunger and shock to pull him into another restless sleep, the fox's last grim thought was how much easier it would have been if he had forgotten about Flynn and saved himself.

Chapter Two

Something sharp was poking Saxton just above his right eye. He twitched and shooed the disturbance away with a mild swipe of his paw. The poke came again, gentler this time, and he forced himself to open his eyes.

Above him, and upside down from his angle, stood the crow with a most impish grin.

"Ah," said the crow. "Still alive, I see. You're either incredibly lucky or truly foolish, or perhaps a little bit of both."

Saxton rolled over, winced at his screaming left ankle, and backed away from the crow with his teeth bared.

"Go away!" He growled. "Leave me alone!"

"Well, good morning to you *too*."

Not sparing any courtesies, the fox struggled to climb up the sandy embankment in an attempt to get away. The crow craned his head to the side, curious.

"It appears you have sprained your ankle," he noted. "With a fall like that you should be happy you didn't crack you head open like an egg against a skillet."

"You talk strange." Saxton grumbled. Try as he might, the sand kept giving way beneath him, and he slid down the slope repeatedly.

"You're going to make your leg worse if you keep moving around like that." The crow looked around. "Where are your parents?"

"*Nowhere!* And anyway, Mother said not to talk to strangers."

"Sound advice, very sound. Perhaps if I give you my name, we won't be strangers then?"

As he slid down for the fifth time, Saxton sat and sighed. At least, he thought, the crow didn't seem to want to eat him. In fact, he stretched out his wings and bowed.

"The name's Quill," he said. "Quite original, I know. Feathers and all that. What is yours?"

"Saxton," he answered reluctantly.

"Saxton? How intriguing. I was expecting something more traditional ... something along the lines of Russell or Copper ..."

"Russell's my brother's name!" He exclaimed, then paused. "... Flynn's my sister's ..."

"Well, your mother did well by you, I must say. A unique name, truly! What does she look like? You've obviously been separated, perhaps I can locate her."

The crow's friendly offer, especially after his earlier nastiness with the eagle, took Saxton aback. He narrowed his eyes and pulled back his ears.

"What do you want? Are you gonna eat me *and* my mother?"

Quill burst out laughing. "*What?* No, no. Don't be silly! I prefer much smaller fare."

"But you attacked us!" The fox argued. "You said you were going to 'return the favor' by stealing me!"

"Ah, yes," the crow said with a sigh. "I had a rather ... troublesome altercation with Mrs. Eagle a few days ago. Thought I would spoil her day as she had spoiled mine. As for you, well, you're too big for me to kill, much less carry."

"That doesn't mean anything! Ants can carry and eat almost anything, and they're a lot smaller than *you* are!"

At that remark, Quill raised one of his brows. "Cunning *and* observant. My, my ... your skulk ought to regret losing you." The crow thought for a moment and then conceded, "I won't lie, I *have* eaten foxes before, but only the ones unlucky enough to be crushed by cars and trucks. Road carrion isn't really my favorite, too burnt for my tastes. My friend Cecil, on the other wing ..." He cleared his throat, realizing he was babbling. "At any rate, if I was going to eat you, I would have done so already. As you can see, I have not, and as I hate the idea of orphans so very much, I will ask again: what does your mother look like?"

Saxton hesitated. Though part of him thought he should continue on his own, he also knew that his twisted ankle would set him back a few days. An extra set of eyes, especially those that can see from the sky, was a miraculous stroke of luck.

Yet a voice nagging in his head, one that sounded uncannily like his father's, convinced him that he had pushed his luck already. Conflicted, he asked, "How do I know you're telling the truth?"

This time, Quill addressed him gravely. "You *don't*."

That, Saxton decided, was the most honest answer any creature could give him.

"She's red," he began, "has golden eyes, and a big, soft tail with a white tip on it."

"Yes, I figured as much." Quill drawled. "Anything else? Her name?

"Scarlett. Um … she has a scar on her left shoulder. Got it from a snare. She smells sweet, like milk and honey."

"Very good. Stay put, then. I shall return by sunset, whether or not I find her."

"And if you don't come back?"

"Then I must have lied."

With that, Quill batted his wings and took to the air. Hoping he wasn't a fool for resting his welfare in the clutches of a crow, Saxton resettled beneath the shrub, and spent the rest of the day thinking about what to do next. One thing he knew for certain was that he needed time for his ankle to heal.

As the sky turned orange and pink, and cooler winds began to blow, Saxton grew anxious. His eyes darted about in search of Quill, fearing something might have happened to him, or worse, that he had wasted his time doing nothing. He was about to abandon the shrub and look for a way out of the embankment, when Quill fluttered down before him, kicking up dust as he landed.

For a brief moment, the fox found himself smiling, but his ears and eyes quickly fell when he noticed that Quill didn't return with any of his family.

"I'm afraid you'll be staying with me tonight," Quill said. "We'll resume looking for your family first thing tomorrow morning."

"We will?"

"Yes," Quill nodded. "I've already invested my time in this task. I may as well see it to the end. I can't stand loose ends, you see. Come on, then. There's a quarry of rocks not too far away. You can use it to climb out of here."

The fox moved to do as he was told, but paused. "Why are helping me, really?"

"Well, I do feel quite bad about that fall you took. I'd like to help you get home safely in recompense."

"Recom—"

"Restitution, er ... *Amends*. You understand?"

"I think so ... "

"Good! Let's be on our way then!"

Saxton followed Quill around the lake shore, and every so often needed to stop and rest his left foot. The crow would wait patiently for him to recover, and once he was ready to move again, they walked at a more comfortable pace. By the time they reached the quarry, it was nearly dark.

Saxton hopped onto the closest stone – keeping his weight on three feet instead of four – and examined the trail rocks for the easiest path uphill. Quill flew to the top and monitored his progress.

"No need to hurry," he assured. "It will be a while before the bobcats will be on the move."

"*Bobcats*?" The urge to hop stones instead of treading them became tempting.

"Careful. You don't want injure *another* leg."

The fox panted as he worked his way to the top. Quill took three steps back to give him room to stand.

"Bravo. If I could clap, I would."

"Do you live far from here?" Saxton asked, breathing hard from the climb.

Turning around, the crow led them through the woods. Crickets were chirping, frogs were croaking, and the hoot of an owl or two echoed into the night. "Yes and no. A crow can make his home anywhere he pleases. We're travelers and storytellers, you see, teachers and scholars. I suppose you can call us vagabonds, although personally I prefer the word 'bohemians'— has a more fanciful ring to it." He caught himself rambling again, and forced himself to stop. "There's a tree in which I like to roost that has a cavity between its roots. It will be a good place for you to stay tonight."

Once more, the crow's thoughtfulness struck Saxton as odd. "You're really ... I don't know ... nice to me, I guess. How come?"

The good humor in Quill's eyes flickered. "I'm old and alone, Saxton, and I've plenty of time on my wings." He brightened again. "And since I have time, why not use it for good?"

When they reached the tree Quill spoke of, he pointed to the cavity where Saxton could rest. "Stay in here. I will call if there is any danger. I'll be over there, on that branch."

Saxton paused, feeling as though he had forgotten something important. "Um ... I feel like I need to say something ... to you ... but I don't know what."

"I believe the word you're searching for ... is 'thanks.'"

"... Thanks ..." He repeated slowly, testing the word. Quill grinned.

"Sleep well, Saxton."

He flew to the top of the tree, closed his eyes, and bowed his head. Saxton entered the cavity, wondering what he had gotten himself into. He pondered if the crow was thinking the very same thing.

Dawn rose with a smile. Saxton awoke feeling refreshed and, to his surprise, quite calm. He crawled out from between the tree's roots, leaned forward, and stretched his back. His sprained ankle was still throbbing with pain, and he thought about how long it would be before he could run again.

A fox that couldn't run, he knew, was doomed.

Caw! Caw-caw!

He looked up. On top of the tree, Quill called out to another crow that was flying past. The fellow crow turned around in midair, flew to the tree, and perched before him.

"I'm sorry, I missed that," she said. "What were you asking?"

"Foxes," Quill said. "Seen any recently?"

"'Fraid not many. A few here and there, but they are all so quick; I may have mistaken a great many for shadows. I imagine most of them have left the immediate area, what with hunting season and all. Some abandoned Montana all together. Nervous creatures, aren't they?"

"That's too bad. What about vixens? One with a scar on her shoulder?"

"My apologies, no. But if it helps any, the foxes have probably moved east toward North Dakota. The state border isn't too far from here. It may be worth a shot."

"Thank you, that's very helpful. What was your name?"

"Avon. And yours?"

"Quill."

"Pleasure," she bowed. "I believe Cecil spoke of you once."

"Ah, yes. An affable fellow."

"Well, good luck. I hope you find what you're looking for." Avon launched off her perch and continued her flight.

Quill looked down at the fox. "Eavesdropping? You seem surprised."

Saxton flinched. He thought his stealth was better than that. "I didn't know crows were so... kind."

"Well, not all of us. We're also known for our mean sense of humor, though generally we try to be polite."

The fox gazed at his paws, a little embarrassed.

"Thank you again," he whispered, "for helping me."

The crow flew down to him. "Not at all. Let's get started."

He led the way east in hopes of finding an animal who might have sighted Saxton's family. Saxton, for his part, followed Quill and tried to make sense of what Avon had said.

"Avon said something about 'North Dakota,'" he began. "What's that?"

"It's a neighboring state, a human territory if you will," Quill explained. "The territory we're in is Montana. Both states, and forty-six others, comprise the entire land our feet are resting upon. That land, this *country*, is called the United States. Of course, there are many more countries in the world, Italy and France, for instance; I'm a bit sorry that my wings can take me only so far."

"Do all you birds know this stuff?"

"Not all, but many see human language as a very useful thing. In fact, there are other creatures that also use it, like the rats."

They stopped before a modest sett tucked beneath two rocks. Quill turned to Saxton. "Now, before I knock, you must promise me not to pounce, maim, or otherwise harm and eat the neighbor with which we are about to speak. Do you think you can do that?"

As if it was listening, Saxton's stomach grumbled. He sighed. "All right, I will."

The crow raised his right leg, balled his foot, and knocked on one of the stones. From within they heard the sound of rustling leaves and mildly irritated squeaking. Before long, a gray face with small ears and a narrow snout poked out.

"Yes?" The shrew's eyes widened upon seeing Saxton. "Oh! Oh, goodness!"

She immediately darted back into her burrow. Quill peered inside, and hollered, "Didn't mean to startle you, Mrs. Shrew! I assure you this fox is well-behaved. May I borrow some of your time?"

Mrs. Shrew peeked one of her eyes out. "You sure he's docile?"

"Docile … might not be the right word. Perhaps respectful would be more appropriate."

Saxton lowered his head with as much respect as he can muster.

"Good morning, Mrs. Shrew," he greeted. "We're looking for my family. Have you seen them? I promise you can trust me, I just want to go home."

The shrew stepped out further and eyed him up and down. She sighed and made a light 'tsk.' "Mama warned me there's nothing sadder than a baby carnivore all by its lonesome. It's the big eyes and big ears that do mothers like me in." She huffed. "All right, kit. You got me. Where'd you see 'em last?"

"In a field at the forest's edge, near the lake."

"Sounds like that could be anywhere," Mrs. Shrew groused.

"Uh …" Saxton panicked. He turned to Quill.

"Do you remember anything else?"

He tried to recall what the lake he fell into looked like. "There are three rivers that pass through the lake," he elaborated. "We lived by the shortest river, by a road that Father told us never to go near."

"That might be Two Hundred." Quill shifted his attention to Mrs. Shrew. "His family lived just south of here, before the freeway. They entered the forest heading east. Does that help?"

Mrs. Shrew scratched the back of her ear. "Well, if memory serves, I do believe Mr. Badger was in the area. As a matter of fact, he lives just five burrows down, near the rabbit warren."

"Thank you, Mrs. Shrew."

"Sure thing, Mr. Crow. Please give Atticus my regards when you see him."

Quill and Saxton bowed their heads in farewell, and then set off to see Atticus. The crow counted the number of burrows they passed while Saxton obeyed his order to keep his eyes open for rabbits.

"I didn't know different kinds of animals actually talk to one another," the fox commented.

"Not all creatures are solitary. Some of us depend on one another for survival."

"Why?"

"There is strength in numbers. Beyond that, we've found there is a certain joy in having a friend by one's side. Perhaps one day you'll have one of your own."

The idea was rather difficult for Saxton to grasp. "But how do you eat? Don't crows *eat* shrews?"

"Crow mostly scavenge the dead. That being said, you can't be friends with everyone. Such a title is meant for someone special. I, for one, pick and choose my meals, my enemies, and my allies."

"Sounds easier to just go it alone."

"That it is," Quill agreed. "But do not forget that you are not without enemies more powerful than yourself, young fox. One day, you may be grateful if a predator chooses to show you kindness ... Ah, here we are."

They stopped at another hole in the ground, one that was significantly larger and surrounded by grass. Quill dipped his head inside.

"Hello? Atticus, are you home?"

From within, they could hear grumbling and the sound of claws scraping along the dirt walls. Two large paws emerged from the badger's sett, followed by an angry face afflicted with mange. The mange was so severe that the badger had lost three-quarters of the fur on his face, and the exposed skin was red and weeping with foul-smelling pus. Combined with yellow, saw-like teeth and a squinty pair of eyes whose whites were blood red, Atticus had to be the ugliest, meanest looking creature Saxton had ever seen.

Apparently blind, Atticus sniffed about, detecting his visitors. His nose stopped before the fox.

"I can smell that you're frightened," the badger said in a short, gravelly voice.

"I am," he replied, trembling

"Must be tempting to scratch me up good and make a run for it, ain't it?" The badger smiled. It wasn't friendly. "But here you stand, with your feet planted firmly on the ground, as determined and steadfast as a red wood. Is it the fear freezing you? Or is it my face that you can't stop lookin' at?"

He swallowed, but answered honestly. "It's your face. It's ... hideous."

Quill balked at Saxton's words, but Atticus laughed.

"You must want somethin' pretty bad, don't you? Bad enough to look at somethin' like me?"

He nodded, and then remembered Atticus couldn't see well. "Yes."

"Well, why should I help a scared *Lonely Thief* like you, hm? You're afraid of me and you hate my face. That's enough to get any creature's blood roiling, and rest assured, I can tear you apart easily."

Quill was about to intervene, but Saxton answered.

"But I didn't run away. That means something, right?"

The badger grinned, but it looked more like a sneer.

"Go on."

"Mrs. Shrew told us you were near the field my parents lived in about seven or eight days ago. We were chased out of our home by two hunters and their dogs. Do you know where my family went?"

Atticus' nose twitched. "It's plain that my eyes are useless, but I do recall everything I smelled and heard. Around sunrise, I detected a male fox runnin' north. His woody scent said he was about four years old. He had a slight limp in his forepaw that might've been from a recent run-in with the hounds. Does this sound like your father?"

"No," Saxton replied. "My father smells like straw and rain, not wood."

The badger frowned as he concentrated. "Around midday I came across the scent of two kits, one male and one female. Think they were separated from their parents."

Saxton sat up straighter, wondering if Atticus was describing Russell and Flynn.

"Bitter scent, new but a bit rough. Smelled like they've just grown-in their red fur."

"No," he said again, disappointed. "Russell and Flynn are younger than that."

Sighing, the badger scratched the back of his head, careful to avoid the open sores. Quill and Saxton waited with baited breath. At last, Atticus set down his paw.

"It was sunset when I picked up a most sweet scent," he said quietly, "like milk and honey."

"Mother … That sounds like Mother."

Atticus nodded. "Yes, it belonged to a vixen, and if my ears were right, she was accompanied by three other foxes."

"That's them!" Saxton exclaimed. He turned to Quill in excitement, who returned the sentiment with a mild grin.

"They were heading east," the badger went on. "Her mate mentioned settling down somewhere southwest of a big lake in the neighboring human territory."

"Sounds like Lake Sakakawea." Quill murmured with thought. "They could be in Watford City or Van Hook. Probably Van Hook."

"So does that mean all we have to do is search those two places?"

Not wanting to disappoint the fox, yet not wanting to him to get his hopes up either, Quill answered, "It will take us at least ten days to reach North Dakota by foot, Saxton."

At that, Saxton felt his heart drop. "Oh."

"Don't get discouraged," Quill said. "We'll begin our journey in the morning. Now, what do you say to Mr. Atticus Badger?"

Turning to Atticus, he bowed in gratitude. "Thank you for your help."

The badger snorted. "Honor for honor, kit. Although yours could use a lil' more work."

"Enjoy the rest of your evening," said Quill. "Mrs. Shrew says 'hello.'"

The crow and fox departed, and as soon as they were out of earshot, Saxton released the shudder he had been suppressing. "Ugh! He was so mean and ugly."

Quill looked at the fox in surprise. "What's this? You're complaining now?"

"I wish we could've talked to someone else, but we didn't have a choice, did we?" He wrinkled his nose. "And his *smell* ..."

The crow abruptly flew before him, his eyes sharp.

"Saxton, that 'mean, ugly' creature helped you just now. Is he really so mean and ugly?"

"You saw him. If Mrs. Shrew didn't act like she liked him, I probably wouldn't have trusted him."

Clearly disappointed, Quill sighed and shook his head.

"Listen to me carefully: there are many cruel creatures and there are many good ones, but rare are those that are truly evil or righteous. If you give someone a chance, regardless of their temperament or their appearance, more often than not you will bring out the good in them."

"So you're saying I gave him a chance?"

"No. He was the one who gave *you* a chance. It would serve you well to think about that."

They walked in silence, Quill, as ever, leading the way. After a few hours had passed, it occurred to Saxton he didn't know how the crow knew where to go.

"How do you know we're going in the right direction?"

"North, south, east and west," the crow replied, pointing in four directions in quick succession. "North Dakota is east of Montana."

"But where's east?"

"The sun rises in the east and sets in the west. A quick glance at the sun or at a shadow can tell you what direction you're going. North and south are perpendicular to east and west. Moss usually grows north, as do evergreen trees. At night you can also find north by looking for the star, 'Polaris.' Deciduous trees, that is, trees that lose their leaves, grow south."

As Quill guided Saxton further east, in search of tonight's shelter on their way across the Montana border, Saxton found he was having second thoughts. "What if they're not in North Dakota?" He asked anxiously. "What if Atticus was wrong?"

The crow remained calm. "If they're not there, then at least you will have had a most interesting journey. You need to be more optimistic, Saxton."

He looked to the ground as he walked. "I don't know what that means."

"It means to hope, to believe that everything will fall into its proper place. I can't tell you with any certainty what tomorrow holds, but I can tell you that whatever happens was meant to happen, for better or worse." Quill stopped walking and turned to Saxton, making sure their eyes met. "There is no use stewing over what we can't control. For now, we can simply choose to be happy."

Without another word, he marched on. Despite the complaints of his sore ankle, Saxton skipped a few steps forward to keep pace by the crow's side.

Chapter Three

"How is your leg?"

"Better. Still hurts a little, but I think I can run."

It had been four days since they had first set off on their journey, and Saxton's hind leg had healed well enough that they were covering more ground as time went on. Crossing a field, Saxton stopped when the sea of grass ended without warning.

"What's this?" Saxton asked as he tentatively set his front paw on a hard, black surface.

"It is a road, the very thing I'm sure your father taught you to avoid," Quill explained. "Whereas animals such as you and I walk on natural dirt paths, humans create roads for their vehicles."

Intrigued, he was about to take another step forward, when Quill stopped him with an outstretched wing.

"Whenever you come to a road," the crow warned, "you must exercise extreme caution."

"Why?"

The instant he asked, a car whooshed past them with alarming speed, nearly toppling Saxton over with its force. Glancing at his companion, Quill chuckled, for the fox's fur had puffed out in fright.

"I assume that answers your question. If you get hit by a car, a van, or, skies forbid, a *semi-truck*, you will be crushed, and that will be an unfortunate end to your story."

"I see," Saxton said shakily. "Can we walk around it?"

"I'm afraid not. Roads tend to stretch for miles."

"Miles?"

"A mile is about five thousand, two hundred and eighty footsteps, give or take a few."

Saxton grimaced. He could only count up to ten, and he knew right away that anything bigger than ten must be a lot.

"Now, now, cheer up. It's really not as bad as all that. Wait here, I'll show you a useful trick my uncle taught me."

Quill flew off before Saxton could argue, but returned within seconds with a nut in his beak. "Now watch."

He looked both ways before flying to the middle of one lane and dropping the nut. Then he returned to Saxton and waited. Moments later, a truck drove by, running over the nut and crushing its hard shell. Quill flew out to the road again, retrieving it.

"You see?" he said. "If you use your head, you can use human creations to your advantage. Now, if you cross the road with me, this little treat will be your reward. What do you say?"

Saxton hesitated. "I don't think my life is worth risking for a nut."

"Well, you're no squirrel, so I suppose not." He chuckled. "Don't worry. We'll cross together."

"Okay."

Saxton peered left and right, and when he found that no vehicle was approaching, sprinted across the road. Quill flew alongside him and landed on the grass. As promised, the crow set the nut before him, and he ate it with one bite.

"There now, that wasn't terrible, was it? Come on, then. We should keep on the move while the sun is still up."

They continued traveling east until they grew tired and hungry, and decided to settle down near a small farm. While Quill satisfied his appetite with berries and insects, Saxton's nose caught a whiff of a delicious and intoxicating scent that made his stomach growl in happy anticipation.

In a nearly hypnotized state, he abandoned the half-eaten frog he had captured and followed his nose toward the farm. Distressed by the abrupt change in the fox's disposition, Quill yelled, "Saxton! Saxton, where are you going?"

But the fox would not, perhaps could not, hear him. Instead he ventured onward, ensnared by a most irresistible smell. Quill tried to fly before him and block his way, but the fox simply walked around him, unseeing.

"Oh, no," Quill murmured, noticing for the first time just what stood near the center of the farm. "A chicken coop."

Saxton came upon a tall fence made out of wooden poles and barbed wire. Driven by raw instinct, he dug a hole beneath the fence, creating just enough space to keep his fur from catching on the wire's sharp spurs.

Once on the other side, he prowled toward a small, rectangular structure where a cacophony of *cluck-cluck-cluck* sounds emanated from within. Not far away slept an enormous dog, and Saxton took care to not stir her awake.

Finding the door to the coop, he climbed up the wooden ramp and squeezed inside.

There, having beaten Saxton to the chickens by flying, Quill stood at the center of coop's floor, panicked and furious.

"Saxton, wake up!" he cried. "Wake up this instant!"

Despite the crow's pleas, Saxton licked his lips and eyed a particularly fat hen perched on a roost. The hen looked at him dumbly, cocking her head and clucking away as if nothing was amiss.

"Don't! The farmer will hear!"

Quill batted his wings over the fox's face in an effort to snap him out of it, but to no avail. Saxton simply lifted his paw and smacked the crow out of his way as he readied to pounce.

Snap! White feathers and a few drops of blood fell onto the wooden floor. He had a chicken's neck between his teeth without knowing when or how it got there.

All at once, the chickens fluttered and jumped and shrieked in chaos. "Fa-fa-fox!" The hens screamed. "Fa-fa-fox!"

Finally coming to his senses, Saxton shook his head and bolted out of the coop, only to come face-to-face with an angry dog.

"*Lonely Thief!*" the dog growled.

She lunged at Saxton, who dodged and sprinted the way he came in. With the dog barking after him, it wasn't long before the farmer ran out the front door of his house with a rifle in hand.

One eye closed and gun perfectly aimed, the farmer was about to squeeze the trigger when a crow descended upon him violently.

Caw! Caw! Caw! "What the hell? Get off me!"

Ducking down, the man waved his arms back and forth and unwittingly dropped the gun.

Bang! A bullet fired into the air and zipped past Quill's right wing. With one eye on Saxton and the other on the man beneath him, he continued to pummel the farmer with his wings and talons until the farmer ran off the porch and back into his house, the door slamming behind him.

Saxton dropped the chicken and dove into the hole he dug by the fence. The dog skidded to a halt before the barbed wire, but continued to bark incessantly.

Gasping, Saxton ran until the dog gave up and returned to her post. He collapsed in a heap upon a mound of grass, and Quill landed beside him, out of breath and equally shaken.

"You reckless fox!" he screeched. "Didn't your parents teach you anything? You could have gotten us killed!"

"I'm— I'm sorry!" Saxton cried, his ears lowered and his tail curled between his legs. "I didn't mean it! I just— I was so hungry!"

"Never let your hunger take over your better sense! Don't ever do that again!"

He nodded, his eyes watering. Quill shook his head and exhaled.

"Your life depends on your choices. You must make wise ones, or you will pay a very heavy price. Do you understand?"

He silently nodded again. The crow wasn't satisfied.

"I said, 'Do you understand?'"

"Y-yes," Saxton stuttered. "I do."

Huffing, Quill straightened his feathers. "Good. From now on, you won't do anything without my instruction."

These being his last words, he took to the air to cool his anger. Numbed by a mixture of fear, humiliation, and another emotion Saxton could not identify, he remained where he was and dared not move a single inch.

Two more days passed, and in that time, the fox and the crow barely exchanged a friendly word with one another. Saxton wondered every day what it was that angered Quill so greatly, but each time he found the courage to ask, his bravery was flattened by the crow's cold stare.

At midday, they stopped at a brook for rest. Gingerly stepping into the shallow stream, the crow threw a few drops of water over his feathers and fluttered his wings about. Saxton watched him curiously. "What're you doing?"

"Cleaning my feathers. Hard to fly when they get too dirty, you see."

Glancing at his fur, Saxton realized it had been a while since he last bathed. He started licking his forearm, but immediately spat.

"Yuck!" He pawed at his mouth, brushing away the wads of brown hair that stuck to his tongue and face.

"What's the matter?"

"Nothing. My fur's shedding again."

Quill froze. He swallowed his apprehension and peered at the fox's fur. Indeed, shades of copper red, white, and black were beginning to grow from beneath Saxton's outer coat. Quill flew out of the brook.

"Let's go."

"But you didn't finish washing your wings—"

"I'll take care of it later. We must make haste if we are to find your family."

He obeyed and took one last lap from the brook before climbing up the ravine.

They were walking for hours and Saxton yawned widely, dragging his feet without paying attention to the scenery he and Quill passed. His slightly improved diet of fish and field mice kept him afoot, but whenever he saw his reflection in the water, it was clear he had grown thin.

As Quill flew or walked ahead, Saxton couldn't help but notice that he was salivating and itching to pounce. He forced his eyes to the ground. So intent on his self-control, he failed to hear a sharp *hiss* just beneath him.

"Watch out!"

Quill pushed him aside. Startled, he staggered, barely missing stepping on a snake's head. Furious, the snake rose off his belly, bared his fangs, and struck.

But the crow intervened. Saxton watched in amazement as he danced around the snake's to and fro attacks. A strike to the right, and Quill gracefully flitted up and landed to the side. A strike to the left, and he spun, moving toward the snake's back. His wings were outstretched in a protective gesture, blocking Saxton from the snake's range, and his beak was wide open, ready to bite.

Pushing the reptile back, Quill cornered the snake between a rock and a broken tree branch. The snake bared his fangs again, only to have his neck snapped in two by the crow's powerful beak.

Panting, he glanced at Saxton with a wary smile. "I do believe lunch is served."

"Is he safe to eat?"

"Yes. This one's not poisonous, and even if he was, you should know you simply avoid consuming the head."

"That was amazing!" Saxton exclaimed through chewing. "You're really good. Maybe you can teach me how you did that."

As the fox continued to eat voraciously, Quill wondered if there would be anything left for him. But Saxton stopped eating halfway down the snake and gave the remainder of the meat to the crow.

"Thank you." He tore the snake into smaller shreds and gulped down the food by raising his neck. He noted that the sky was becoming dark. "We should settle in for the night. We've already made it across the state border. Van Hook should be about three to four days away if we keep moving at this pace."

"Really?"

He nodded.

"That's great!" Saxton happily skipped about in a circle. "I'll be with my family soon!"

Though he would never admit it out loud, Quill was relieved. When they sought haven beneath a cottonwood for the night, Saxton fell asleep almost instantly and Quill watched him from his perch. What would he do, he thought, if the kit's family was nowhere to be found and he would be hampered by this fox forever?

A hoot and flutter of thick wings descended from above him. Quill looked up. It was his friend Echo, the owl. He greeted her with a small bow of his head. She returned the gesture in kind.

"May I speak with you?" Echo whispered, "Away from sensitive ears?"

He glanced at the dozing fox. "Yes, but not too far away."

They flew three trees over, just close enough that Quill could watch for any danger approaching Saxton, and just far enough away that Saxton would not be able to hear their conversation should he rouse from slumber.

"His fur is turning red," she said, a frown forming between her large, orange eyes. "Before long, he'll be fully grown. If he decides to eat you, what will you do then?"

"He will not eat me." He said this defiantly, but without true confidence.

"Well, that's quite a leap of faith. Must I tell you the cautionary tale of the man who owned a giant python?"

"Watching the news through the windows again?" Quill asked dryly. "These days it's a load of rubbish."

Echo rolled her eyes. "Be that as it may, a dead man is a dead man. He was partially digested, no less. Imagine the mess the landlord had to clean-up when the tenants noticed the horrible stench seeping through the floors!" She shook her head. "At least in the wood, you can die with dignity."

"You make it sound as if my premature demise is a foregone conclusion."

"Keep in mind a fox's nature."

"A fox's nature is cunning, self-reliant, and opportunistic." Quill frowned. "I had been hoping my influence might sway his view of things … I seem to have taken on a task far greater than I thought it would be."

"Yes, well, that always seems to be your problem. You should end this, *now*, before it's too late."

"Too late? Please, I have time to waste."

"You're getting old, Quill. You ought to fly home now. This year might be your last chance to see what's left of your family."

He grew silent.

"… Perhaps," he finally allowed.

Unbeknownst to the two birds, Saxton had awakened upon sensing he was alone. Alarmed, he softly called out Quill's name. When no reply came, he raised his nose to the air and soon found the crow's distinct scent. He followed that scent until it grew stronger, and discovered the tree in which the crow and owl conversed in secret.

But Saxton's large ears were powerful, and his chest tightened upon hearing the owl's truthful words. Echo was right, he was growing larger and hungrier, and every so often felt enticed by the notion of attacking and devouring his one and only friend.

His eyes narrowed at the word: 'friend.'

Quill had mentioned that he might one day make one. Though the word was completely alien to him, somewhere inside him Saxton knew what it meant. He couldn't define the word with speech, but he could define it by the complicated feelings it left inside him.

When he thought of Quill, he thought of his father: a protective and practical figure familiar with the ways of the world. But unlike Father, he was kind, patient, and possessed knowledge that never ceased to amaze him. The fox felt not only safe, but happy, happy even when the crow was a little cross with him. And that, he thought, was quite odd.

It was then that Saxton realized he couldn't— *wouldn't*— remain.

Treading lightly on the dry leaves beneath his feet, Saxton scurried away before the birds could notice that he was ever there.

When Quill returned, Saxton was nowhere to be found. He circled the cottonwood two times. Nothing.

He felt a sudden wave of dread. He took to the air.

"Saxton!" the crow hollered. "Saxton, where are you? Saxton!"

Hearing his cries, Saxton ran faster, bounding east, hoping beyond hope the crow would never find him.

Quill spent the remainder of the night and well into morning flying around the forest. Every so often he would catch stray clumps of brown fur tumbling in the wind. He followed the haphazard trail, not at all caring that it would lead him not to a kit, but to a fully grown fox.

Saxton took to digging burrows, hiding within them, and waiting for the crow to fly past. When he was certain that Quill was out of sight, he would reemerge and head further east. The terrain morphed from soft fields to rocky paths. It was midway through this crossing that a deep, ethereal howl reverberated in the evening and made Saxton freeze.

He had been warned about wolves before, but he had never had the misfortune of seeing one. Lowering his head and body to the ground, Saxton darted his eyes about in search of potential danger.

A light fog had descended over the rocks and grass. Through the mist, a pair of eyes, bright as lightning, glowed not far away. They were not so much menacing as they were regal, though the howl that accompanied those eyes made the fox tremble.

The wolf, a lone creature with a large build yet surprisingly uncertain posture, sat on the grass to sing. He closed his eyes and raised his voice to the moon, releasing a beautiful entwinement of howls.

There was something about his song that caused Saxton to lower his defenses and quietly sit up in interest. Although he could not explain why, he knew that the wolf was singing about sadness, shame, and regret.

Before he knew it, the howls disappeared altogether. Saxton opened his eyes. The wolf stared at him, unmoving.

Saxton didn't know what to do. His heart was racing, but his feet were rooted to the ground. The wolf, with his head lowered, approached him with mild curiosity.

Shaking, he realized he should have set off running a long time ago. Yet here he was, standing nearly face to face with a creature that could kill him in an instant.

Howooooooo…!

The wolf's ears twitched. He raised his head and turned in the direction of his pack's call. Losing interest in Saxton, he trotted away with his back hunched over and his tail between his legs. It was only then that Saxton noticed this wolf did not seem very coordinated. He lumbered forward and almost tripped over his own feet a couple of times.

"*There* you are!"

The breathless crow took him by surprise. Quill landed before him, his eyes tired and his demeanor more than a little incensed. He made a cursory assessment of Saxton's physical condition. Deciding the fox was all in one piece and in good health, he let him have it.

"Why did you run off like that?" he scolded. "I searched everywhere for you!"

The feathers behind his neck were bristling. Saxton looked away, not sure of what to say.

"Well?" Quill went on, clearly expecting an answer. "I was so worried! Do you have any idea of the things that went through my head? What if I had *lost* you?"

Saxton opened his mouth and closed it, struggling to find the right words. Realizing he needed to calm down, the crow took a deep breath and let it go. The fox tried again.

"You're my friend," he said hoarsely, "My *only* friend … I don't want to hurt you."

All emotion washed off Quill's face. "You heard."

He said nothing.

"If you wanted to, you would have taken my life a long time ago. You did not."

"But I thought about it—"

"And you didn't act on it."

He looked at the crow, who tried his hardest to smile.

"Everything will be fine."

"You think so?"

"I know so," he replied firmly. Clearing his throat, Quill redirected the conversation to lighter ground. "It looks like you did a good job of heading toward Van Hook on your own. Let's continue tomorrow, shall we? I haven't slept in a while."

They found shelter beneath a pair of boulders that were leaning against each other. The two animals crawled beneath the small shelter. As Quill rested, Saxton tried to quell a question that had been buzzing faintly in the back of his mind. The owl had mentioned Quill had a family, but where were they? And why did Quill never speak of them before?

The crow blinked his eyes open and saw that the fox seemed troubled. "Penny for your thoughts."

Saxton looked at him in confusion.

"Human saying. It means, 'What's on your mind?'"

He sighed. "The owl said you should return 'home.' How come you never told me you had a family?"

Quill stilled his features, careful not to react. "I was a mate and a parent once, had three darling chicks and a lovely spouse." His eyes grew distant. "That was a long time ago."

"Where are they now?"

"Gone. I have a sister, but I haven't seen her in years." He paused. "Perhaps someday, I will see her again. I'd like to see home one last time."

It sounded as though it was too upsetting a topic for the crow to discuss. Saxton decided not to prod any further.

"When we were apart," he began, "I was thinking you would have made a great father."

The crow was both warmed and embarrassed by the comment.

"Thank you."

But the fox did not end there.

"Can we ..." He hesitated, unsure why he was asking this. "Can we ... be family?" The crow was astonished. Saxton quickly amended, "Just for a little while?"

Quill closed his eyes.

"Yes," he whispered. "For a little while."

Chapter Four

In Van Hook, North Dakota, there were wooden fences lining both dirt and paved roads, and little farms appeared every few miles along with the occasional tall-standing silo. Hoof prints left braided patterns across the horse trails, and every so often a vehicle would drive by carrying horses or cattle.

Between their swift reunion and entering of Van Hook, Quill had watched with silent pleasure as Saxton grew healthier, happier, and more inquisitive each day. Their journey was punctuated with numerous questions by the fox, all of which Quill patiently answered.

"What are clouds made of?" Saxton once asked.

"Water."

"Is that why clouds make rain?"

His quick reasoning made Quill blink in surprise. "Why, yes."

"I used to hate rain," he thought out loud. "But recently I've been thinking it's nice to have when there aren't any streams around. I didn't know there was so much land and so little water."

Quill had laughed. "Actually, my friend, most of the world is made of water."

"It *is*?"

He nodded. "It's called the ocean. A long time ago, everything came from there. That is why everything that lives and breathes needs to drink."

The fox frowned, bewildered. "Then why'd we leave the ocean?"

"We were curious. Isn't the world so much more interesting when you get to see more of it?"

Saxton stopped to look around them, admiring the morphing landscape beneath their feet. "Yes."

At night, Quill would tell Saxton stories the crows overheard from humans for many centuries; stories about gods and demons, fairies and trolls, war and peace, good and evil. Though Saxton enjoyed the adventures of Zeus and Snow White, he much preferred the stories the crows created themselves. His favorite was one that Quill learned from his father, and his father from *his*.

"Long ago," Quill would always begin, "there were a flock of cranes that lived peacefully together in a marsh. One day, an egg hatched, and a crane with pure silver feathers was born. Despite her perfect beauty, she was born blind. The world, to her, was a big and dark place, filled with lovely sounds and wonderful smells, but always vastly mysterious.

"The other cranes, all of whom looked alike, treated the silver crane with spite. They envied her beauty and considered her blindness an oddity to be laughed at.

"So the poor silver crane spent all of her days alone, and mourned not having a single soul to speak to. At night, when the others were asleep, she wept.

"One evening, when autumn had laid down her red and orange blankets upon the ground, the silver crane's small sobs were heard, and someone spoke to her for the first time in years.

'Pray, why do you cry dear Crane?'

'I have no one to talk to,' she said, 'and I have no one to see.'

'I will talk to you,' said the stranger.

'Why? Don't you think I'm terribly different?'

'Everyone is different,' said the stranger. 'And everyone is the same. Everyone wants to be happy, and everyone wants their wishes to come true. Tell me, dear Crane, what wish can I grant you?'

"Little did the silver crane know that she was speaking with none other than the moon. 'I should like to see who has been so kind as to listen to me, when no one else would.'

'Then fly, dear Crane,' said the moon. 'Fly as high as your wings can take you.'

"So the silver crane raised her powerful wings and took to the air. She flew up, up, and up until the darkness faded into bright light, and at last she could see. The moon greeted her with a crescent smile and said, 'Dear Crane, it is so good to have company where no one can reach me. Would you care to stay?'

"Happy at last to have a true friend, the silver crane quickly agreed. To this day, she flies around the moon, dropping her feathers in the pitch black sky. She serves as the moon's messenger, granting those too shy, too small, or too lonely a single wish, and lighting the way for those who cannot see the path before them.

"That, my dear Saxon, is how stars are born."

Quill told him this story at least once a day, and he often requested it again before sleep. With a pang of regret that the crow had not foreseen, he realized that one day soon, he would no longer have someone to tell such stories to.

They crossed an expansive bridge that embraced a river and asked a mallard, who was just slightly behind his flock, how much farther they had to walk before reaching Lake Sakakawea. The mallard politely indicated that their intended destination was not too far away, and they should reach it by sunset. Overjoyed with the prospect that their travels may very well be coming to an end, Saxton hummed himself a cheerful tune as he walked.

He stopped humming when they heard the sound of someone singing. It was a female's voice, warm and loving and so very tender. They looked around until they saw an enormous bear several yards away, playing with her cub.

"Little cub, little cub, who loves you most?
No one, but Mama Bear with her grizzly coat

"She'll clean your ears and feed you honey
And when you cry she'll make it sunny

The cub giggled and squeaked as his mother gently pushed him onto his back with her massive paw and tickled his belly with her nose.

"She'll cover you from rain and hold monsters at bay
She'll never, ever go running away

"And when you're grown up and ready to leave
She'll shed a single tear, but will never grieve

Her little one squirmed from the tickles, trying to wriggle free. She stopped teasing him and gently licked his forehead before pressing her muzzle against his.

48

"Because Mama Bear, Mama Bear loves you most
As long as you're happy, she'll always boast

"Little cub, little cub, who loves you most?
No one, but Mama Bear with her grizzly coat"

Saxton stared. "Is that ... a bear?

"Yes," Quill whispered. "The *Terrible Beast*, as some might call them. They are rare around here. Most of them are further north. You should treat them with great respect."

Saxton tip-toed slightly closer, but Quill blocked his path with an outstretched wing.

"Not too close. You don't want to frighten the cub."

Nodding, he held back, but continued to watch the two bears, fascinated.

"Do you remember your lessons from yesterday, my honeycomb?" Mother bear asked.

"Um … be careful crossing rivers and watch out for traps. Eat lots for the winter. Clean my paws every day."

"And?"

"And fight for yourself and fight for your family."

She beamed with pride. "That's right. Very good, Tarlo."

Her son beamed back. "I'm hungry," he said with an impossibly little voice for a creature his size. "Can I have something to eat?"

The mother bear surveyed the trees around them. She ambled toward a tree, stood, and reached into its branches. A bees' nest crusted over the juncture between two tree limbs, and she broke a small piece of honeycomb off with her mighty jaw. The bees buzzed and stung, but they didn't seem to bother her one bit.

She returned to all fours and gave Tarlo the small treat.

Tarlo slurped and chewed enthusiastically. He ate so fast that the honeycomb soon became an empty husk. He looked at his mother, clearly still hungry, and said, "Can I get some more myself?"

"All right, but you'll need a little help."

Her cub stood against the tree and tried to climb up it. She gave him a boost by the rear with her head, slowly lifting him up until he could reach.

"Don't take too long or move too much," she said. "The bees will sting more if you do. Does it hurt?"

"Nah," he said with self-satisfaction. "I can take it!"

Tarlo grabbed a fistful of honey, and his mother gently lowered him to the ground. They looked so close and happy, Saxton felt himself growing terribly jealous. He didn't realize until this moment how badly he wanted his family back, and how painfully he missed his mother.

The moment was broken when a male bear walked through the bushes. The mother bear was enormous, but the male that had just appeared was gigantic. He grunted and growled as he moved about, and Quill and Saxton hid behind the grass on instinct.

"Mama!"

She whirled around and nudged her son behind her. "Stay behind me." Then she growled at the intruder. "You again. What do you want?"

"What do you think, Napowsa?"

He stepped forward, but Napowsa bared her teeth.

"Come any closer, and you'll regret it."

A mean smile drew up his lips, and he lunged for Tarlo. Napowsa stood upright, blocking his path, and smacked him across the face with her claws.

His head swung to the side with the force, revealing long red lines along his face. His eyes slid to their corners as he stared at her, furious. He turned back to Napowsa, roaring, and grabbed her around the torso with both arms.

"Mama, no!" Her little one squealed. He ducked and moved away as the fighting drew too near. His eyes were fearful, helpless.

Napowsa slammed her body to the ground, taking the other bear with her, and the earth shook. She rolled them over until she was on top of him, grabbed the skin on his shoulder with her teeth, and pulled until it ripped clean off his back.

The bear screamed.

Saxton screwed his eyes shut and lowered his ears. He felt Quill cover the top of his head with his wing.

"I warned you!" Napowsa bellowed. "Stop following us! Come at me and Tarlo again, and I'll *kill* you!"

She pushed him away from her, and rose shakily before retreating back into the woods. Napowsa looked behind her, her face swiftly transforming from ferocious to loving in seconds.

"Are you all right, honeycomb?"

"… Uh-huh," her son said, shaking a bit. "You were strong."

Napowsa licked his nose and rubbed the side of her head against his shoulder, taking Tarlo into a hug.

"She beat him," Saxton said. "He was *huge* ... and she *beat* him."

"Never underestimate the love a mother has for her little one," Quill replied. "It is a fiery thing, warm and bright, and sometimes violent.

He glanced at his friend. "How long do they stay together?"

"Eight seasons, or about twenty-four full moons."

They watched the two bears leave the clearing.

"That's a long time."

After two days, Quill could not get the images of Napowsa and Tarlo out of his mind. He looked at Saxton, whose scent, once woodsy and fresh, now carried traces of adult musk. Yet despite his physical maturity, Saxton was still only as capable as a reasonably talented cub. 'Well,' the crow thought, 'that simply won't do.'

He lifted Saxton's tail with his beak and showed him its now-white tip. Seeing his confusion, he dropped the tail and explained, "Your fur is fully red now, and soon you'll stop growing. You must learn the basics of living on your own, and fast."

"That's all right," the fox replied. "My family can teach me when we find them."

"That's just the problem; by the time we find them— *if* we find them— I'm not sure your mother and father will take you back. *Especially* your father; he is male and territorial. He'll see you not as a son, but as a rival or possible threat. Perhaps worse, if he finds you can't pull your own weight ... he'll see you as a burden."

Saxton swallowed the lump he found rising in his throat.

"What happened to optimism?" he weakly joked.

"At this point, it's time to be realistic," Quill said sternly, "by preparing for the worst possible outcome." Glancing around them, the crow nodded to himself. "I will teach you some survival skills. Fortunately, you're a bright young fox and a lot of what I will teach you should come naturally."

"You're going to teach me *now?*"

"I know you're eager to see your family, but your siblings have no doubt received continuous training in the time we've spent looking for them." With that, he broke course. "Come, now. I'm going to teach you how to hunt more sizeable prey."

Impatient, but unwilling to disobey Quill, Saxton reluctantly followed the crow until they came to what appeared to be a rabbit warren. Hopping on a rock, Quill looked down at him.

"You, Saxton, are no less than *Vulpes vulpes*, which is Latin for the renowned, the crafty, and the willful red fox. Though you're from the same family as the wolf, your lineage is very different. You are a solitary hunter, not a pack hunter, and your kind prefers to stalk their prey rather than give chase. In many ways, you're similar to a feline. Do you understand what I'm saying?"

"I guess so ..."

"Second, foxes, however reclusive, must learn to speak well. Please say, 'I suppose so,' rather than 'I guess so.' While other animals depend on brawn or poison or flight, foxes depend on their intelligence and stealth. When you find yourself cornered by a stronger animal, you have only two choices. The first, as you are well aware, is to flee. The second is to convince your hunter *not* to eat you. You can only do that with confident speech and ingenuity."

Lifting one of his feet, he pointed to one of the rabbit holes. "Now, I want you to capture a rabbit."

He stared at the crow as if he'd grown an extra wing. "But how?"

"Saxton, I just told you, use your inborn skills. Begin!"

Jumping to his feet, Saxton lowered his nose to the ground and inspected several rabbit holes. When he came upon one that was occupied, he began to dig, only to have the rabbit burrow deeper into its complex network of tunnels.

"You must think like your prey," Quill coached. "When your family was being forced out of their home, what did they do?"

Abandoning the hole, Saxton ran across the field in search of the back end of the tunnel. To his surprise, the rabbit popped out of a hole several feet across from the first hole he had previously examined.

"Not all animals behave the same way," explained the crow. "A fox might require nothing more than a single escape exit, but a rabbit, which has countless enemies, will require more."

Saxton barely heard Quill's lecture as he scrambled to change direction and pursue the rabbit. The rabbit zigzagged around the field, dodging at precisely the right moment.

"You are *chasing*, Saxton! You will tire yourself out if you continue to do so!"

The rabbit changed directions again. Not reacting fast enough, Saxton skidded along the dirt and tumbled into a trough. Laughing, the rabbit turned to him from a safe distance and teased, "Give it up, *Lonely Thief*! You're too slow for me!"

She then batted her white tail and jumped back into her burrow.

Grumbling, he tried to run after her, but Quill flew before him. "No good. Let's try again. Remember, you need to *stalk*."

And so, Saxton spent the remainder of the day patrolling the warren, attempting to nab a rabbit. The sun turned orange, and through all the waiting, Quill sat on a soft pile of leaves and fell asleep. Frustrated with his lack of success and Quill's loss of interest, Saxton sat on his haunches and threw dirt into the air with his paws.

"Stupid rabbit," he growled. That was it. He was tired and fed-up with this nonsense. If Quill could take a nap, then so could he, he thought petulantly. He curled up to do just that.

He woke up later to the sound of crickets and nightfall. As his eyes adjusted to the light, Saxton almost gasped when he discovered the rabbit had emerged from her burrow to feast on clover. Lowering his head and ears, he crawled from behind, careful not to make noise. Despite his extra care, a twig snapped beneath one of his feet, and the rabbit sat up, alert. She rotated her head and twitched her long ears, searching for the source of the sound. Saxton held his breath and remained unmoving, waiting for the rabbit to return to eating.

After a moment, she let down her guard again and continued where she left off. Saxton moved forward, inch by inch, until she was within jumping distance. He forced his hind legs flush against the ground, arched his back and sprang forward.

The rabbit was dead before she even knew what had hit her.

He had finally done it.

Saxton's heart fluttered with excitement. He carried the limp rabbit to Quill, who was still sleeping, and gently nudged him awake with his nose. The crow groggily stirred, blinking several times before recognizing the fox standing proudly before him.

"I cawp wun!" he grinned, his eyes mischievous and wide.

"Ah, good." Quill yawned. "I knew you could—" another yawn. "— do it."

In spite of his tiredness, Quill offered him a warm smile. "Now you may enjoy your reward. Eat up, Saxton."

The following morning, the crow taught him a new skill. After providing breakfast, Quill requested that Saxton catch a gopher. Next, he showed him the method and importance of caching spare food. The key was to dig just deep enough to prevent other animals from sniffing the cache out, but high enough that Saxton would be able to locate it above ground.

"Don't hide everything in one spot," he added. "Chances are one of your stashes is going to get nabbed by another fox or wolf too smart to pass up a free meal. Tear your food into pieces and spread your caches around. The further apart you spread them, the more likely you'll have protected food for a rainy day. It's simple mathematics."

"Mathematics?"

"Never mind. Waste of time for creatures without opposable thumbs anyway."

Saxton practiced hunting and burying food, and before they knew it, they had finally reached Lake Sakakawea. The crystal blue waters, which stretched as far as the eye could see, and the lush, abundant greenery took their breaths away. They both sat down to take in the marvelous view.

"What a beautiful place," Saxton whispered.

"Yes."

"Can— *May* we look for my family now?"

"Yes, you are ready."

"That's good. I miss my mother and sister. It will be nice to see them again."

Quill cocked his head to the side. "What about your father and brother?"

Saddened, Saxton lowered his head. "Father believes I'm a fool, and my brother believes anything my father says."

"Why?"

The fox worried his teeth against his bottom lip.

"I ... didn't tell you the whole truth about how I got separated," he began. "That day, my sister was so scared, she could barely walk. Father said I should run ahead instead of waiting for her, but I- I couldn't leave her to die. So I left my family to distract the hunters. It worked, but now I'm the one who is left behind."

Stepping closer to Saxton, Quill raised his wing and draped it across the fox's narrow shoulders.

"You are no fool, Saxton."

Chapter Five

Saxton circled the lake. He knew that if this was his family's primary water source, at least one of them must have left their scent behind recently. Quill remained unusually silent as he observed Saxton's progress, reminding him now and then if they had already covered an area.

They reached a formation of red rocks overlooking one of the lake's shores. It was there that Saxton detected the scent of milk and honey.

"Mother was here," he said. "They must be somewhere close by."

Quill seemed anxious, but he rallied his enthusiasm. "Wonderful! I'll look around from above."

"That's a good idea. Let me know what you find."

While Quill flew, Saxton probed the area for Mother's scent. It was fading, but seemed to lead northeast. Within minutes, the crow returned.

"I saw two foxes heading southwest. I think they might be your mother and father."

Saxton wasn't so sure. "I don't know, I think the scent is heading northeast."

"They must have circled around."

He frowned. "I suppose you're right."

He followed Quill as he led them into a forest at the foot of a hillside. Though they found the smell of a fox, it did not smell like any member of Saxton's family.

"Maybe they've moved on," Quill suggested.

"Maybe."

Quill saw Saxton's disappointment. It was rather hard to miss. "I'm sorry, my friend."

The fox shook his head. "It's all right. Now that we're here, we can try again tomorrow."

They turned around to search for a place to call it a night, when Saxton heard a twig snap.

"Did you hear that?"

"Hear what?"

Without warning, a fully-grown cross fox leapt for Quill and pinned him by the wings to the ground. Baring his teeth for the killing bite, Saxton ran at the bigger fox and head butted him off his friend. The fox rolled along the soil, but quickly found his footing and stood up.

"He's mine!" The fox barked. "I caught him first!"

Furious, Saxton pulled back his ears and showed his teeth. Quill had never seen him like this before, and the sight of this suddenly very feral creature chilled his blood.

"Hurt him, and I will make you regret the day you came upon us," he hissed.

They barked at one another, creating a pair of haunting sounds that echoed all about them. The older fox stood on his haunches, snarled, and attacked Saxton with his front paws. Saxton fought back, matching bite for bite and scratch for scratch. They circled one another, ran after one another, and bounded off rocks and tree trunks. The fox bit him on the tail and continued to chase him across a fallen log, where Saxton quickly swirled around and pounced.

The two fell off the log and tumbled down a ravine. Saxton bit the cross fox on the shoulder, forced him down, and moved his teeth to the jugular. The fox whimpered.

"Please! Please, don't kill me!"

"Do you yield?" Saxton growled, pressing his teeth more firmly against the fox's vulnerable neck.

"Yes! Yes, I concede! Please don't kill me, please!"

Saxton released him, but pressed his front paws on the fox's chest. "Hunt the crow again, and next time you will not be so lucky."

With that, he stepped off him, and the other fox bolted away. Calming down, Saxton climbed up the ravine to find Quill watching him from the ledge.

"Are you all right?" he asked, all of the fury gone from his eyes, replaced instead with concern. "Did he hurt you?"

Quill swallowed and answered hoarsely. "No, no I'm fine. Thank you."

He sighed with relief and nuzzled the crow's shoulder with his nose. "Good, that's good. I don't know what I would have done if you weren't."

Alarmed, but at the same time grateful, Quill could only nod.

The fox and crow spent the next few days following the same routine. They would rise and survey the land for any sign of Saxton's family. Once Saxton found a scent, Quill would take to the skies to determine the proper direction in which to continue their search. One day, they stumbled upon a circular arrangement of rocks that Quill told Saxton to avoid stepping on. When Saxton asked why, Quill grabbed a long stick with his beak and set it down where the rocks were arranged. SNAP! A leg trap that had been buried by leaves and soil broke the stick in two.

"Humans arrange rocks in a circle to warn their own kind there's a hunter's trap hidden beneath," Quill said. "It's not easy to do, but you can open it by putting all your weight on the release here." He pointed to a flat paddle on the side of the trap. Saxton pressed both of his front paws on the paddle and leaned forward. The trap's mouth opened minutely.

Saxton let the steel jaws snap shut again, shuddering at their strength.

After five days of searching, Saxton grew wary that their efforts had been fruitless and it was time to search Watford City. Quill reassured him they would try again, yet Saxton couldn't help but wonder if he would have better luck searching on his own.

The following day, when Quill was still asleep, Saxton decided to continue his search by himself. He traveled to the formation of rocks he had visited yesterday, and his nose caught another vague but familiar smell. It reminded Saxton of honeysuckle flowers that had been dried by summer sun and fresh grass on a misty morning. Pursuing the scent, he came down a sheer wall of rocks around the lake's river bend. He stopped at the sight of a dainty vixen fastidiously cleaning her tail, ears, and paws. She sensed she was being watched and ceased licking her fur, glancing around.

The sight of her brother, standing before her and nearly fully grown, caused Flynn to blink. When Saxton did not disappear, she blinked again and crept forward.

"Saxton?" she asked quietly, her eyes wide with shock and joy. "Is that *you?*"

She had, in Saxton's opinion, grown to be very beautiful. Her eyes were golden, just like Mother's, and her fur was a paler, softer shade of red that recalled a durum wheat field.

"Flynn?" he asked, though he knew without a doubt it was her.

Delighted, she nodded, and they rubbed shoulders against one another in affectionate greeting.

"I thought you were dead." There was a quiver in her voice, warm and worried, and Saxton remembered why he protected her. "We all did."

Before Saxton could reply, their brother, Russell, appeared through a curtain of reeds.

"It was supposed to be for the best." He had a fierce look about his face. The corner of his lip was slightly curled and the middle of his brow seemed to be permanently furrowed in distrust. His fur was darker, almost russet, and his build was significantly larger compared to his siblings. With a swagger that foretold his pride, Russell prowled up to Saxton and eyed him up and down with disgust. "Guess you have the kind of luck that only fools have."

Saxton stood straighter. "I see being brothers still means so little to you."

"As it should," Russell scoffed. "We live alone and we die alone, that we're born from the same mother is merely circumstantial."

"Russell," Flynn interrupted gently, "we should be happy to see him alive and well."

"Ha!" He responded with a humorless laugh. "Happy? This just means more competition for the rest of us; one more fox to fight for land and food."

"I didn't come all this way to fight or steal your food," said Saxton. "I came because I wanted to be with my family again."

"Well, you've come too late. None of us want to see you."

"Nonsense!" Flynn rebuked. "I thought about Saxton every day!" She turned to him, her eyes all but pleading that he forgive their brother. "How'd you survive?"

"Quill," Saxton replied with pleasure, a smile crossing his mouth. "He's a crow, and he found me the day—"

"A *crow?*" The hair on Russell's back bristled, and the pupils of his amber eyes narrowed. "You mean a *Sky Murderer?* You can't trust those birds! They're all liars!"

"Don't say such things— they're unkind," Saxton said as he stepped forward, his mood growing cross. "And you don't know that *all* crows are liars."

"Of course, they are. Father said so."

"And Father isn't always right."

In a flash, Russell pounced on Saxton and pinned him by the chest onto the cold soil.

"Don't talk about Father that way!" He growled.

"I am merely stating a fact." Saxton returned calmly.

Russell dug his paws further into Saxton's flesh. Saxton resisted the urge to wince under the sharp pain.

"You don't know anything."

At that, he smiled. "I believe you mean, 'I don't know *everything,*' in which case you are right: I don't, and neither do you, nor our father, nor our mother, nor our sister."

He clawed the soil with his hind feet and pulled himself upward and over, throwing Russell aside with force. His brother tumbled a few feet away, landing clumsily in a murky puddle. Flynn barely suppressed a giggle, and the sound of it brought Russell to his feet and running at Saxton for a second strike. He stepped aside, allowing Russell to miss him and run past.

"Coward!" Russell barked as he turned around. "Fight me like a real fox!"

He arched his shoulders, pulled his ears back, and swung his tail side to side. Saxton regarded his stance with legs ready to jump and paws ready to block.

Russell made the first move. He leapt to his hind legs and thrashed his claws across Saxton's face. Saxton stood and countered many of Russell's scratches with ones of his own. A few drops of blood flew across the air in faint, bright lines that disappeared into the grass. Despite the injuries, neither withdrew, and they proceeded to run and chase one another through the reeds in an effort to bring the other down. With each attack, they opened their mouths wide, baring long rows of sharp teeth, threatening to bite and never let go.

Flynn backed away from the brawling in fear and dismay. Russell bit Saxton's left wrist, but he countered by clamping onto his neck, positioning his teeth against the jugular. Feeling his brother's delicate pulse just beneath his canines, Saxton knew that any rash move could tear Russell's throat apart and kill him.

Russell must have understood this, for he released Saxton's wrist and remained still, waiting for the teeth against his skin to pierce.

Instead, Saxton shifted his teeth to the scruff of Russell's neck, gripped there, and flipped him over, exposing his vulnerable abdomen. Russell lay on his back, eyes crazed and breath panting.

"The fight was yours! Why didn't you finish it?"

Instead of replying, Saxton gently closed his jaw around Russell's muzzle, silencing him.

"Yield." He ordered. Russell struggled beneath him.

"*Yield*," he repeated, losing his patience.

When his brother refused again, Flynn crept forward and spoke into his ear, "That's enough. No more."

"Fine!" Russell bit out. "I concede."

Saxton released him. His brother refused to look at him.

"Where are Mother and Father?"

"At the den," Flynn replied. "We were just about to have our midday meal. Please join us; I'm sure we have a lot to catch-up on."

Russell snorted, but cleared his throat when Flynn glared. Their sister led them along a winding path until they reached a clearing not unlike the one in which they used to live when they were in Montana.

"Mother!" Flynn called out gleefully. "Mother, we have a surprise for you!"

A pair of big, pointy ears emerged from the den, followed by sharp eyes and a slender face. "What is it, Flynn?" The second vixen asked, but before her daughter could answer, Mother's eyes roamed to the third fox standing to the right of Russell.

"Saxton," Mother said breathlessly.

He timidly moved to greet her. "Hello, Mother."

That was all he needed to say. Mother broke into a run and embraced her lost son with nuzzles and kisses. She rubbed her forehead beneath Saxton's chin, closed her eyes, and sighed.

"You're alive," she said. "You came all this way, and you're *alive*."

The commotion caused Father to emerge from the den as well. Saxton felt his heart skip a beat upon seeing him, and he quelled the disappointment he felt when his father's face expressed no emotion.

He gently extricated himself from his mother's loving grasp and bowed. He would not be cowed.

"Hello, Father."

Father nodded. "Saxton."

This was not the type of reunion Saxton had dreamt of, though he could not say he was surprised. Flynn and Russell nervously stood aside, waiting to see how their brother would be received, when Mother dispelled the tension.

"We were just about to eat," she said. "You must be so hungry. We have duck, rabbit, and several rodents."

"Darling," her mate said in mild warning, "we can't eat all of our stores."

But Mother would have none of it. "Our son has returned. That's just cause for celebration! Besides," she went on. "I'm sure with one more fox, our hunts will be more prosperous."

And so, the fox family unearthed their captures and laid them upon the grass, where they ate in a circle and asked Saxton about his travels. He began his story from when they were first separated, explaining how he had evaded the hunters by digging a hole beneath a hollowed out log, and then tricked an eagle into dropping him into a lake.

"After escaping the eagle, I landed in the water and sprained my ankle. I had trouble walking, and if it hadn't been for Quill, I probably would never have survived."

"Quill?" Mother inquired.

"A crow," Flynn elaborated.

Pointedly ignoring his father's look of disapproval, Saxton continued, "Yes. He's very kind, and quite wise. He offered to help me find all of you, and so, here I am."

"Seems very odd that a crow would go out of his way to help you," Father commented. "Surely he must have named a price."

"No, not at all. He mentioned having free time on his wings, nothing more." Saxton censored the fact that he and Quill had nearly separated. His father, as always, sensed there was more to the story he was telling them.

"Wasn't he afraid that you might eat him?"

He inwardly cringed. "No, I was just a kit when he found me. Later on, we…" He searched around for the right words. "… came to an understanding."

"What understanding was that?" Russell prodded, picking a duck's bone from between his teeth.

"That we're friends."

All at once, Saxton's family ceased eating.

"I know it's hard to believe," he went on, "but it's true. I *like* Quill. I … care about him. I think he feels the same way."

"I can see that," Father said curtly. "You speak more like a crow than you do a fox."

He wasn't quite sure what Father was talking about. "What do you mean?"

Licking his paws clean, Father looked up with a critical eye. "Foxes speak well," he said, "but they do not speak with any emotion or poetry before a stranger. To do so is a sign of weakness."

Embarrassed, Saxton looked away. "I didn't know that."

Mother noticed the shift in her son's mood, and once again decided to smooth any mishandled hairs. "That's perfectly understandable," she mollified. "You've been away all this time."

They finished the rest of their meal, after which Mother requested Flynn and Russell help clean up the bones so as not to attract any roaming enemies. She excused Saxton, which made Russell grumble. Father took this as an opportunity to take Saxton aside.

"You're almost an adult now," he said. "Why did you bother searching for us?"

'Why *wouldn't* I search for you?' Saxton thought. Instead he said, haltingly, "I wanted to be home … and I wanted to know if you were all well and safe."

Father turned to him, sitting down and wrapping his full tail around his feet. "We're all in good health, as you can see. Your brother and sister will be with us until mid-fall. Do you want to stay with us until then?"

His question did not feel like an invitation, and even if it was, it hurt Saxton to understand that he needed one to begin with.

"Maybe," Saxton replied. "I don't know yet."

Father raised his brow and shifted his gaze to the sunset on the horizon. "Well, your mother would be happy to have you."

Saxton could not help himself. "And you?"

Rising from the ground, Father walked toward the den.

"Whatever your choice, I am fine with it. Good night, Saxton."

Watching his father go, Saxton wondered briefly if Quill would have said the same thing.

Chapter Six

Saxton awakened next to his sister, who was still lightly dozing. Stretching his limbs, he climbed out of his family's den to greet the morning.

Mother rose not long after him, and she joined his side, rubbing Saxton's chin with her nose as she sat down. "Look how much you've grown," she said with pride. "Your fur is a lovely shade, too; copper and ginger, just like your father's."

He tried to smile. "Thank you. I'm afraid our similarities seem to end there, though."

"Don't mind your father," she grinned. "He's a very stubborn fox who never lets his guard down. Deep down, I know he's pleased to see you." Her stomach gurgled, and she laughed. "Looks like my stomach knows what time it is. Care to hunt for breakfast with me?"

He smiled again, honestly this time, and followed his mother to the lake for fish. It was a slippery affair that ended with them being soaked to the bone, but the brisk temperature of the water and the adrenaline of catching bass and Northern Pike left them in high spirits.

As they feasted, Father, Flynn, and Russell approached, all of them carrying some sort of rodent in their mouths.

"No fish today?" Mother asked.

"Too cold!" Flynn replied.

"And I hate fish!" Russell added.

They settled on the sand. Father eyed Saxton's catches.

"Two bass, one Northern Pike, one catfish, and one trout. You're quite good at fishing, it seems."

"I caught one for each of us," he said, "in thanks for last night's feast."

Flynn and Mother happily accepted one fish each, Russell declined, and Father seemed uncertain. Eventually, his opportunistic tendencies won out over his pride. He took the pike.

The rest of the day was spent lazily napping beneath the sun with sporadic trips to the lake or the hunting grounds. By afternoon, Saxton became restless and bored.

"Have you explored outside this area of the lake?" He ventured. "The open land seems almost endless. We should look around."

Russell yawned. "We spent days just trying to get here. Why would we waste time walking around when we've already claimed our territory?"

"Aren't you curious?"

"No! Curiosity gets bears stuck in hunters' traps, wolves chased by angry mother cougars, and deer stuck in the mud. I'm perfectly happy here, safe and sound, thank you very much."

Saxton turned to Flynn, who merely shook her head. He tried to think of something else to pass the time with. "What about a story? Have you heard of 'The Tale of the Silver Crane'?"

"Sounds like a waste of time," Russell grumbled.

"Oh, come on, Russ,'" Flynn chided. "It might be interesting. Go on, Saxton. Tell us about it."

He recited the story in the same way Quill had told it to him. He remembered where to place the pregnant pauses and where to raise his voice in excitement. Halfway through the story, Russell rolled off his back and nudged Saxton with his paw, interrupting him.

"That's all a bunch of lies. No bird can fly as high as the moon."

Huffing, Saxton resisted the urge to roll his eyes. "A story doesn't have to be true in order for you to enjoy it."

"Then what's the point?"

"To imagine— to imagine something *greater* than what's out there."

"Oh, ho … that crow of yours really did you in."

"What is that supposed to mean?"

"That you've got a whole bunch of stuff in your head that's useless." Stretching his back, Russell started to leave. "Well, you kits enjoy whatever it is you're enjoying. I'm going to do something useful, like hunt."

"I thought that story was nice," Flynn said, though Saxton detected a small note of humoring. "How does it end?"

Instead of continuing, he stood. "You don't have to be polite, Flynn. It's only a silly fairytale."

That night, it occurred to Saxton that he hadn't seen Quill in nearly two days. Part of him worried that something might have happened to the crow, but the greater part of him sensed that Quill knew where he was and chose to stay out of his way. When he suggested that his family should meet the bird, his father declined and shifted their dinner conversation to techniques in staking out territory. Though Saxton listened, he found himself quickly losing interest.

When the stars began to twinkle and the air grew cooler, he hunted down two rabbits, a toad, and a duck to replenish his family's caches. His mother, of course, was more than delighted, but her disappointment was apparent when Saxton announced:

"Thank you for having me. I must be going now."

"You won't stay?" Mother asked. He shook his head.

"I don't want to change the way things are for you," Saxton explained. "And I think I have changed too much as well."

Mother glanced at her mate. When he did not argue, she courteously accepted her son's answer.

"You're always welcome to visit," she said.

"Please do," Flynn added.

Saxton rubbed shoulders with each of his family members, though he thought it was for the best if he simply bowed before his father. Having said his goodbyes, Saxton set off once more, surprised to find that the home he was looking for was not home at all.

His footsteps came to a halt when he saw a shadow streaking across the pebbles and soil. He turned around.

Russell had followed him.

"Let me guess: you don't want to leave the *Sky Murderer* behind?"

"Stop using those words. They're cruel."

He gave a derisive snort. "They're just words."

"And they are cruel," Saxton insisted, but he realized this battle would be as productive as arguing with a basin wall. "You're right, though. I'd rather stay with Quill if this is how you turned out."

To his amazement, his brother was not incensed. Rather, he looked inquisitive. "You'd rather be dependent on others instead of self-reliant and strong?"

His tone was neutral, and if Saxton were generous, he would say Russell almost sounded concerned. Regardless, he shrugged off the sentiment, thinking that he was hearing what he wanted to hear.

"I would rather think for myself than believe everything I'm told," he retorted.

"Well, that's funny. *You* believe everything that crow of yours tells you. So tell me, how does that make you any different from me?"

"I don't want to be alone in life," he said.

"Our kind is selfish. We have to be." For a moment, it seemed as if Russell wanted to express something that he could not put into words. At a loss, he fell back on old habits. "One day, you'll see ... "You'll see that you'll choose yourself first, and you'll do it to *live*."

Since he did not know what the future would hold for the both of them, Saxton chose not to argue. "Good luck, Russell," he said at length. "I doubt we'll see each other again, but if we do, I'll stay out of your way if you stay out of mine."

He set forth, toward the settlement he and Quill had created not too long ago, when his brother called out:

"Saxton."

He stopped again, and looked back.

"If the crow hurts you," Russell said gravely, "kill him."

When Saxton came upon familiar ground, a voice from above softly asked, "Why didn't you return to them? Your brother, however brusque, has good intentions."

He winced. "You weren't supposed to see that."

"I asked you a question."

Too tired for another lecture, the fox gave in. "*You're* family, Quill. I can't simply leave you."

The crow seemed pained by this. "Not only are they your kind, they are your family by *blood*. I am short on both counts."

"And neither of those things matter, not to me." He frowned and shook his head. "My family ... they are so hollow and cold. Seeing the way they live, it saddens me."

"Don't judge them too harshly, Saxton," Quill said with a measure of caution. "There is no right or wrong way to live. Whatever our choices, we are all simply trying to get by, and there really isn't much difference between us and them, you and me." The crow paused. "Are you sure you do not wish to return to them? I don't want you to regret your decision."

"Unless you want me to leave, I've made my choice. I'm happy to be your friend, your family. It's enough for me."

For a long time, Quill didn't know what to say, or perhaps, how to say it. "And I am happy to be yours."

They climbed up a ridge that faced the North Star. They gazed up at the sky, talking as they pleased.

"Quill, what happens when we die?"

"We go back into the earth."

"What about after?"

The crow raised his brows, but he looked at his companion and answered steadily.

"I don't know, to be honest. No one does. Some creatures think there's nothing after. Others think it's like being asleep without a body. And some think we have spirits that go up into the sky."

"And you?"

"I think we all have souls, but I'm not sure where they go. Immortality, Saxton, is achieved not by avoiding death, but by being remembered after it. Parents leave their legacy behind in the knowledge they share with their children, and the children pass on everything they know to theirs. It's always changing, this knowledge, this wisdom, but it never dies. Crows believe in this wholeheartedly, that's why we share everything we've learned with one another."

Quill's words made Saxton remember something that had bothered him earlier. "My brother called your kind *Sky Murderers*. Where does that name come from?"

Though the moniker was one of those pesky remnants of corvid history, it never ceased to ruffle Quill's feathers. "For the longest time, crows carried with them an air of doom and gloom. I suppose it's because, like vultures, we have a tendency to capitalize on the dead. That's probably why a flock of crows is called a 'murder.'"

"Many animals feed off the dead," Saxton pointed out. "I don't see why your kind needs to be singled out."

He shook his head and sighed. "Crows are everywhere, and so we've developed a dark reputation. The same thing happened to the wolves. You won't meet more honorable creatures, as a promise from a wolf is a promise kept, and yet they're called *'Viscious Howlers'*."

"And *Lonely Thief*?"

"Foxes are solitary creatures. They steal, lie, and cheat at any opportunity for the sake of survival."

Saxton knew Quill wanted to qualify his statement. He prompted him. "But?"

"But for all of your species' acts of selfishness and deceit, only you can choose how you want to lead your life. *Lonely Thief* can describe any number of foxes. Do you want that title to describe you?"

The fox lay on his back and yawned widely.

"No more than I'd like to be called a *Sky Murderer*."

Quill smiled. He playfully poked the fox's belly with his beak. Saxton flinched and recoiled.

"Ow! Hey! What was that for?"

"Your name is Saxton, and you have a soul. Treasure it, for you only have one."

Chapter Seven

"I don't see why you're being so stubborn about this," Saxton said, and the crow withered beneath his scrutiny. "You helped me find my family; I don't know why you won't let me help you get back to yours."

They had been arguing since high noon, and it didn't look like the barbs they traded were about to end any time soon. Their conversation had started amicably enough during breakfast, when Saxton reminisced on the brief, but sweet moments he shared with his mother and sister before everything went south. Talking about Flynn reminded Quill of his sister Fiddle, one faded memory led to another, and before he knew it, he was found himself being pushed toward going home— his *real* home from which he came.

"It's too far," he said. "If you think walking from Montana to North Dakota was a challenge, think again."

"Whatever happened to being optimistic?" Saxton grinned.

Quill shuddered. "After a certain age, optimism becomes one of the most cringe-worthy things in the world."

"I hope you realize you're being a hypocrite."

"Then do humor an old bird by kindly looking the other way."

Realizing he was losing this battle, Saxton finally relented.

The apex of summer had given way to the first tides of fall. Flowers wilted and died, and leaves transformed into hues of yellow, orange, and red before falling off their brittle branches. Saxton and Quill spent their days peacefully sharing meals, conversations, and the occasional stroll along the lake or through the woods. Quill taught Saxton everything he knew, and in return Saxton protected him from danger and provided him with a share of his food.

But just as Quill was growing comfortable, and the first bit of frost made its arrival, the fox ambushed him.

"Aren't you getting bored of this?" he ventured. "You always encouraged me to see more of the world— experience new things. Well, finding Fiddle would do just that, wouldn't it?"

"No, no … Not this again—"

"Oh, stop! You're the one who keeps going on and on and on about how important family is!"

"This is different. This is—"

"Quill," Saxton began, his tone darkening, "you're being ridiculous. Do you really want to regret not seeing your sister again?"

"I never thought you'd actually use *guilt* against me—"

"*Quill.*"

The crow sighed deeply, and Saxton knew his friend well enough to understand he had something important, perhaps difficult, to say. At length, Quill began.

"I didn't exactly leave on good terms. I'm not sure she wants to see me again, much less speak to me."

Saxton blinked. Quill was such a sociable bird; he didn't think it was possible for him to have a bitter relationship with anyone.

"You don't think I felt the same way when we came here? It didn't turn out the way I hoped, but I'm glad I came. It was nice to see Mother and Flynn's smiles." He gazed at his friend, saw that he looked uneasy, and tried to be kind. "Listen, would you at least think about it? I'll let it go if you do."

"Very well. But I make no promises."

Saxton grinned.

That night, when the fox was already dreaming, Quill shifted back and forth on his tree branch, unable to settle thanks to the torrent of thoughts that wouldn't leave him alone. He thought about Fiddle's musical laugh – a laugh that inspired her very name – and realized that he'd like to hear her so happy and playful again.

He wondered what they would talk about. Surely by now she would have had many chicks of her own. And what might her mate be like? Knowing Fiddle, she surely would have beaten some responsible sense into the poor fellow. Maybe she missed him after all. Maybe she would welcome him back.

Had the town in which he grew up changed much since he had left it? He could already imagine the human children bundled in their fall clothes, playing in the leaves and smelling of cinnamon and chocolate. There would be colorful galoshes, yellow duckling raincoats, pumpkins, cornucopias and snowmen adorned with baseball caps and crochet mittens. He hoped none of that had changed.

But he had changed, somehow. He felt that he had, deep in his bones … the old soreness finally beginning to fade away.

He allowed for the possibility that he'd finally forgiven himself.

Quill didn't sleep. By the time the sun rose, he was already sitting by Saxton's nose, eagerly waiting for him to wake-up.

He blinked awake, and with the crow's face being so close, he nearly jumped off the patch of leaves he was curled upon in fright.

"Whoa!" he exclaimed. "What's happening? Why're you up?"

"When you called me family," Quill began, "my life wasn't the same anymore. It's better, bigger, because of you. I've been teaching you everything I've learned from my youth, and you have taught me in return."

Even though he was groggy, Saxton felt his face heat. "Don't be silly—"

"No, it's true," he insisted.

The fox yawned until he thought his jaw would snap and stood. "What are you … You're not making any sense."

"I've been thinking. I don't know why I never saw it before. It's so obvious, really. Maybe that was why things ... happened the way they did. Maybe it was fate."

"What was fate?"

"That everyone's gone." Though Quill's eyes were bright with tears, his voice happy. "Now I understand: you can lose all your ties by blood, every last one, but new family can find you too. Life does not move when one dwells on what is gone. It moves with change and love and forgiveness. I nearly wasted my life, and then you came along."

"Quill."

"I'm ready! Let's go! To Exeter. To New Hampshire. I want so much to see my sister again, and if I can return to the soil that I came from, well … my life would be complete."

It took some time for Saxton to absorb what he was saying. A slow grin crept its way across his lips.

"I *knew* you'd come around!" And his grin turned into a bright smile. "So how do we get there?"

"East, once again," Quill replied. "Although, it might help to consult my friend Cecil along the way. He can probably give us the best route to get there."

After eating breakfast, they headed east, leaving Lake Sakakawea, and it occurred to Saxton they were merely continuing a journey they had already begun when he was only a kit. They took a coiling trail up a rocky mountain, and Saxton remembered to scent mark along the path to make sure they didn't get lost.

"Dear skies!" Quill coughed, "you smell like a skunk!"

"It's not my fault that's what grown foxes smell like to others."

The crow fanned his feathers and held his nose up in disgust. "And what do you smell like to vixens, I wonder?"

"Probably like a bunch of roses."

"Praise mother earth for small miracles. I think I'll fly, if you don't mind."

"Ha ha. Thank you for your unshakable support."

"Don't mention it."

They continued to banter as they went onward, and it cheered Saxton to see his friend in such high and hopeful spirits. Quill talked and talked and talked about the wonderful scents and sounds of the northeast, describing the salty yet creamy aroma of Boston Clam Chowder and the joys of snowshoe hare.

"Hare?"

"Yes, we've had rabbits, but never hare. It won't be long before winter will be in full swing. I'm sure the snowshoes are beginning to come out. Speaking of which, we need to move fast. The crows in Exeter have begun migrating ever since a big winter storm hit years ago. We have a year to get there, but that might not be enough time." His face grew serious. "We could miss her."

"We better find Cecil quick, then," Saxton agreed.

Traveling south toward the badlands, Quill anticipated encountering a flock of vultures despite the chilling weather. At the very least, he thought, a condor might point them in the right direction.

The environment changed drastically. The terrain consisted of beautiful, but deadly formations of land that either had sinking sand or slippery clay that would crumble beneath Saxton's weight. He experienced the unpleasant sensation of nearly falling no less than seven times, and rather than trying his luck any further, he decided to take the long way by traveling at ground level. Quill flew just ahead of him, warning the fox of any terrain that might prove more than just a little challenging. The nights in the badlands were terribly cold, and the harsh wind blew up sand and frost that stung Saxton's eyes and ears.

Luckily, it was not yet cold enough for the frost to stick and become snow. Quill thanked Saxton for putting up with such discomfort for his sake. The fox merely laughed it off and said he 'loved the thrill of sleeping on' – what might as well be – 'a slab of ice.'

They had been on foot for two weeks when, to their great fortune, Saxton saw a flock of vultures feasting upon what appeared to be a deer carcass. The smell was revolting, and there was a billow of flies hovering about. Saxton flicked his ears at the buzzing little pests, and took caution as he and Quill approached.

"Excuse me," said the crow. "By any chance is there a Cecil here?"

One of the vultures took his head out from between the carcass' ribcage.

"Cecil? Why, there are three of them, actually. Common vulture name, very common."

"Yes, well … if there *is* a Cecil in your flock, may we speak with him?"

"Just a second, mate," the vulture craned his neck to his flock. "Oy! Cecil! You got yourself a couple of guests 'ere!"

Three vultures raised their heads, each of them with various degrees of dried blood on their heads and torn meat snared between their beaks.

"Guests?" one asked.

"You mean that foxy one and that dapper little crow ova' there?" Another pointed with his wing.

"Wait just a minute, mate … Quill, is that *you?*"

The last vulture stepped forward, his surprise and delight causing his mouth to drop open. A shredded ligament hung sloppily from his beak.

The crow laughed and stepped forward with his wings outstretched. "Cecil!"

They hopped towards one another before moving into a hearty embrace. The vulture patted Quill briskly on the back, laughing. "Great skies, how long has it been? Two, three years?" He eyed the fox who awkwardly stood aside. "'Ello! Now who's your friend there, mate?"

Trying to be polite by not cringing at the smell of decay, the fox stepped forward and said, "I'm Saxton."

Cecil slurped up the ligament. "Don't mind me now, I'm just havin' lunch. Or what's left of it, at any rate. Fancy a tendon?"

Saxton twitched. "No. Thank you."

"I'll have a bit."

"Then help yourself, Quill! Help yourself! Now, what're you doing around here? I fancy you're up to one of your old adventures again?"

"You can say that," he smiled as he tore at a particularly putrid bit of muscle.

"We were hoping you could give us good directions to Exeter," Saxton added. "I heard it's a long way …"

"Well, that's the understatement of the year, innit?" Cecil turned to Quill. "You planning on going home?"

Despite himself, the crow looked a bit embarrassed. "It's about time, don't you think? I hope I'm well-received."

"Nah, don't worry about all that. I reckon Fiddle would say you're a sight for sore eyes. Honestly, I have to say, good for you." As Quill brightened, Cecil cleared his throat and glanced at Saxton. "Now, if it were me walking on all fours, I'd head toward the road just past the riverbank, and look for a big sign that has 'ninety-four' on it."

The fox frowned. "Ninety-four?"

Cecil moved closer to the fox and crow with his foot balled into a fist and one talon outstretched.

"Looks like this, mate."

Using his sharp nail, he drew on the sand:

"Just keep following the signs that say 'ninety-four' and head east," he went on. "Ninety-four ends in Wisconsin. There'll be a junction. Follow the signs that say 'ninety' after that. This is ninety"

Again, he drew on the sand:

"Ninety ends in Boston. When you get there, go north. You'll hit New Hampshire eventually. Just ask the birds."

Saxton and Quill stared at the figures the vulture had drawn.

"Thank you," Quill said. "This is very helpful, Cecil. Thank you."

"Much obliged, dear friend!" Cecil politely bowed his head. "And it was a pleasure to meet you, Saxton. Good luck, and walk safely!"

74

Chapter Eight
WINTER

Winter fell, and it was cold and bright and bitter. Saxton's fur had grown thicker, protecting him from the blistering winds and the snowflakes that would settle upon his back. Ninety-four, it turned out, was a seemingly endless road that left Saxton and Quill feeling as though they had taken on a fool's errand. Cars and other vehicles would speed past, either drenching them with splashed puddles or choking them with exhaust. Whenever they grew tired or hungry, they abandoned the road to hunt and sleep. And when they were full and rested, Saxton and Quill would return to the road and continue where they left off.

The walking itself was not as bad as the monotony. Ninety-four never truly swerved, bent, or turned. It went in a straight direction and cut through scenery that began to all look the same. With the both of them frequently falling into long gaps of silence, Saxton thought he would go mad with ennui.

It was on the fourth week that Quill decided it was time to make a change in plans. Although they would continue to follow the road, they would no longer walk upon it, and would instead traverse the lands parallel to it.

The change in pace seemed to do the fox and the crow good, for the altering terrain, the sounds of wildlife, and the scent of different trees were refreshing. In the middle of caching the leftovers of a squirrel, Saxton raised his head and froze.

They were being watched.

"Something wrong?" Quill whispered.

"Maybe. Better stay close."

Looking around them, they quickly buried their meals and set off. Saxton couldn't hear or see anything following him, but knew intuitively that he was being hunted. He kept his stance poised and his nose to the air, searching.

His nose found something. It was a pungent smell he had only discovered once before. His heart pounded and drifted up his throat.

"Quill," he rasped. "There's a wolf nearby."

The crow darted his eyes about for a safe place to hide. Out in the open, however, there was nothing but a sea of snow. 'What a terrible mistake,' Quill thought, 'walk where there are no trees, and you have nothing between you and your predator!'

Slush ...

It was the distinct sound of a foot sinking into snow.

Saxton refused to look behind him. He took three steps when he heard it again.

Slush ... slush ...

Four more steps. He paused and glanced at Quill, who looked ready to fly at a moment's notice.

Slush ... slush ... slush ...

The fox exhaled slowly, his breath turning into mist. Another step, and then he broke into a run. Footsteps raced behind him, followed by a chilling howl. Quill cawed and took to the air.

He ran, looking for obstacles to throw in the wolf's path. When he found none, he zigzagged across the field as he had seen deer do when pursued by a cougar. The abrupt changes in direction taxed Saxton's precious energy, but adrenaline kept him moving against his aching muscles and frantic gasps for air.

"Keep running, Saxton!" Quill called. "Don't look back! Run!"

Left, right, left, and right again. Saxton kicked up snow as he ran, but the wolf continued to gain ground and swiped with his paws. He dodged the wolf's attacks and fell into a deep pocket of snow. In a split second, he saw daylight and sky, and then pure white. The snow seemed to be swallowing him up, and clawing at it seemed to only make it worse. Beneath ground, he could feel the vibrations of the wolf slowing down and inspecting the immediate area with his nose. He stilled and waited.

The wolf plodded around, dipping his muzzle into the brittle snow and quickly withdrawing. When the wolf moved in the wrong direction, Saxton heaved forward with all his strength and dragged his body out. The wolf barked and leapt to where he had emerged, but Saxton escaped his grasp like a slippery trout.

It was a close call, but now the wolf was directly behind him. With no cover in sight, Saxton knew the chase would soon be over. He could hear panting, and as he felt the predator's hot breath upon his tail, he closed his eyes. Just then, a furious screech pierced the sky.

"Don't you *dare!*" The crow screamed, diving at the wolf and clawing at his face with his talons.

Saxton swung around and watched in amazement as his friend fended off the large beast with nothing more than feathers and nails. The wolf growled and barked and stood on his haunches, swatting at Quill with his overlarge paws.

"Quill!" The fox shouted. "What are you doing? Get out of there!"

It happened nearly too quickly for Saxton to see, but the wolf swung his paw at the crow's fragile chest and sent him hurtling into a tree trunk. The tree rattled and snow shook off its gnarled branches as Quill fell onto the ice below, unmoving.

Sprinting for his friend, Saxton slid between the wolf's legs and gently picked Quill up with his mouth. Then he changed directions and raced across the powder white.

In the distance, Saxton saw a large, red structure. It was a farm He glanced behind him. The wolf was hot on his heels again.

If all farms were similar, and he hoped they were as his and Quill's lives depended on it, a large fence should surround the perimeter. As the farm came closer and closer into view, Saxton all but let out a victorious laugh.

The farm was enclosed with a barbed-wire fence.

Saxton jumped on a stone, and from there he hopped atop one of the fence's wooden poles and leapt to the other side.

The wolf had been running at full speed. He did not see the barbed wire and plowed straight into it.

CRACK!

One of the poles fell to the ground, and the wolf whimpered as strands of wire entangled around his neck. Out of breath, Saxton watched as the incapacitated wolf kicked his legs and struggled to pull his head out of the wires. This only served to dig the barbs deeper into his throat and draw blood.

He was trapped.

Saxton stepped away from the damaged fence. When the wolf made no attempt to rise and chase him further, he turned on his heels and bounded to the horse stable, carrying his friend and his weakening heart with him.

Slipping inside, he ignored the curious snorts and whinnies of the horses, and laid Quill upon a half-empty sack of oats. Saxton brushed the crow's matted feathers away with his nose to search for injuries. It didn't take him long to find broken ribs.

"Quill ..." Saxton said softly, unable to suppress the tremor in his voice. "Can you hear me?"

"Saxton ... I'm so sorry ..."

His eyelids were drooping. He seemed delirious with pain.

"Stop talking," Saxton said urgently, "Everything will be all right, understand?"

The crow groaned and continued to mumble incoherently. Saxton looked around him, assessing how safe they could possibly be this close to humans, and found a golden mare and her foal watching him intently.

"Don't just stare!" Saxton demanded. "He's in pain. He needs help. Maybe water—"

"Oh, darling," the mare sighed. "It might be too late for that ..."

"Too late for what, Mama?" her little one asked. The mare gently pushed her to the back of the stall so she couldn't see what was happening.

"What went on out there, fox?"

"A wolf chased us down ... hurt my friend." He stared hard at the horse before him. "What do I do? His heart ... I can hear it. It's so weak ..."

For a moment, the horse said nothing. Then she ducked her head behind her stall and came back up with a mouthful of straw. She stretched her neck and dropped the bundle by the fox's feet.

"Lay him there," she instructed. "It's softer than oats. At least he'll be a little comfortable."

"What about water?" Saxton repeated.

"It might hurt him more than help him," she replied. "Anything broken?"

The fox nodded faintly. "Ribs."

Quill started coughing, needlepoints of blood dotting the straw beneath him. The horse shook her head.

"No. No water for him."

"Then what else can I do?" He asked helplessly. "He's going to— he might ..."

The mare closed her eyes. "Keep him company. Keep him warm. Understand?"

Shaking, Saxton nodded and remained at Quill's side, wrapping the crow with his lush tail. He'd whisper some words of encouragement into Quill's ear, though whether he was encouraging himself or his friend, he was uncertain.

The fox waited and waited, hoping for Quill to get better, but instead he only grew worse. Time seemed to grind to a halt, when the crow's eyelids suddenly fluttered open. He looked at Saxton, who sat beside him with a large crease between his brows. What would happen soon, they both knew, was inevitable.

"I lied to you," Quill rasped, "I wasted so much time ... keeping you from them ..."

At first, Saxton thought he was delirious again, when it occurred to him what the crow was talking about.

"Mother's scent ..." he murmured, remembering the day he was certain of where his family was, but decided to defer to Quill's judgment. A string of days and numerous failures in finding his family had followed. It was only when Saxton sought his family on his own that he found them. He swallowed. "Why?"

The crow looked at him, suddenly looking very old. "I didn't want to be forgotten."

He let the words sink in slowly. He should have been angry, but found he wasn't.

"Don't— don't be silly. I'd never—" He tried to laugh, but instead what came out was a bit of a sob. "This ... this is ... it's *my* fault. If I hadn't pushed you—"

This time, the crow snorted and actually smiled.

"Then I would have died with the regret ... the regret of knowing I never even tried to get back home. As it is, I only regret I didn't do it sooner ..."

A racking cough overtook him, and he went silent.

Saxton felt his eyes burn and looked away, but he could still hear uneven breathing. He couldn't stop himself from saying:

"You shouldn't have saved me."

Quill gazed at him. "Why not? You're my friend. You're my family. You're my *son.* Why *wouldn't* I?"

He couldn't think of an answer for that, not unless the word 'wouldn't' had been the word 'shouldn't.'

"Does it hurt?" Saxton asked instead.

The crow didn't even blink. "Slow deaths always do. But at least I have my dignity … I'm not out there, wailing and alone, thanks to you."

"Don't— don't thank me for anything."

Quill regarded him for a moment. "You have so much kindness in your heart … more than you realize … I wish you would be … more kind to yourself."

Saxton's mouth snapped shut. He didn't want to tire his friend by arguing, so he ceased saying anything more and lay his head down by Quill's side. When night came, he fell into a fitful sleep.

Quill remained awake, savoring the feel of night air that blew in between the wooden planks of the stables and the smell of horses and hay. He didn't make it, he realized; he didn't make it to Exeter, but perhaps that didn't matter. Perhaps home turned out to be somewhere else.

He looked at Saxton: a most unique fox with the whole world now waiting before him; a fox who filled his chest with love and pride. With barely any strength left to speak, Quill whispered the last of his wisdom through sharp, ragged breaths. Saxton roused, his mind foggy and in between dreaming and wakefulness. His ears twitched as Quill spoke:

"Open your heart to others.

Never fear journeying long and far.

Live with truth and humility."

And the last words Quill uttered before everything would change were thus:

"The world is unkind, but you needn't live and die alone. You are Saxton, and you have a soul."

PART II

Chapter Nine

Saxton sniffed at the unmoving body and stared at the black eyes that no longer sparkled. He sat down, and he wailed.

It was a long, awful sound that recalled an infant's scream. It made the horses neigh and the birds in the rafters flutter about, but the fox could not stop himself. He continued to wail and sob and whimper for hours until he was too tired to do anything more.

He fell asleep again.

Something soft and warm was nudging him against his side. He opened one eye to find the golden mare touching him gently with her nose.

"You best take care of him now," she said, tipping her chin to the stable doors. "If you don't bury him, either Mr. Fitzgerald will throw him out with the garbage, or the hounds will eat him up."

Saxton's stomach churned at the thought, but he picked up Quill. He was astonished with how stiff and cold his friend was— so unlike what he used to be. Pushing the door open, he slid outside and explored the farm yard. He found a thick evergreen, tall and beautiful, standing all by itself in the white of winter.

He dug a hole at the foot of the tree, digging as deep as he could to prevent other creatures from finding the body. Laying Quill to rest at the bottom, he took a single stray feather as a memento before burying him.

That was it. Saxton didn't know what to do next. He lay on his belly by the gravesite and mulled over the feather he held between his paws.

Before he knew it, it grew too cold to stay outside any longer. He returned to the stables with the feather between his teeth.

"I'm sorry you lost your companion," said the mare.

He set the feather down. "He was my friend."

"You look tired and thin," she commented. "You should eat."

The fox sighed. "I'm not hungry."

"I doubt your friend would appreciate you starving on his account." She paused. "Might I offer some advice, darling?"

He shrugged, and she took that as a 'yes.'

"You might feel better if you say goodbye to your friend properly." Seeing that Saxton was about to interrupt her, the mare rushed the rest of what she had to say. "Maybe you can fulfill your friend's final wish, whatever it might be."

The fox looked away, wounded. "What's your name?"

"Twenty-Four Karat Gold," she replied with a hint of pride. "Used to be a racehorse back in the day, but I've earned my keep and now I'm retired. You can call me Goldie for short." Turning to her side, she nosed her daughter's forehead. "And this is Diamond Dust."

Saxton smiled warily at the little quarter horse, awkward but lovely on her still too-long legs. "Very pretty, just like your mother."

"What's your name?" asked the foal.

"Saxton," he answered. Then, thinking of Quill, he remembered his manners. "Thank you for letting us – *me* – stay here. Is there any way I can return the kindness?"

Goldie looked at him in surprise. "You're certainly polite for a fox, honey. But really, you don't need to worry about us."

"I'm not like other foxes," he said absently. "Are you sure there isn't anything I can do for you? I'd feel better if there were."

The mare glanced at her foal. "Well, I'll tell you what, why don't you bring me and my daughter some extra blankets without causing a ruckus?"

"Sure," He agreed. "What does a blanket look like?"

Goldie turned around to give the fox a better view of the thick cloth draped over her back. "Looks exactly like this. Mr. Fitzgerald keeps a bunch of extras in the tool shed. Word is there'll be a cold snap today, and I'd rather not have my daughter and I catch pneumonia."

"All right. Where's the tool shed?"

The two horses directed him to the small, wooden structure standing to the left of the barn. Saxton stealthily crossed the yard, careful to not draw attention from the chickens and the dogs. Once he reached it, he found that the door was locked. Walking around it, he found a gap between two of the shed's wooden planks and squeezed inside.

It was dark and musty, and filled with all sorts of sharp objects Saxton didn't recognize. Glancing around, he noticed a stack of blankets sitting on the very top shelf.

"Of course it would be that high," he sighed.

Climbing the unsteady shelves, he grabbed one of the blankets by its corner with his teeth and pulled. All the blankets, and Saxton, fell to the ground.

He shook his head, but wasted no time grabbing one of the blankets and pulling it through the gap in the wall. Since the blankets were large and heavy, he would have to make two trips.

The mare was surprised by the fox's swift return. He came in through the stable doors, turned around, and dragged the blanket inside. The blanket was covered with snow and dirt, but otherwise appeared fine.

"It's just one," Saxton said, panting as he crossed the threshold. "I have to go back for the other."

He pulled the blanket to Diamond Dust, and Goldie lowered her long neck to pick it up and cover her filly.

"I'm impressed. How'd you get inside?"

Saxton shrugged. "I have my ways."

He then went out to retrieve the mare's blanket as promised.

When he returned once again successful, the mare kneeled down and allowed the fox to pull the blanket over her. "Thank you, Mr. Fox. While you were out, I got you a bit of something to eat."

"I'm not hungry," Saxton repeated, "but I could do with some water."

Goldie grinned. "Come with me."

She led Saxton to her stall, where a trough of water was mounted along the wall. She gestured to it, tilting her head.

"Help yourself."

He jumped up the rectangular bundles of hay, and lapped greedily at the water until he heard something cumbersome dragging along the floor. Hopping down, Saxton cocked his head to the side and watched as Goldie pulled forth a giant bag with a dog's face printed upon its surface. Small, brown pellets fell to the ground when she tore the bag open with her teeth.

"Eat. Your friend would want you to take care of yourself, you know."

He still had no appetite, but he humored the mare and began nibbling. The pellets were crunchy and dry, but they were palatable enough and smelled of beef and lamb.

"What's this?"

"Dog kibble. I took one of these from the barn while you were in the shed." Saxton stopped chewing and stared at her anxiously. She only chuckled. "Don't worry. We have bags and bags of these. I doubt anyone will notice one going missing."

"Thank you."

"Don't mention it," Goldie smiled. "You were right, though. You certainly are different."

They enjoyed one another's company as the day wore on, the mare doing her best to soothe the fox's troubles with light conversation. When night fell and the cold snap hit, Mr. Fitzgerald, the farmer, came to seal the stables. Saxton hid within a pile of hay.

"Hey, there, Goldie. Hope you sleep tight tonight." Mr. Fitzgerald stroked the mare's mane and noticed the second blanket. "Huh, that's funny. Don't remember getting another one of these for ya." He looked at the other horses. "Better get more for the others."

He went out and returned with more blankets in his arms.

"Good lord, the wind's a mighty beast this year!" he exclaimed. "Knocked the blankets clear off the shelves."

The farmer covered each of his horses, making sure they all had two. Before he left, he locked the stable doors.

Saxton reemerged when the farmer was gone.

"He seems like a good man," he commented.

"He is," Goldie affirmed. "A little absentminded sometimes, but he means well. His wife and children are quite charming too."

They tried to sleep through the shrieking wind that pounded against the doors. Beneath the wind, they heard something much more eerie: the low song of a wolf's howl.

"He's certainly making a lot of noise, isn't he?" Goldie whispered. "If he keeps that up, Mr. Fitzgerald'll notice and it'll be curtains for him."

"Mommy, what does 'curtains' mean?"

"It means the farmer will put him to sleep for a long, long time."

Saxton stood and pressed his right ear against one of the stable walls. The howls were desperate, and he could tell that the wolf was hurting his own vocal chords calling for help. Just hearing him alone and in pain made his stomach churn. He wanted it to stop.

He began digging a hole along the wall.

"What are you doing?" Goldie inquired.

"Going outside."

"You're joking."

He didn't respond. Once his tunnel was complete, he slipped into it and he turned to the mare, "I'll be back."

"Well, all right," she snorted. "Just don't do anything stupid, darling."

Outside, Saxton squeezed his eyes shut and lowered his head. The wind was so unforgiving, it almost sent him sailing backwards. Nevertheless, he followed the wolf's voice, moving closer and closer to the fence with each stiff step. It was a terrible walk, but he almost wished it lasted longer, for now he was face to face with the very creature that had tried to end his life, but took Quill's instead. The wolf looked up at him. He had only one, yellow eye. The left one was missing and had scar tissue all over it. His left ear was torn in half and in similar shape.

"I should let you die here," Saxton said. "An eye for an eye, maybe. Although, it looks like you only have one left."

The wolf snarled, saliva dripping down the corner of his mouth and melting the snow. "If you want to laugh in my face, get it over with and leave me alone, *Lonely Thief.*"

But there was no humor in Saxton's eyes, none at all.

"There's nothing to laugh about. You killed my friend yesterday."

"What're you talking about? I wouldn't've gone after you if you weren't alone—"

"I *wasn't* alone!" He snapped.

The wolf stared at him with genuine confusion, which only angered the fox further.

"You don't remember? You honestly don't remember?"

"I'm gonna die," the wolf sighed. "What more do you want from me?"

Saxton looked at the wolf with rage so hot he thought he might catch fire. But the blood that collared the wolf's neck caught his attention, along with his frayed breaths and erratic heartbeats, and he knew all too well the pain of a slow death. Calming himself, he breathed through his nose and closed his eyes.

"Where is your pack? You've been howling for help for a long time now."

"Why do you care?" the wolf snarled.

"I *don't*," he said hotly, "but Quill would want me to."

The wolf frowned, and then it hit him. "The crow?"

Ignoring him, Saxton noted the wolf's wounds. "That looks painful."

"Thank you for the reminder," he groused, tugging at the barbed wire around his neck. "I was beginning to forget."

"I meant your face," the fox corrected. "What happened to it?"

The wolf had the audacity to smile and bare his fangs. "Run in with a bear," he bragged. "I left him a memento to remember me by too. Keep talking and I'll give you the same."

But Saxton was unimpressed. "You're hardly in any position to do so. Continue to twist like that, and you'll entangle yourself further. Stop moving. You'll die."

"As if I have a choice."

Coming closer, Saxton inspected the web of wires. "Perhaps I can help …"

At that, the wolf gaped at him. "I tried to *eat* you, then you accused me of killing your *friend*, and now you want to *help* me? Do you have squirrels nesting in your ears?!"

"You did kill my friend. And no, I don't *want* to help you. Unfortunately, my friend wouldn't want you to die like this …"

For a moment, the wolf fell silent. "Why?"

Saxton fought back the tears he felt, determined to stay angry. "Because that's who Quill was."

In a flash, he remembered the day he and the crow first met. He remembered how scared he was, how desperate and frustrated and helpless. The wolf looked no different.

"So ... do you want my help or not?"

The wolf's face softened. Saxton noticed the change.

"I was only after you. I didn't mean to hurt your friend … to kill him … It was an accident. Please … get me out of here. I don't want to die."

The fox turned to look at him. He studied the wolf's face, which seemed grave with sincerity.

"I'll be back."

Dashing to the tool shed, Saxton squeezed inside and perused the tools for anything useful. Most of the items, which consisted of strange wooden sticks that ended with a row of metal teeth or a single sharp blade, were far too large and heavy for Saxton to carry. He would need something small, but strong enough to cut through wire.

At the bottom of the shelf, he investigated the small rectangular compartments that had wooden, mushroom-shaped knobs growing sideways on their flat surface. He pulled on one of the knobs with his teeth, revealing what appeared to be a square-shaped nest, and he found an assortment of tools he couldn't begin to imagine what humans used for within it.

"This won't do," he groaned, realizing he was in over his head.

He squeezed through the gap again and ran to the stable. There, he consulted with Goldie.

"Goldie, what do humans use to cut something strong?"

"Well, that depends," the horse replied. "Are we talking about paper? Rope? Wire?"

"Wire."

"Wire, huh? I suppose shears of some sort will do."

"What do shears look like?

Goldie paused, sensing something was afoot. "Now, wait a minute, darling. You're not planning to cut Mr. *Viscious Howler* free, are you?"

"I told him I would."

She whinnied in dismay. "Oh, no. Honey, please tell me you're pulling my reins!"

"If I don't free him," the fox explained, "he'll die an avoidable death, and without any dignity."

"And what about us? Did you think that part through?"

"He's injured. At this point, I'd say he's fairly harmless.

The mare laughed. "Harmless? Saxton, you are the most naive fox I've ever met."

"I could kill him," Saxton suggested darkly. "I could snap a chicken's neck and leave a blood trail straight to him. The farmer would shoot him dead despite the storm. You don't think that crossed my mind?"

Her lips formed a thin line. "Grim as that sounds, that would solve more than one problem."

"Would it? I don't think Quill would agree."

"He meant that much to you, did he?" She snorted, blowing several stray strands of hair out her eyes, and relented. "If that wolf kills any of the farm animals, I'm holding you responsible."

"Name your price."

"That's easy: your life." When she was met with silence, Goldie elaborated with, "If even a single egg gets crushed because of the wolf, I will likewise crush your head with my hoof. And don't think I can't track you down and keep up with you. Just because I don't run no more don't mean I lost my legs. Am I clear?"

Saxton felt his breath catch, but steeled himself. "Done. Now, what do shears look like and how do they work?"

Minutes later, Saxton returned to the wolf. The wolf eyed him, unsurprised the fox came back without help. "Not as easy as you thought it would be, huh?"

Saxton ignored him. "Before I release you, I need you to make a promise."

"Anything."

"Promise me not to hurt any of the animals on the farm, and that you will never hunt, maim or otherwise harm another fox or crow ever again."

At first, the wolf said nothing, allowing the weight of the fox's words to sink in.

"I haven't eaten in days. I'm not so sure I'll be able to control myself."

"If you don't," replied the fox, "the horse will snuff out my life with one footstep. Not a very honorable way to repay a good turn, is it?"

"I understand." Yet the wolf couldn't help but frown. "But what I don't understand is you. Why are you doing this?"

"Because ... I believe in choices, and I choose to be kind."

The wolf considered his words.

"Then ..." he said slowly, "I choose to honor your wishes."

Pleased with the wolf's response, Saxton darted for the shed. Once inside, he rummaged through all the drawers until he found two knives that were attached to one another, and when their handles were compressed, their curved blades would close together like a bird's beak. Carefully taking one of the shears' handles into his mouth, Saxton sprinted to the fence. There, he crawled over the wolf's back and slipped one of the tangle wires between the shear's blades. Holding the lower handle down with his paws, Saxton closed his mouth around the upper handle and forced it down with his teeth.

TING!

A wire snapped, and the hold on the wolf's neck loosened. Saxton moved around to find another wire.

TING!

And then another.

TING!

One more snip and the wolf would be free.

TING!

The wolf rose to his feet. Dried blood crusted around his throat, and more blood stained the snow. The pain stung, but the wolf was nonetheless relieved. He stood with his back arched over and his tail curled between his legs.

90

"Thank you," he whispered. His lips twitched, as if he wanted to say more, but he had nothing to add.

"Don't thank me," Saxton replied. "Thank my friend."

Chapter Ten

Saxton watched as the wolf walked away, purposely distancing himself from the farm to prevent any temptation. Once the wolf disappeared into the vast, snow blanketed field, Saxton reentered the stables and shook his thick coat.

"Well?" Goldie asked.

"He's gone now. You and everyone here are safe."

She shook her head in disbelief. "A merciful fox and a grateful wolf? Next thing you know, chickens will be the smartest birds on earth."

"I wouldn't go that far," Saxton chuckled as he settled himself atop a bag of horse feed. Goldie smiled at him from her stall.

"To be honest, I'm relieved he kept his word. Would've pained me to step on you."

Exhausted but growing comfortable in the stable's warmth, Saxton closed his eyes with a yawn. "Goldie, believe me … that would have pained me even more."

She laughed, in that bright, cheerful way that horses do.

The following morning, the cold snap eased and Saxton filled his stomach with kibble before bidding Goldie and Diamond Dust farewell. Goldie remarked that despite his short stay, Saxton would be missed.

"Where are you going?" she asked.

"To Exeter," he replied, and then he laid his paw upon Quill's feather. "I'm taking Quill home, so he can rest the way he wanted."

The two horses peeked out of the stable as Saxton crossed the farm yard and slipped under the fence, carrying Quill's feather between his teeth. When a soft wind blew, it erased Saxton's footprints from the ground until there was not a trace of them to be seen. It was as if the fox had never been there at all.

Trotting at a leisurely pace, Saxton would stop on occasion to let his feet rest and set down the feather. Though the feather weighed nearly nothing, continuously carrying it seemed to make it heavier. The feather had grown weather worn and dirty, and Saxton would force himself to ignore the bitter taste of dirt and melted ice each time he picked it up and resumed his journey.

It wasn't until the next day that Saxton sensed that he was, yet again, being watched. While the stare aimed at his back didn't feel predatory, it was enough to make the fox uneasy. He stumbled upon a herd of deer and decided resting near so many pairs of eyes would serve him well, provided he hid his presence from them.

Nestled against a rock, he nearly nodded off, but grew alert when a new scent entered the air. Blinking his eyes open, Saxton sat up and gazed in the direction that his nose guided him. There was a foul, fishy smell, the kind of smell that recalled the scent of bobcats and lynxes. He shifted his ears around until he heard a low, throaty rumble.

A buck paused in the middle of his grazing and lifted his head. He moved his front feet back and forth anxiously, as if he were debating between fleeing and preventing panic from overtaking the rest of the herd. There was the faint sound of big feet pressing down on the snow. From the corner of his eye, Saxton saw a wisp of warm breath.

The buck would not wait any longer. He leapt away, hollering: "Cougar! Cougar in the field! Cougar!"

Like thunder clapping, the herd took off after the lead buck. Saxton ran astride them to avoid being trampled and escape the danger he hadn't yet seen. But just as he jumped over a large boulder, the feather fell from his grasp, caught in the wind, and flew back.

Horrified, Saxton back flipped from the stone and ran against the relentless waves of deer. Their hooves plodded straight through the snow and pierced the hardened mud. The fox dodged their legs, but fell and tripped and rolled over as the stampede continued on.

The feather landed several yards away, but was kicked up once more when a young doe ran with the cougar just behind her tail. Determined to retrieve it, Saxton changed directions and flitted across the field. Grabbing the feather with his teeth, his chest seized when he looked up and saw a stag's front hooves looming over him.

Before Saxton could react, something big and powerful grabbed him by the scruff of his neck, snatching him to safety in the nick of time. The fox looked back and watched as the buck stomped over where he had been standing only seconds before. When they were a safe distance away, the grip around his neck loosened, and the fox fell to the ground in a heap. Shaking his head, Saxton did not expect to find the one-eyed wolf standing before him. The wolf looked more than a little peeved.

"You ran against a stampede for a *feather?*"

"What business is it of yours?" Saxton snarled.

The wolf snorted.

"Seeing as I saved you from being turned into a footprint on the ground, I say a *lot.*"

"Did saving me bring my friend back?" Saxton retorted, and the wolf winced. "No? Then do me the favor of shutting your mouth and leaving me be. My life will never be the same again, and it's all because of you."

The fox took his leave, but when the wolf followed him, Saxton grimaced. "Why are you still following me?"

"I might have saved your life, but I haven't fixed it."

"You cannot. Fix. This." he replied through gritted teeth.

"I can try. At the least, I can protect you until your life gets better, and maybe then you can forgive me."

Exasperated, Saxton tried trotting faster. "Don't you have your own pack to care for?"

The wolf seemed to flinch, but he quickly put on his best game face before Saxton noticed. "I'm on the drift," he replied. "But I still have my honor code as a wolf, and I swear to follow it."

The fox wasn't sure if he liked the sound of that.

"Wolves have unrealistic expectations."

"No, we just have high ones." The wolf eyed the crow's feather in Saxton's possession and grew serious. "That was his, wasn't it?"

"No, I like collecting feathers for *fun.*"

The fox meant his words to come out biting, but instead his voiced cracked, dulling the sting.

"The things you do for him …" the wolf began, "I'm breathing because of them. I'm sorry. I mean it, truly."

Saxton lowered his head, unable to look at the wolf. It hadn't been easy to free him, but it was even harder to hear him remorseful.

"Please, please just … go away. I don't want to look at you. Understand? You can't make anything better. Not ever."

94

The wolf hesitated, shifting his weight from side to side. "If that's what you want."

Turning away, he abandoned the fox as requested and vanished into the shadows of the trees. Saxton waited a moment to be sure he was gone for good before continuing on his way.

The back of his mind, however, wouldn't leave him alone. After a few days, he couldn't help feeling as though he made the wrong decision. But Saxton held onto his anger, his outrage, and convinced himself that he had done well enough by Quill in sparing the wolf's life.

Hungry, Saxton ferreted out several field mice from the snow. The mice were more skin and bone than meat, no thanks to the winter, but they quelled the fox's stomach pains for the time being.

As Saxton settled beneath a barren tree not far from a pond, he nearly jumped back in surprise at the sight of the wolf once again crossing his path. Once he realized the wolf was minding his own business, Saxton watched with mild interest as the wolf tried and failed to capture even a single waterfowl. Observing him, the fox realized it was not unlike watching his younger self struggling to hunt rabbit and failing over and over again until Quill was bored to sleep.

He grinned a little, almost chuckling to himself, and as he continued to watch the wolf's movements. He noted that the wolf's hunting would have been more successful if he corrected his posture and relaxed his constantly curled-in tail.

The wolf nearly snatched one goose by the tip of her wings when he took one too many steps forward and went sliding across the ice on his belly, his legs outstretched and his body spinning like a pinwheel. The surrounding birds squawked with glee before taking flight. One of the geese left a fresh parting gift on the wolf's nose. It hit him with a stinking splat.

It was too much. And though he knew it was a cruel thing to do, he tumbled forward and burst out laughing.

He laughed and laughed, tears running down the corners of his eyes. Unable to breathe, the fox rolled side to side until he was on his back, shaking with amusement.

The wolf rose to his feet, wobbling, and pawed his muzzle.

"Ha. Ha. Yes, let's all laugh at the wolf with bird scat on his face!"

Saxton continued to chuckle as he turned and went on his way, thrilled to have seen the wolf humiliated and to be at no fault for it. It was a nasty feeling, a spiteful feeling, but he held onto it just a bit longer because it made him a little less bitter.

He didn't quite realize how quiet the world could be without Quill at his side, nattering away about this or that. It was annoying at times, but he found he missed the cadences of Quill's voice – a warm comfort in the wind. Some nights, when Saxton dwelled too much on his death, he would enter a vicious cycle of crying and wallowing that exhausted him until he was angry. And when he was angry, he couldn't stand to be angry at himself, so he pooled all of his hatred and focused it on the wolf instead.

Saxton frequently reimagined the wolf making a fool of himself chasing geese, and it made him laugh until he grew bored with it. He then imagined the wolf falling through ice and freezing to death. It's a terrible thing to wish upon anyone, and Quill would scold him for it surely, but thinking about it didn't give Saxton the time to regret.

He traveled miles this way, not really paying attention to the world around him. Somehow, it made the long walk easier.

A low, rumbling sound pulled him out of his daydreaming. It shook the earth just a little, and caused some snow to drop off the branches. He wondered for a moment if the earth was stretching or yawning, as Quill said it sometimes did, when he caught sight of a large, brown bear moaning in agony.

The bear lay beside a naked bush, the foot of his right hind leg twisted abnormally between the teeth of a hunter's trap. The fox cautiously stepped forward. The bear was not quite a cub, but not quite an adolescent either. He growled at Saxton as he set down Quill's feather and approached.

"Easy," Saxton said in soothing tones. "I mean no harm. How long have you been here like this?"

The bear groaned and sniffed. "Three days. I'm– I'm lost. I don't know where Mama is."

Saxton stepped around the bear's paw, scrutinizing the metal device. "I recognize this trap," he said. "If you give me a moment, I might be able to free you."

"Don't do it."

Startled, he turned and saw the one-eyed wolf standing a safe distance away. Saxton growled, peeved that the wolf had followed him once again despite his wishes.

"You can't trust him," the wolf went on. "You heard what he said, no food for *three* days. He'll eat you the first chance he gets."

96

Saxton rolled his eyes.

"I seem to recall someone in a similar position, wolf."

"Don't be cocky, fox. You were lucky I am a keeper of my word. But *him* ..." he stared at the bear and revealed his fangs. "... the most dangerous beast alive, no you can't trust him."

The bear looked at Saxton, his eyes big and pleading. "Please, Mr. Fox, don't listen to him! I wanna go home! I wanna find Mama!

"Liar!" growled the wolf.

"Stop it!" Saxton snapped. "That's enough! I can't treat you one way and him another. It wouldn't be fair!"

"Life isn't fair!"

"Then we must try and make it just!" He turned to the bear. "Give me your foot."

The bear obeyed him and the chains rattled as he moved his leg. Saxton's eyes roamed the device until they found the release lever Quill had shown him long ago. He wiped off the snow and pressed his paws against the lever, putting all of his weight onto it. The leg trap sprung open, revealing jagged silver teeth, covered in blood. The bear roared in pain, then swung his front paws, knocking Saxton to his side. Saxton shook his head and gaped at the bear, dazed and betrayed.

"What are you doing? I *freed* you!"

"But I'm hungry!"

He raised a paw, armed with nails the size of cougar's teeth, and swung.

The wolf leapt forward and bit the bear hard on his injured foot. The bear reared backwards, roaring. Saxton dashed out of harm's way, but the bear lumbered forward, throwing the wolf off him as if he were nothing but a fly.

"Go!" yelled the wolf, "Head for the mountains!"

Dumbstruck, Saxton backed away slowly until his brain finally snapped to attention and told him to snatch up his feather and sprint for the mountainside. He glanced behind him as he ran, watching as the wolf snapped his jaws ineffectually before making an escape himself.

The wolf stumbled as he ran, but he managed to catch up alongside him, and together they ascended the mountain path with the bear not too far behind.

But the path they had taken lead to a cliff with a drop no one could survive. The wolf looked around until he found a small crevice between a pair of boulders.

"Hide in there!"

Saxton did as he was told and squeezed inside, dropping the feather to his side.

"What about you?"

"Don't worry about me. Just stay in there!"

He turned around in time to catch the sight of the bear snagging the wolf's legs and upending him. The wolf landed hard on his back with a cloud of snow. He tried to scurry away, but the bear laid his paw on his chest, pinning him to the ground.

Saxton heard his heartbeat pounding between his ears. He watched, knowing the wolf would die if he did nothing.

The fox bolted out of his hiding place, feeling every bit the fool his father said he was. He jumped on the bear's back, climbed onto his shoulders, and pulled as hard as he could on one of the ears with his teeth.

The bear's growl thundered through the air, and he raised his arms to swat the fox off him.

The sudden turn caused the bear to lose his footing. His feet slid against loose gravel and ice, taking him right over the cliff side. His weight dragged him down, and Saxton with him, until he was hanging off the edge by his front paws.

Saxton held on for dear life, forcing himself to look away from the fall below. He dug his nails into the bear's fur and pulled himself up as the bear continued to slide down.

He jumped off the bear and onto solid ground.

He didn't mean to kick the bear in the face.

He didn't mean to make the bear lose his hold and his life.

He watched in horror as the bear plummeted, with a haunting moan, until he disappeared from sight altogether.

The sound he made hitting the rocky canyon below was like a bunch of shattering eggshells.

"TARLO!" A voice screamed at the top of her lungs.

That name sent ice creeping through Saxton's veins. He looked to where the voice had come from, and saw mother bear Napowsa standing on another cliff high above them.

"Tarlo!" She screamed again. "*TARLO!*"

Napowsa scrambled down the mountainside, going as fast as she could without risking her own life. Pebbles and rocks rolled down in her wake. The click-clack noises they made barely masked her sobs. Saxton felt sick to his stomach.

He grabbed Quill's feather from in between the boulders and made to follow her.

"Hey!" the wolf called. "Where're you goin'? You out of your mind?"

But he ran with him anyway.

Chapter Eleven

They reached the bottom of the canyon and found Napowsa hunched over Tarlo's unmoving and unrecognizable body. She heaved cries so loud that the birds were startled from their trees and took to the air in a fright. There was dark blood pooling around Tarlo's head.

Saxton tried not to look into those unseeing eyes.

He dropped his feather and gently patted it instead.

"Napowsa?" he whispered.

Napowsa's head jerked up, her eyes red and nearly as dead as her son's "You!" she bellowed. "I saw what you did! You killed him! You killed my son!"

"I— I didn't mean to," he croaked, his words tripping over themselves in his throat as though he had hiccups. "I was trying ... I was trying to help ..."

"I don't believe you!" she seethed, spittle flying out of her mouth. "You killed him! You took him away from me!"

"No, no that's not ..."

"You're walking dead, *Lonely Thief!*" Napowsa shouted, growing even more hysterical. "I'm going to get you! I'm going to get you and rip you apart limb by limb until you beg me to rip your heart out and *end* you!"

Saxton's feet were trembling, numb and on fire, when the wolf nudged him gently on the shoulder with his cold nose.

"She's not in her right mind," he said. "Leave her be. She needs to be alone."

The wolf stepped away from the scene, beckoning Saxton to follow with a cock of his head to the side.

He didn't want to leave her like this, but the wolf had proven right more than once already. He followed him out of the canyon, but that didn't stop him from hearing Napowsa's tearful song.

"Little cub, little cub, who loves you most?
No one, but Mama Bear with her grizzly coat"

"I knew her," Saxton explained once they were a safe distance away and settled on a clearing of snow surrounded by naked trees. "Not well, but I knew her. We crossed paths. I remember thinking how lucky Tarlo was to have a mother like her."

"She's dangerous," the wolf said coldly.

"But a good mother."

"I told you, you should have left him be."

"Maybe," but he shook his head. "But when I was a kit, I was lost too. I didn't have anyone until Quill came along."

"Yeah? Well, sometimes you just gotta watch out for yourself. You won't be much good to anyone if you're dead."

"I would be dead if it weren't for Quill," Saxton couldn't help but snap.

The wolf grinned, but there was no humor in it. "Easy, fox. I'm not your enemy. "Not anymore anyway ... I want to make things right, and I can tell by that look on your face I haven't done that yet. Besides, even if you don't want my help, I owe Quill too. I'm not wrong, am I?"

Saxton pulled the feather closer to his chest. He honestly couldn't fathom walking side-by-side with this wolf any more than he already had. He would have to clutch his resentment every day just to keep his peace of mind.

'There are two parts to forgiveness,' Quill had once told him. 'Someone can apologize and mean it, but that is only half of the process. The one who was slighted, the one who was hurt, must let his unhappiness go in turn. That is why it is easier to ask for forgiveness than it is to give it.'

Saxton groaned and wondered, not for the first time, why doing the right thing was always so annoying and difficult. Just as he opened his mouth to reply, the wolf's stomach gurgled.

"Come on," the fox huffed. "We better eat, and I've got an idea."

The wolf blinked. "You're letting me come with you?"

"Apparently."

'Well,' he thought, 'I can try to forgive him, but I don't have to like him.' He picked up the feather and led the wolf through a nearby thicket. After patrolling the surrounding area, they stumbled upon a small family of deer peeling bark off tree trunks and feasting upon them. There were two young bucks, a doe, a female fawn, and an older buck that appeared to be the doe's mate.

"I atched yer hun-ing echnique ..." Saxton mumbled as he set down Quill's feather and placed a small stone atop it. "Chasing those geese around might've worked if you were in a pack, but you're by yourself. You need to stalk your prey so they won't realize you're there until it's too late."

"Are you actually giving me a hunting lesson?" The wolf asked hotly.

"Do you want to eat or not?" Saxton snipped back.

The wolf's stomach complained again.

"Fine. What do you suggest I do?"

"Keep your head low to the ground. Use the trees and stones to your advantage. Pick the weakest of the herd. It will save you time and energy, and you'll be less likely to get hurt." Saxton checked the wolf's posture. "And stop hunching your back over with your tail between your legs. You can't run like that."

"I don't hunt big game by myself," the wolf said, already uncomfortable "That's not how it works."

"Then how does it work?"

"There's at least one pack member who cuts off the path of the target ... and there's usually another member who surveys the land and decides where the cut should be."

"I'll do it, then."

"*You?*"

"Do we have a *choice?*"

"You almost died today. And you almost died getting pulverized seven days ago. You sure you want to press your luck?"

"Well, I guess you're just going to have to save me again if that happens. You *did* say you would."

The wolf rounded on him, his face pinched.

"Y'know, you're really stuck-up."

The fox, despite being so small, rounded on him in return.

"I'm not stuck-up. I'm just *right*."

They stared at one another for a long time, seeing who would back down first, when both of their stomachs grumbled.

"That answers that. I'll look over the area and come back."

While Saxton set off, the wolf studied his prey. The fawn would be too small to satisfy both himself and the fox, and her parents were too big to risk. He focused his attention on the two adolescent bucks grazing several feet away. One of them was smaller than the other, and his antlers were not yet as developed. He thought about what Saxton said and made his choice.

"There's a rocky ridge southwest from here," Saxton whispered upon return. "The deer will probably try to escape through there and use their jumps to their advantage. You drive your target in that direction. I'll cut him off there." Saxton frowned. "And stop slouching!"

Nodding, the wolf straightened his back, lowered his head and waited. A few minutes passed before the targeted stag made the mistake of straying a foot or two away from the others. The wolf charged and the deer dispersed. Chasing the smaller stag, the wolf flushed him out and directed him away from the rest of his family. Unable to reunite with his herd, the buck bounded away in the opposite direction. He zigzagged around, hoping to tire out the wolf and evade his claws. The wolf countered each evasion with a jump and a nip at the deer's hindquarters.

From afar, Saxton left his feather beneath a small stone and watched the chase unfold. Though the wolf plodded across the snow maladroitly, he was doing a fair job of keeping up with the stag and steering him in the right direction. When the stag and the wolf drew near, Saxton readied his legs to pounce. They were coming even closer. Four steps, three, two …

The fox leapt forward, startling the young stag and causing him to jump aside.

The wolf pounced, grabbing onto the stag's rump with his teeth and nails. The stag kicked his hind legs until it was free, but badly bleeding. As he stumbled for escape, the wolf found his footing and attacked once more, opening wounds along the deer's ribcage.

The stag fought for his life, but he faltered on his hooves.

"Knock him down!" Saxton shouted. "Push him to his side!"

The wolf lowered his head and plowed the stag's ribs.

CRACK!

The stag fell over with a moan.

One merciful bite on his throat, and he was dead. His head flopped to the ground, unmoving.

Saxton ran to the wolf. "You did it."

"I … did." He sounded like he couldn't believe it. "I caught him."

Saxton had never eaten such a hearty meal, and it occurred to him that there might be more advantages to having this wolf around after all.

They ate quietly for what felt like too long, and the silence between them made the fox uncomfortable and a little lonely. He pawed for his feather, freeing it from beneath the stone.

"I'm Saxton," he offered tentatively.

The wolf paused, taken aback.

"Dante," he said. "My name is Dante."

Chapter Twelve

The following days continued in this fashion, wherein the fox and the wolf would follow the freeway and break for a hunt. They were not always successful, but Saxton noticed that Dante's coordination was improving bit by bit, and that he was getting better at strategy.

One day, however, they ventured too far from the freeway in the pursuit of gophers and found themselves unable to find it again. Had the winter surroundings not reflected the sun's rays, they would have been able to determine east from west. Unfortunately, the white snow and gray skies made every direction seem the same.

The freeway cut through several small towns before entering yet another deserted field. For the past week, Dante had resisted the urge to ask where Saxton seemed so intent on going. But when the days became increasingly monotonous and it seemed as though their journey would never end, the wolf gave in to his curiosity.

"So how did you meet the crow?" Dante asked with what he hoped was a casual tone.

"Quill raised me," Saxton explained, carefully balancing the feather across the top of his muzzle as he walked. He hated not having hands like a human. "He's not just a friend, he's my family."

"Oh." He replied lamely. "So where are you taking his feather?" When the fox refused to answer, Dante cleared his throat. "Look, I don't mean to meddle in … whatever this is, but I have to ask: where exactly are we going?"

"Exeter, New Hampshire."

"You're joking."

"No."

"Do you have any idea how far that is?

"Yes, do you?"

Dante rolled his eyes. "I'm not an idiot, you know. The crows in Canada like to hang around the packs and chat when we're not hunting. New Hampshire's clear across the continent."

"You said you owed him," Saxton reminded.

"Yeah, but your life matters more because you can still lose it. So, why Exeter?"

Saxton tripped a little, and the feather fell to the ground. He stared at it, and for a second the fox looked as though the true length of his journey was finally dawning on him.

"His family is there," he said. "The last of it, anyway. He wanted to see his sister and spend his last days there, but …"

The fox's throat ran dry, and Dante studied him, thoughtful. "All right," he said. "But there's gotta be a better way of getting there."

They heard a branch snap and swung their heads around.

"Did you hear something?" Saxton whispered.

They looked around them, the world shrinking in.

"Yeah," Dante replied, and lifted his nose. "Smells like—"

A grizzly bear barreled out of the forest, taking down branches and mowing down barren bushes as she went. Mist puffed out of her flaring nostrils as she breathed. Her eyes were bloodshot and wild.

Saxton's eyes widened. "Napowsa."

"Oh, scat! She followed us!"

She bore her teeth, revealing her gums. "*Lonely Thief.*"

Dante made to run, but Saxton remained fixed where he stood.

"Please," he pleaded, "I never meant to kill him. What must I do to make amends?"

"You think you can repair what you've done?" She growled, her rage boiling over as she thudded closer. "How *dare* you!"

Saxton was about to take a step forward, when Dante turned him around with a push of his head and nipped him on the ankles. Saxton yipped indignantly.

"Time to run!"

"But—"

"No time to chat, move it!"

Saxton grabbed Quill's feather, and they darted across the snow, Napowsa hot on their tracks and leaving huge footprints. She was monstrously large and frighteningly fast. She moved across the land like an unstoppable force, but banked poorly whenever the fox and wolf swerved to evade her.

"She's getting closer!" Dante panted as they drew to an exhausted stop. "What do we do?"

Just then, a thunderous roar rapidly approached them from behind. Lowering their ears, they watched as a long vehicle with numerous cars and wheels ran along the steel tracks that ran several yards away from the freeway. The individual cars went *tha-thum, tha-thum* as they rolled passed.

"We're jumping!" Saxton exclaimed. "On *that!*"

"*What?*"

"Do you have any better ideas?"

Dante glanced at the bear that was steadily gaining ground, the earth beneath them shaking more violently as she came close. Bitterly, he shook his head.

"I'll jump first and unlatch the door to one of the cars. Then you can jump inside."

In the back of his mind, Dante wondered if he had been better off stuck in the barbed wire fence. "I don't know where you get your ideas, but they border on suicidal."

Saxton ignored him and focused on their timing. "And ... now!"

He clenched his teeth tightly around his feather, and chased the train's caboose. Leaping on, he climbed up the train's ladder and ran across the rooftops of the cars.

Finding a car with a sliding door on its side, Saxton stopped. He watched as Dante caught up with him, barely keeping ahead of Napowsa's claws. The second Dante was running alongside the door, the fox leapt down and grabbed the door's latch. The door slid open, and Saxton held on tight.

Dante ran and ran and ran.

Napowsa snarled and pulled fur off his tail.

He whimpered and tucked his tail securely between his legs.

He glanced at Saxton.

He stared at the feather.

He closed his eyes and took what could be considered a literal leap of faith. Dante landed in the car, tumbling over and hitting a wall.

With Dante inside, Saxton swung his body forward and used his weight to take the door with him. Napowsa was less than a foot away. She roared and sprung forward –her breath hot on his toes – but Saxton managed to slip inside the car as the door slammed shut before her face.

106

The sudden silence within the car was broken by their harsh breathing. Saxton collapsed on his side; his feather dropping to the floor, and his tongue sliding out of his mouth unbecomingly as the adrenaline drained away and the weariness seeped in. He peered at Dante, whose lone yellow eye was big and wide, and his legs were shaking like leaves in the wind.

"We made it." he gasped. We're alive."

Chapter Thirteen

"What is this thing?" Dante asked.

"I think Quill once called it a train."

Saxton tried to stand, but he was still trembling and felt sick to his stomach. Dante noticed.

"Saxton? What's wrong?"

He shook his head. "Why? Why would this happen?"

The wolf frowned, impatient. "Why would what happen?"

"I took the most important thing away from her. It was an accident, but it happened, and now I'm no better than you." Saxton laughed, but it was mournful. "Why would that happen? Things happen for a reason, don't they? It doesn't make any sense. It's like a terrible joke."

Dante bit back the outrage he felt at the words 'no better than you', and tried to be reasonable. If his tone was a touch sharp, he felt entitled to it. "Life can be a terrible joke," he said. "Don't expect it to do you any favors just because you think you've got the moral high ground."

Saxton winced and tried not to look at him.

"We should be well out of reach now," the wolf added pragmatically. "I don't think we'll be seeing her anymore."

"Do you think she'll follow us?"

He shrugged. "It's a bear on the warpath. Maybe, but she'll probably lose track eventually."

Dante sat on his haunches to regroup while Saxton explored the inside of the boxcar. The walls were made of sheet metal, drowning the interior in near darkness save for the little cracks of light that stole in between the gaps. There were large, cardboard boxes stacked on top of one another, and the fox detected a tasty aroma trapped within. He licked his lips.

"Smells like... dried meat... and salt," he declared with a second sniff.

"It's beef jerky, Red," a small, nasally voice spoke, "Hundreds of pounds of it."

The wolf and the fox looked around until they both spotted a black rat sitting atop one of the cargo boxes. He was a rather greasy fellow, with a crooked snout and a pair of sharp buck teeth. The rat casually swayed his naked tail side to side as he licked his nails clean with his narrow tongue.

"Looks like we got ourselves a couple of interlopers. What're you two doin' on the BSNF?"

"The BSN— what?" Dante asked.

Rolling his eyes, the rat lay on his back and gestured to the walls around them.

"This train, genius. Where you two headin'?"

"Exeter," Saxton replied. The rat snorted.

"Have fun gettin' lost in Wisconsin."

"You ride this train often?"

"Often? I live here." The rat's tone turned severe. He stared at them with a crease between his brows. "In fact, I'm not a fan of the idea of sharing my food and space, and I'm even less of a fan that I might be on your dinner menu. A word of advice: hop off the train before I push you off."

"Pretty large threats for a little guy," Dante snarled, but the rat remained undaunted.

"What I lack in size I make up for in brains, but seein' as wolves are nothin' if not brawny, I guess you can't appreciate that."

Dante bristled and growled. Saxton stepped in front of him.

"I hope you realize that by angering my 'brawny' companion here, you're only tempting him to tear you apart. For all your so-called intelligence, your attitude is foolish. Tell me, have you ever heard of manners?"

Intrigued, the rat raised his eyebrows. "I'm a *rat*. I've got no use for niceties, and tempting danger is par for the course." He pointed at Saxton. "You are a fox. What d'you know about manners?"

"Certainly more than you," Saxton scoffed.

"Huh." The rat glanced at the crow's feather by Saxton's feet. "You know, I heard crows have a lot to say about etiquette. Did your lunch give you a brief lesson before you ate him?"

At that, Saxton felt his blood boil and his eyes narrowed. "What did you say?"

"Ah, hit a sore spot, I see." The rat hopped down from his box, landed upon a lower one, and hopped down once more before he reached the floor. "You are interesting. You weren't raised by your own kind were you?"

His astute words took Saxton by surprise, and he took an unconscious step back. Dante cut in, ready to fight.

"You've got some nerve," he growled. "Maybe you should shut your mouth before I tie it up with your own tail."

"Oh, I'm so scared," the rat taunted before turning to Saxton again. "Foxes never travel far from their birth home, and they never talk to strangers unless they have to. Funny how you broke both rules, Red."

"What difference does it make to you?" The wolf asked.

"Knowing thine enemy is all part of the game, One-Eyed Jack."

"Y'know, we have names, if you cared enough to ask!"

"There's the rub: I don't," the rat sneered. "You've been taught to listen, haven't you? And not just listen, you've been taught to understand. No Papa Fox in the world would think about teaching his kits more than how to survive. But a crow, a Papa Crow at that, now that's a different story."

Watching Saxton's growing ire, and the underlying sorrow that accompanied it, the rat dared to press further. "Oh me, oh my, compassion is a double-edged sword isn't it, Red? Your gut says, 'Kill that *Sewer Beggar*, but your silly lil' mind says, 'give him a chance'."

"You won't provoke me, Mr. Rat," Saxton said stiffly, "I'll neither hop off this train nor snap your neck, though the latter is more than tempting."

"Yeah? Why not? Got your silly honor to preserve?"

"Don't talk to me about honor," he hissed. "I am going to Exeter, and I only have until next snowfall to get there! This train is going east, and it will get me there faster than on foot. Unfortunately, you said it's going to stop in Wisconsin. I want a train that goes farther than that. So here's the problem: I need to find that train, but I don't know how to read. You, however, *do*."

At that, the rodent froze. Saxton grinned almost wickedly as he assessed him with an unkind gaze.

110

"To know how the trains operate, where they go, and what they carry, you *must* be able to read. You're a clever one. You took one look at this feather –" he patted it thoughtfully "– and you knew, instantly, that no ordinary fox would take such a meaningless item with him. So you goaded me to confirm your suspicions and assume the upper hand."

Saxton circled the rat and tauntingly dragged his thick tail across his nose. "Nothing concerns the enemy more than having his secrets known. What you didn't know is that I figured out your other talents, and I have use for them."

The rat batted Saxton's bothersome tail away and bared his front teeth. "I call your bluff, Red. Threaten me all you like, I ain't gonna teach you one thing about the rail system, let alone how to read."

"I'm sorry, Mr. Rat," the fox replied. "You might be really good at sniffing out facts, but I don't threaten when I can bargain."

Dante interrupted, nudging Saxton roughly on the shoulder. "Hey, trusting a stranger didn't exactly work out last time."

"I'm not in trouble yet, Dante. No need to get so anxious." He looked at the rat and repeated himself. "So Mr. Rat, what is it that you want?

"What do I—?" The rat cut himself off, not knowing how to reply. Bit by bit, the rat's hardened features waned as he fell into deep thought. Saxton and Dante waited, until finally, the rat shrugged.

"What're wants anyway? They're nothin' but luxuries. My kind's been reduced to hiding in sewers and landfills, and I ain't fool enough to believe you can do anythin' to change that. *Sewer Beggars* are what we are, that's what we'll always be. You can't offer me a thing."

But Saxton understood what it was the rat wished for and offered, "I can't change the name that burdens you and your brothers and sisters, but I can tell everyone I will ever meet about the rat that was so intelligent, he figured out how to read human words."

"You have no way of proving that," he scoffed.

"He doesn't," the wolf confirmed, "but I promise to make sure he'll do it."

"And a wolf's promise is a good one," Saxton added. "He promised never to hunt another fox again, and as you can see, I am alive and well."

But the rat shook his head. "That ain't enough. I want somethin' I can actually see and touch on top of your offer. Call it insurance."

"He's demanding too much," Dante said, not liking the rat's gall. "And how do we know he'll even hold up his end of the bargain?"

"We don't." But that didn't stop him from asking to the rat: "So ... What is your price?"

The rat blinked, actually surprised. "Food from the kitchen. There's only so much beef jerky I can stand before it starts tastin' like nothin.' The train crew stays in the caboose at night. During the day, it's mostly empty, but there's usually someone in there on break."

"You've tried to get in there yourself?" Dante asked.

"Yeah. Easier at night when they're all asleep and the train ain't movin.' But they lock all the cupboards up, so I can't get to any of their stores. I need the keys to unlock them."

Saxton cocked his head to the side. "Keys?"

"Small metal things. They got teeth on one end and are round or square on the other." Using the layer of dust on the floor, he outlined the shape of the object with his paws. "The engineer usually keeps a ring of 'em in his pocket."

"Where's the engineer?"

"At the head of the train. He's usually so focused on drivin,' he won't notice someone walkin' in. Tried to get to him a few times, but the crew got smart about it and started layin' traps."

"I see. Well, then, I'll retrieve the keys for you."

"How can I help?"

Saxton cringed and tried to hide it. While Dante meant well, his earnest desire to be helpful was sometimes cloying.

"You're too big to go unnoticed," said the fox. "I'll take care of this. You stay here and take care of the feather while I'm gone."

The wolf's disappointment was apparent, but was quickly replaced with frustration. "I'm supposed to make things right between us. How can I do that if you keep pushing me away?"

He was supposed to be patient, but something snapped.

"Because you're always in the way!"

The wolf's mouth clamped shut, and Saxton momentarily felt guilty. He shoved the emotion aside and climbed up the boxes.

Once he was high enough to touch the car's ceiling, the rat showed Saxton a hatch he could exit through. He poked his head out, squinting as powerful wind blew across the speeding train. He jumped out and broke into a run before he could be blown backwards.

Saxton ran across the car rooftops, jumped down into an empty flat car, then climbed up and tumbled into a coal hopper. He coughed – soot dusting his nose – and struggled to crawl across the coal without sinking down into it. Once he made it to the other side, his heart sank when he saw two more coal hoppers before him.

By the time he reached the locomotive's rear platform, Saxton was no longer copper red, but black and gray.

He climbed the platform ladder, and maneuvered around the radiator fans' whirring metal blades. He made it to the top of the engine room when the air horn decided to blare, nearly deafening him. Saxton ducked his head and lowered his ears, waiting for the horn to silence before jumping over the engine's exhaust pipe. Hot, burning air singed Saxton's tail and underbelly, and he resisted the urge to scream.

At last, he made it safely to the top of the locomotive cab. After peering inside and making sure the engineer wasn't looking, Saxton slipped in through the cab's side window. The engineer was too busy monitoring the train's controls and eating a sloppily made sandwich to notice he wasn't alone. Examining the engineer's pockets, Saxton spied several small objects with teeth hanging from a metal ring.

He tried to reach for them, but was wary of drawing the man's attention. He searched around for a distraction, when his eyes fell upon a bag of potato chips sitting on top of the dashboard. Quietly moving toward it, Saxton tugged at the bag's corner, yanking it down and spilling its contents all over the floor. The engineer turned and looked down at the mess.

"Dang it! What a waste!"

He leaned over to salvage what was left in the bag. While he was preoccupied, Saxton ran to the other side of the engineer's seat and carefully hoisted the key ring from the engineer's baggy left pocket with his teeth. By the time the man was sitting up again, the fox was no longer there.

Atop the train, Saxton navigated his way back across the locomotive, taking care to avoid being burned or deafened. He was crossing the third coal hopper when the air horn blew.

Startled, he dropped the keys.

"Perfect. Just … perfect."

He dug through the coal, tossing piles of it overboard. His stomach clenched at the thought that the keys had sunken to the bottom of the coal heap, but just as he was about to give up, a bright glint between two coals caught his eye. Saxton knocked the coals away, grabbed the keys, and ran the rest of the way back to the box car before anything else could happen.

Crawling through the hatch, Saxton leapt down the boxes. The rat and the wolf were waiting with baited breath.

Saxton tossed the keys on the floor.

The rat snatched up the keys – greedy, so greedy – and perused them until he found one he was certain was for the food cupboards.

"You did it!" The rat cried. "Holy smokes, Red! You did it!"

Dante said nothing, and in fact hardly looked impressed. Saxton pawed the side of his front leg. The wolf looked down on him, and he worried at his bottom lip with his teeth.

"… Sorry."

It came out mumbled and half-hearted, borne from guilt more than anything else, but he could see that Dante heard it. Dante sighed and turned to the rat. "Now it's your turn."

Chapter Fourteen

The rat excused himself to retrieve a couple of items for their lesson. He returned dragging a long cord with his mouth. At one end of the cord were three prongs of metal, and at the other end was a strange object that looked like an egg trapped inside a small iron cage. Ever curious, Saxton asked, "What's that?"

"A power cord," the rat replied as he inserted the end with the prongs into a vertical panel lined against a wall. "We need more light to be able to see."

Once the cord was properly plugged in, the egg-shaped object instantly emitted light.

"And what's that?" Dante gaped.

"It's called a light bulb," the rat muttered, rolling his eyes. "Now obviously, you're not gonna read full sentences after just two days of learning. That would take a miracle. The most I can teach you is how to read names and certain words so you can figure out how to use a rail map. So let's start with the alphabet."

The rat tore a piece of cardboard off one of the cargo boxes and dipped his right paw in black grease. Using the cardboard as a tablet, he began writing the letters of the English alphabet. Saxton and Dante watched over his shoulder, fascinated.

"How'd you learn to read?"

The rat threw his head back and laughed, his red eyes glittering in the shadows. "You don't hang around humans all day without figuring out that skulls and bones are bad news. Illiterates don't survive long, not with man running amok on our land."

He finished writing the alphabet and lifted the cardboard to lean it against one of the walls.

"Okay. These here are letters. Letters are symbols for different sounds in the English human language. The main sounds you need to know are 'a,' 'e,' 'i,' 'o,' and 'u.'" He pointed to the corresponding letters. "These sounds, and their matching letters, are called vowels. You need these puppies to put the other letters together and spell words. Vowels are kinda like glue."

Taking a step back from the alphabet, the rat peered at his students and noticed the glazed look in their eyes. "Am I going too fast? Am I losing you?"

Neither the fox nor the wolf answered. They continued to stare blankly at the alphabet. The rat sighed.

"I lost you. Oh boy, you two are gonna be a whole lotta fun. All right, let's try this again. We'll start with sounds this time. And grab me some jerky, will you? It's gonna be a long night."

Indeed it was. With no windows in the cargo car, it was difficult to discern what time of day it was, and Saxton was certain they had lost one night of sleep. As the hours continued to pass, the fox, the wolf, and the rat grew bored and weary. What started as a loud and excited discussion devolved into yawns and barely intelligible mumblings. Even the light bulb, which once glowed brightly, began to flicker. The rat had grown haggard by the endless repetition, and was grasping at straws to stay patient. Fortunately, they had mastered memorizing the alphabet, and were ready to move on.

"Here's the easy part," said the rat, "the trains. Every so often, a train needs to make a stopover at a freight facility or a train yard or whatever, and that's where you can switch rides if you need to. Lucky for you, they name trains with no more than four letters tops, and the first train you need after we stop in Wisconsin is spelled 'C N.'"

"That doesn't sound like a word," Saxton commented through drooping eyes.

"Yeah," Dante yawned. "Where's the vowel?"

"It's not a word!" the rat snapped. "It's the abbreviation for Canadian National! Do you want me to spell those two words out for you? They're eight letters a-piece, you know!"

Startled, they shook their heads.

"Good. Abbreviations are easier to remember, aren't they?"

They memorized the alphabet and the rat tested them, over and over again until he was certain they recognized all of the letters in both

116

capitalized and lower case forms. When Saxton and Dante thought they were finally finished, the rat disappointed them greatly.

"Not so fast, you two," he said. "You haven't even started memorizing numbers!"

They groaned as the rat turned the cardboard sheet over, dipped his paw in more grease, and wrote the figures '0' through '9.'

"Okay. Numbers are important when you want to use the freeways or find an address."

"What's an address?" Dante asked.

The rat rubbed his palm across his face, smearing motor oil all over his fur. "It's a number for a house or a building along a street. Trust me, wolf, you'll probably never use it, but better safe than sorry, I always say."

He forced them to memorize the ten figures, and once they did, he began to show the numbers put together in pairs, threes, and fours.

"Look, it's not that complicated," the rat grumbled. "The most important thing is to remember what the numbers zero through nine look like by themselves. If some bird or rat or whatever gives you a number that's bigger than nine, just ask for what it looks like. Okay, now I'm gonna test you again. Ready?"

He pointed to each number written on the cardboard, and Saxton and Dante would shout out what the number was. When it was clear they had finally studied everything to exhaustion, the rat turned off the light and settled into his nest of shredded newspaper for sleep. Saxton and Dante settled down as well, though the wolf noticed that the fox was restless.

"You're gonna make it to Exeter," he said. "I'll make sure of it."

"How?"

"I don't know. I'll do whatever it takes. Just give me a chance to prove myself, okay?"

When Saxton's eyes closed, he saw Quill, alive, chatty, and smiling, and for a moment he thought everything had been an awful nightmare.

In dreams, he usually caught on to the fact that what he saw wasn't real fairly quickly, but the sound of Quill's laugh was so warm, he thought nothing of it as they scampered through lush grass and up a mountain path.

Then Quill took to the air, graceful as always, and dived toward the canyon below.

Saxton laughed, his breath taken away. As a kit he always wished he could fly, and his father reprimanded him for such trivial fancies.

But the crow's daring flight turned into a heavy plummet. His feathers fell away from his wings, the wind carrying them away in a great black billow, leaving nothing but bone.

Saxton screamed Quill's name, but nothing came out of his mouth. His dear friend fell and fell, until he disappeared into the rocks.

He ran down the mountain and searched the canyon— desperate, frightened, and nauseous. He turned over rocks, looking for any sign of life. What he found was a young bear, covered in blood.

Their eyes met.

It was Tarlo, but his painful sobs sounded disturbingly like Quill's. The bear turned to him and cried:

"You killed me!"

Saxton woke up with a start, feeling much too hot, and panted. His eyes not yet accustomed to the dark, he patted his paws around until he located Quill's feather. His ears twitched when he heard a faint snarl, and then a whimper. Dante appeared to be having a fitful night as well.

"No … No, Rush," he mumbled. "… We can't leave them …"

The wolf kicked his legs as if he were running, and a moment later he stopped. His good eye continued to shift beneath its eyelid.

Unable to return to sleep, Saxton remained awake while his companion slept, wondering what kind of troubles the wolf had been hiding during daylight.

The train drew to a halt around dawn. As the crewmen unlocked the boxcar doors and slid them open one by one, Saxton, Dante, and the rat climbed up the hatch and jumped to the ground on the other side of the train. Saxton looked around them and, seeing multiple train tracks, realized they had reached a freight facility just as the rat had described.

"Thanks for everything, Mr. Rat," Saxton said.

"Yeah, whatever," he replied with a nonchalant wave of the paw. "Now remember, you wanna take the CN down south, get off at Illinois, and then get on the NS going east. You got that?"

"CN south then NS east," Dante repeated. "We got it."

"And you gotta get off at Illinois."

"Thanks, we heard you the first time."

As Saxton and Dante were about to depart, the rat ran up to the fox with a thin piece of twine in his paws.

"Keep carrying that feather around like that and you're eventually gonna lose it, Red."

Gently taking Quill's feather from Saxton's mouth, the rat tied the twine around the feather's shaft and then looped the twine around Saxton's neck. The fox looked down on the feather, which hung just over his chest.

"Thank you ...?"

"*Scratch*," the rat filled in. Scampering away, Scratch turned back and said, "Don't do anything I wouldn't do."

Chapter Fifteen

Saxton and Dante separated ways to cover more ground in the train yard. They were careful to hop across the tracks and not catch their paws or tails on the rails, and were even more cautious when the occasional engineer or crew member crossed their path. Upon finding a red and black train, Saxton squinted at a peculiar symbol painted in white across the train's side.

At first, the fox didn't immediately recognize the symbol as any of the letters the rat had taught them. He cocked his head to the side, and thought, perhaps, that the symbol was a sideways 'S,' yet that couldn't be right, as Scratch had explained to them that all trains are branded with at least two letters. He looked at the symbol more closely, and it slowly dawned on him that the symbol was actually the two distinct letters, 'C' and 'N', with hardly any space between them.

"Ah, it's this one." He turned around and barked for his companion. "Dante!" he hollered, "I found it!"

Abandoning the train he was studying, the wolf trotted over. He frowned at the writing Saxton was staring at.

"Are you sure?"

"Positive. Nothing else looks close to the letters we're looking for."

Dante tilted his head to the side. "Looks like a sideways nine to me."

"Really? I thought it looked more like an 'S.'"

Dante squinted. "Wait … wait, I think I see it now." The wolf stepped closer and snarled. "Humans! What's the point of learning to read when the writing is *unreadable?*"

"I don't know, but if we're going to start our journey to Illinois today, we better board now. It's already midday, and the trains are due to depart soon."

Running to one of the box cars further behind the locomotive, Dante selected a car that smelled of cardboard and preserved food. Standing upright on his hind legs, he laid his forepaws across the car's door latch and used his weight to force the latch down and the door open. The door rumbled as it slid aside, and Saxton wasted no time jumping in. Dante followed suit and pulled the door shut with his teeth.

Sniffing about, Saxton located a power cord and iron-caged light bulb coiled against one of the car's corner walls. He picked up the pronged end of the cord with his teeth and plugged it into an outlet. The car filled with soft incandescent light.

The train's horn gave an earsplitting blow, and the car they were in began chugging forward.

"Hungry?" Dante asked, as he tore open one of the boxes and threw several packets of tightly wrapped smoked sausage on the floor.

"Starving."

Saxton ripped open the plastic and eagerly dug in.

Satiated and sleepy with fullness, they stretched themselves out before curling up on the floor. Just as Dante settled his chin upon the top of his front paws, Saxton suddenly remembered—

"Dante?"

"Yeah?"

"Who's Rush?"

"What?" Startled, the wolf raised his head.

"You called out that name while you were sleeping the other night."

"Oh." He paused, "Rush is my brother. We used to scuffle a lot."

"I see."

He looked at the fox, and by the pinched look on his face, saw that he doubted that was the whole story.

"Rush always got into a lot of trouble," Dante added. "He'd slow down the pack during our hunts and make so much noise he'd scare the deer or the caribou away. One time, he had the gall to walk right into a bear's den. Now look at my ear and eye." He shook his head. "It was a pain trying to keep him in line."

"You were pack leader?"

The wolf hesitated. "Not exactly, more like second in command. My father's pack leader. He's the Head, and I was one of the Fangs. My siblings are the Legs, and Rush is the Tail."

"Why did you leave?"

"I thought it was time to strike out on my own." He yawned and swept his tail along the curve of his body. "I've outgrown the pack."

"I see ..." Saxton said again. "You must be looking for a mate, then."

"Yeah, eventually. Kinda like being on my own for now, though."

The conversation ended there, leaving Saxton with questions he never considered before. What was your pack like? What were your parents like? What does it mean to be a wolf? What does it mean to be a lone wolf? But he reminded himself that Dante was neither friend nor family, and that he best not cross that line.

And yet, it suddenly occurred to him that perhaps they were not so different. It was possible he assumed too much, but he was fairly certain that Dante quietly missed his family— even the mysterious brother who vaguely reminded Saxton of his own.

"I'll stay up," the wolf offered as the fox's eyelids began to droop. "I'll wake you when we reach our next stop."

Saxton murmured something unintelligible, but nodded with understanding. When he woke again, it was not because Dante had roused him, but because the wolf had dozed off and was once again kicking and growling in his slumber.

They had several more hours before the train would reach its next stop. He supposed he would be able to stay awake until then.

He let the wolf sleep, trying to be kind to him for once.

The light bulb had died and the train wasn't moving. Natural sunlight peered in between the sliding door and its frame, stretching across the car floor and pestering Dante's good eye. He twitched and, a second later, jumped to his feet.

"No!" Dante exclaimed, startling Saxton awake. "No! I fell asleep! Where are we?"

Alarmed that he had fallen asleep as well, Saxton swallowed before replying, "I don't know. It's all right, Dante. Let's look at the rail map and find out where we are."

They pulled the door open and hopped out of the car, scurrying across the numerous train tracks toward a small, single story building standing in the middle of the train yard. Leaping onto the building's porch, Saxton scanned the wooden wall until he found a large cork board with a map and other fliers pinned along its surface.

The fox squinted. "It's high up and the letters are tiny. Can you see any better?"

Dante rose on his hind legs and leaned his front paws atop the map's surface. He frowned as he tried to sound out the words scattered about the graph. "It says we're in a state called 'Miss-oh-ree.'"

"*Missouri*," Saxton corrected. "We missed it. Well, it'd be a waste of time to backtrack. We might as well head east from here. When's the next train?"

"I don't know. Where should I look?"

"Try looking for the word 'schedule.'"

Dante bobbed his head up and down the cork board until he came upon a pad of paper with more writing on it. "This thing says sk-he-do-lee. Is that it?"

"I think so. Do NS trains go through here?"

With the tip of his nose, Dante flipped the pages. "No. I don't see NS anywhere."

The fox grimaced. "Lovely."

Lowering himself back onto all fours, Dante bowed his head and curled his tail in. "It's my fault," he said bitterly. "It was my duty to stay awake and I failed."

"Don't say that. You were tired. I let you sleep."

Dante looked at him in a piercing way that made the fox feel very small and nervous.

"You *what?*"

"You needed to rest. You were exhausted."

"And so were you!" The wolf turned in circles, clearly beside himself. "You should've just woken me up!"

"I was trying to be nice!"

"Why?"

"Why not?"

"Because nothing is easy to forgive, and what I did is unforgivable! You should've woken me, yelled at me, and forced me to do my job!"

123

Saxton stared at him incredulously and shook with anger. He was tired and frustrated, and letting this wolf – this insecure, cynical, combative wolf – follow him around was eating him up from the inside-out like acid. He had lost his temper before, and staring at the wolf's solitary eye, lightning bright and stormy, he felt his hackles rise.

"I'm trying! I'm *trying* to forgive you!" He barked. "You say I push you away when you try to make things right, but when I try to be friendly, you throw it back in my face! What's wrong with you? Back hunched, tail between your legs, head lowered to the ground ... hardly the demeanor of the second in command you claim to be. What happened? Did your pack throw you out? Because I'm truly thinking about doing the same!"

With those last words, the spark that lit Dante's yellow eye dulled and disappeared.

"My past is none of your business," he said in a low voice. "Pull your nose out of it."

He abandoned the porch. Saxton watched as he clumsily trotted out of the train yard, and though he wanted to stop the wolf, he found that his feet were stubbornly rooted to the ground. He took a breath, searching for his composure, and glanced at the feather hanging around his neck. He wished he could somehow hear Quill's calming voice.

'Apologize,' Quill would say. 'And mean it this time.'

His feet came back to life, and he dashed to catch up with Dante. He found his scowling companion sitting beside an old, out of service telephone booth that was overrun with spider webs and wild grass. Dante hadn't run too far off, and Saxton could only assume that he had chosen to remain close so as not to break his vow to protect him. The thought made him more than a little ashamed of himself.

The tip of the wolf's right ear twitched, sensing that the fox was behind him.

"I'm sorry," the fox began. "I know you're trying. We're both trying. What I said ... that was uncalled for."

Dante moved his head slightly, just enough for Saxton to see the horrible wounds marring his face.

"Whatever happened between you and your pack is your story to tell, not mine. I won't mention it again."

The wolf snorted. Not at Saxton, but at himself.

"It's not like you need the details. You already know my pathetic story," Dante said sullenly. "You're shrewd, but kinda naive too. Both are good things, in a way. Let's be honest, though: you're not being very honorable when you look down on the wolf you're feigning to forgive."

"I'm not pretending—"

"You only want to forgive me because Quill would have wanted you to, but forgiveness doesn't work that way, Saxton."

A corner of the fox's lip twitched. "We're always coming to blows, aren't we? You're a lot more complicated than you say. You're right, though. I suppose ... I sometimes think too highly of myself. Thanks for being—"

"Blunt?"

Saxton smiled. "Yes, blunt."

The wolf passed a wry grin in return. "You say I owe it to Quill that I'm alive. You're right, I do, but you forget who it was who cut the wires in the first place. You didn't have to do that. Most would say you shouldn't have done that. Your friend is gone, and it's my fault. That's not an easy thing for me, and I know it's definitely not an easy thing for you. I get that, but I'm not gonna give up."

Moving closer, Saxton sat before Dante, seeing him for the first time as someone with a past and a set of ideals that were all his own.

"You're a tenacious wolf, Dante. Your parents did well by you. I wish I could say the same about mine. My father always insisted that foxes should never stray too far from their territory. 'The world,' he said, 'is a cruel and dangerous place.' In some ways, I suppose he was right. If I hadn't been so stupid and stubborn, if I had been more rational and selfish, Tarlo might've survived."

He turned away and gestured toward the vast land full of tall grasses and sprawling roads. The earth was green and gray, a collision of the patience of nature and the brute force of man.

"My other father, Quill, insisted there is so much to see in the world, it would be a shame to not explore it. He believed in kindness and second chances, and wished for me to one day make a friend." He gazed at the filth on his paws before looking at Dante again. "So here I am, far from home and seeing so many things, all because you're here to make sure the world is not so cruel or dangerous. And yet, I don't really know who you are. I've treated you quite poorly, and didn't even think that maybe you were the friend I was meant to meet ... even if I had lost the one I already had because of it." He paused and put as much sincerity into his voice as he could. "So ... can we start over?"

Dante said nothing, but the corner of his mouth quirked up.

The clouds above them thickened and churned. They both looked up as the first drops of rain began to fall.

"It's going to storm," Dante said, getting to his feet. Saxton glanced around. A few hundred yards away, he saw a pocket of desolate land filled with piles of metal and abandoned cars.

"Over there!" he shouted. "Hurry, before it pours!"

They ran through an empty plot of land before entering a scrapyard. With metal all around them, the rain came down with a musical ping-pong-ping, *tah-tah-tah*, and *plip-plop-plip*. Dante inspected the cars, and scratched at the firmly shut doors in an effort to get inside. After circling a van, a coupe, and a convertible that they deemed useless, the fox and the wolf finally came upon a jeep that had both of its left doors torn off. They hustled to get inside.

BOOM!

A large Rottweiler landed on the jeep's hood. Dante and Saxton stepped back as she bared her thick teeth and slobbered all over the car.

"Get out of our yard!" she barked.

Pouncing off the hood, the Rottweiler was about to tear Saxton to pieces when Dante head butted the guard dog aside. Saxton watched in horror as the Rottweiler swiftly rolled onto her feet and jumped. Her teeth sank into the scars wrapped around Dante's throat. Yowling, he twisted and turned until his neck was freed.

The Rottweiler prepared to attack yet again, but Saxton bit her ankle in a vain effort to hold her back. She glanced at the fox, a sardonic laugh in her eyes.

"That all you got, fox? I've had needles that were worse!"

She kicked Saxton off without effort, but failed to notice Dante rushing toward her with his teeth bared.

They hit the ground and rolled in the dirt in a flurry of claws and gnashing teeth. Barking, the Rottweiler shouted, "Sputnik! Get out here, you mutt!"

A white bull terrier with a black patch around his right eye burst into the scene. He stood atop a pile of scrap metal, proudly surveying the yard like the Roman soldiers Quill used to tell stories about.

"Where d'you need me, love?"

The Rottweiler pulled back just as Dante's jaws snapped before her nose.

"I've got the wolf, you get the fox!"

Saxton's eyes widened and he glanced at Sputnik, who was already making his way down to him.

"Run!" Dante yelled, blocking one of the Rottweiler's swipes with one of his own. "Get out of here!"

The fox dashed across the muddy ground and zigzagged through the maze of human refuse, Sputnik not far behind him. He ran until he was cornered between two piles of compacted cars, trapped. His eyes swept the area, and they spied a car with a barely opened window not far away.

He ran for it and slipped through the crack.

Sputnik scrambled to a stop and collided with the car door. Jumping to his feet, he scratched at the window and barked furiously.

Saxton fought to catch his breath, and saw through the rearview mirror that Dante had the Rottweiler subdued. But before he could think of a way to escape the other guard dog, an enormous shadow befell the car and Sputnik ran away. Suddenly, the car shifted. Saxton dashed to the window and peered outside. His eyes filled with terror as he saw the found of the scrapyard receding rapidly beneath him. A giant crane was lifting the car with its magnet!

Saxton ran from door to door in a final bid for escape. All of them were locked. He felt his insides rise as the car fell from a great height and landed between two metal walls.

There was a cold, emotionless growl, and then the walls began to close in and crush what metal and glass surrounded the car.

As the car tucked and the windows burst, Saxton toppled over the steering wheel and banged his head against the parking break. Shaking off the ache, he tried climbing out the shattered window but was forcefully yanked backwards. He turned around.

His hind leg was entangled in what looked like a flat, gray rope.

The walls were squeezing in, and Saxton gnawed desperately at the belt, reducing the edges to frays, which did little to free him.

The metal around him screamed as it folded in on itself like an accordion, and the light from above slowly disappeared.

"Dante!" Saxton screamed at the top of his lungs. "*Dante!*"

Chapter Sixteen

"Saxton!" Dante shouted. He sprinted for the odd contraption making the terrible noises, when Sputnik bit him on the tail and pulled him back. He growled, murderous, his solitary eye gleaming.

"Let me go," he said in a rough voice. "*Now.*"

Cowed, Sputnik dropped his tail. Dante glanced at the machine, then at the two dogs before him.

"Turn. It. Off."

"Don't listen to him, Sputnik," Mars ordered. "He's—"

She didn't see the wolf move. He was too fast. In an instant she was on the ground with one large paw on her chest and a set of razor sharp teeth near her jugular. The bull terrier whimpered.

"Mars!"

"Turn it off!" Dante repeated. "Do it!"

Sputnik scrambled out of the yard and ran toward the control booth stationed on higher ground. There was a cacophony of barks before Sputnik managed to get past the humans and into the booth. A couple of yard workers attempted to pull him back by the collar, but he kicked at their shins and scared them with his teeth. They stepped back, giving him just enough time to hit the power switch.

A moment later, there was a low pitched groan, and the crushing walls ground to a halt. The crane moved over the wreckage and lowered its magnet. The car and other metal debris were lifted from the compactor and lowered to the ground. Dante released Mars and sprinted to the smashed car just as Sputnik returned.

He circled the half-smashed vehicle. Most of the doors were completely jammed, except for the passenger's side. He pulled on the handle with his teeth. The passenger door pried partway open, giving Dante just enough space to wedge his head and shoulders inside. Using the weight of his body, he jerked from side to side until the door popped free.

He looked around and blinked, bewildered.

The car was empty.

"Where is he?"

"Probably dead," Sputnik said, licking Mars on the nose.

"No! I don't believe it. He's too smart to die!"

He scanned the inside of the car again, and this time found that a sealed compartment in front of the passenger's seat was perfectly intact. He entered the car, and slammed the side of his body repeatedly against the compartment. When the compartment door fell open, he didn't know whether to laugh or cry. Tucked inside, a perfectly safe Saxton lay in a tight, furry coil. He lowered his bushy tail from his face, and cautiously opened one of his amber eyes.

"You crazy fox!" Dante howled with an ear to ear smile.

Saxton carefully climbed out of the compartment, shaking all over. "You stopped the machine, didn't you?"

The wolf smiled.

"While I find this all very touching, the both of you have three seconds to get out of our yard," Mars snarled. "Should I start counting?"

"What are you talking about?" Dante growled. "You lost. I won. You gotta do what I say."

"Yeah? Well, dogs don't play by wolf rules!"

Keenly aware that he was the smallest and weakest of the four animals in the yard, Saxton moved closer to Dante. Sputnik glanced at Saxton, then at his mate and the wolf. It didn't look to him like the wolf was going to give.

"Mars, let it go."

The Rottweiler turned on him. "Just whose side are you on?"

"Ours. And I'd rather not see you beneath the wolf's death bite again, okay?"

She huffed. "Fine. What are you doing here? What do you want?"

"We needed a place to stay—" Saxton began.

"I wasn't talking to you, I was talking to the wolf."

"Hey! An answer from Saxton is as good as an answer from me. Show some respect." He turned to the fox. "Go ahead."

Clearing his throat, Saxton continued. "We need to get out of the rain. As it is, we're soaked to the bone, and we can't afford to get sick on our journey."

"Our job is to protect the yard from intruders," Sputnik explained. "We can't let you stay here. Our master's word is heavier than the wolf's."

"His name is Dante," he replied. "I understand. But can we hide somewhere until the rain stops? We promise not to disturb anything."

It was clear that Mars was using every muscle she had to lock her broad jaw shut. She turned to Sputnik, who gave her an apologetic grin. He nodded to a collection of vehicles sitting in the outskirts of the scrapyard.

"There's a truck that's not scheduled to be flattened for a while. You can stay in there. 'Course, I need your word you won't set a single paw on my mate again."

"Done," Dante agreed. "Where's the truck?"

"Follow me."

While Sputnik led the way, Mars brought up the rear, wary the fox and wolf might do something nasty with her mate's back turned. As they crossed the yard, Saxton studied the female guard dog. If he could attempt to make peace with Dante, there was no excuse to not do same with Mars.

"You have a lovely name," he said conversationally, but his compliment only upset the Rottweiler further.

"Master's son named me before finding out I was female. I hate my name. If I could tear it to shreds and bury it in the ground, I would."

Saxton ignored her snip, and added kindly, "From what I've been told Mars is a warrior. In fact, he is the god of war. I think the name fits."

"So what? It's still a male's name." She grumbled.

"Well, I don't think that matters. What matters is what you do with the name you've been given. Mars is a powerful name, but you can make it more so."

Mars lowered the lips that had been curled over her bared teeth.

"Why're you making nice? I don't like it."

"I noticed you changed your mind about killing me when your mate spoke up. He obviously loves you quite deeply."

"I don't see what you're getting at."

"His love for you spared us. We should not be unkind to the female he adores."

"Pretty words from a *Lonely Thief*. You think I buy all that?"

He shrugged. "I don't want to cause any trouble. I just want to get to New Hampshire so I can lay my family to rest."

She looked away from him and observed Dante, who had skipped a little further ahead to walk nearly side-by-side with Sputnik.

"He's your friend?" She asked.

Her question caught him off guard. He hemmed and hawed, then acknowledged the fact that the wolf had saved his life not once, not twice, but three times now. "It's … complicated."

"I've heard wolves are good judges of character. Hope that dead eye of his isn't a big blind spot."

Saxton watched Dante conversing amiably enough with the bull terrier. He walked as he always did, tail tucked and back hunched. Yet upon looking more closely, Saxton saw that he held his head just a little higher, and his gait moved with a more unconscious ease that hadn't been there when they first met. The fox frowned, wondering how it was that Dante truly lost his left eye and ear, and what sort of shadows had chased the wolf into such constant doubt.

They climbed inside the truck bed which had a camper shell installed upon it. The shell shielded them from the rain, and Dante and Saxton took a moment to shake their fur and relish being somewhere dry.

Sputnik and Mars settled near the open tailgate.

"So, Dante said you came in by train. How'd you navigate the rail system?" Sputnik asked.

"It's an amazing story, actually. A rat taught us the basics of reading."

The bull terrier blinked. "No kidding? The only things I can spell are 'treat,' 'walk,' and 'ball.'"

Saxton went on to describe how they met Scratch and what he had taught them. It was sheer luck, Saxton admitted, that they had met such an intelligent rat as Scratch. Had they chosen any other train or any other train car, they mightn't have met him.

"Luck's only half of it." They all turned to Mars, who had remained stubbornly silent through Saxton's account. "The other half is this wolf's … Dante's … muscle and your— how'd our master say it? 'Powers of persuasion.'"

Knowing an olive branch, however small, when he saw one, Saxton sought to return in kind: "Mars, about your name, did you want to know more about it?"

Mars stared out one of the shell's tinted windows, feigning indifference. The rain was still pelting down like little bullets.

"It's pouring so hard I can't patrol. Go ahead. I've got nothing else to do."

At first, Mars half-listened as Saxton repeated the myths Quill had told him, but as the owner of her namesake became a brighter and more real person, she moved to sit a little closer. When the rain continued well into evening, and it was clear to all that the fox and the wolf would be staying the night, Mars did not protest.

"Venus loved him?" she asked, "even after he acted ... the way he did?"

"Of course. Mars might be impulsive and hot-headed, but in the end he is always strong, determined, and brave. Venus adored these qualities in him. Actually, he had many children with her."

Genuine interest fled from her face, and was replaced by bitterness.

"Have I said something to upset you?"

"Nothing that can be fixed," she sighed.

He turned to Sputnik, who also looked concerned.

"Mars and I are, you know, getting on. Pups are out of the question, and she's more than a bit upset about that."

"Out of the question?" Dante repeated. "Why?"

"We're both fixed." Mars spat. Seeing that neither Saxton nor Dante understood what that meant, she explained, "That means the humans ... they took our ability to have pups away."

Saxton frowned. "Why would they do that? How?"

"We don't know why," Sputnik replied. "And as for how, you don't want to know. Anyway, I don't see how human logic works seeing as they get all up in arms about having their own young. Fickle guys, aren't they?"

"That's terrible. It's not right." Dante commiserated.

Mars shook her head.

"Well, life ain't fair. I was born big, brawny, and ugly, I was given a male's name, and I can't have pups. What am I supposed to do?"

"Don't you talk like that, Mars," Sputnik gently scolded. "I love your name and I love you. And don't even get me started on how gorgeous you are when you smile."

His voice sweetened as he spoke, and there was clear look of devotion in his eyes that made Saxton and Dante a touch envious. Mars looked at her mate, clearly in love, but conflicted too.

"Sometimes I just don't know what you see in me, Sput."

"Then let me tell you," he grinned. "You've got the most dedicated heart I've ever seen. You'll do your job to a tee and then some, and when push comes to shove you'll do anything to protect our master and me." He looked at Dante somberly. "Even take down a full-blooded wolf."

Mars smiled weakly, and then glanced at the dark sky. "Better get going before Master wonders where we are."

She lowered her head beneath the camper shell and slipped outside through the tailgate. Sputnik followed her out.

"You two stay out of trouble," she said.

"And sleep easy," Sputnik added, "but you've gotta get out of here once the rain stops. Got it?"

"Yes," Saxton answered. "Thank you."

It wasn't long before the Rottweiler and bull terrier were gone. Dante stretched out his legs and lay on his belly. He peered at Saxton, who suddenly looked very upset. He was about to ask what was wrong, but Saxton beat him to it.

"What have I done?"

It took Dante a second to catch on to what he was talking about. He sighed. "What happened back on that mountain wasn't your fault."

"Not my fault? I took her son away from her!"

"Stop, just stop!" Dante barked. "Listen, sometimes you can do the right thing – the hard thing – and it just doesn't turn out the way you hope. Don't punish yourself over it."

"Is that so? What about you?"

"It's a different situation and you know it. Anyway, didn't you want to start over? What about that?"

Saxton relented, but didn't stop himself from asking, "What am I going to do?"

"If we're lucky, we'll never see her again and you won't have to do anything."

"Dante."

"I mean it, Saxton. You don't want to reach out to her. She won't listen. Sometimes you've just gotta let it go and stay alive."

He turned Dante's words over in his head. "Then why didn't you eat me? You were starving. It can't just be because of your promise."

The wolf stared at him for a moment, and then looked elsewhere, thinking it over.

"You're worth protecting," he said at length. "At least, I think so. It's not often that … someone trusts me with their life, especially after I tried to take it in the first place."

They were quiet for a while, both of them still a bit on edge from the events of the day and unable to settle down.

"Did Mars really make all those mistakes? The god, I mean?"

"Yes, he did."

Dante's ear twitched nervously.

"You were right; I wasn't second in command," he confessed. Those five simple words seemed to have taken the wind out of him. He squeezed his single eye shut, as if expecting some sort of rebuke. When none was forthcoming, he studied Saxton, who looked at him no differently. He opened his mouth, closed it, and then began again.

"I couldn't do anything right," he went on, "so I was the pack's bottom rung, the joke and scapegoat. The *Tail*. When I was little, I used to think I was going to be special by the time I grew up. Maybe I wouldn't be someone like my father, but I could be a key hunter, a strategist, maybe even a storyteller like Grandmother." Cynically, the wolf shook his head. "Pretty presumptuous, huh? Well, here I am. Pretty much all grown up, and I'm still a mediocre member, at best. I haven't accomplished a thing to be proud of."

"You're being too hard on yourself," Saxton objected. "Look at you now; you've left and you're surviving on your own."

"Not because I wanted to." Dante looked away. "I left because I was ashamed."

Chapter Seventeen
SPRING

The following morning, Saxton and Dante bid Sputnik farewell. Mars was conspicuously absent, and her mate made her excuses for her. Asking where to find the nearest train yard through which NS trains passed, the bull terrier directed them to St. Louis. He cautioned, however, that St. Louis was clear across the state, as they were presently in Clay County.

"We pick up scrap from that train line every now and then. If you head southeast along fifty and pass a landfill, you know you're going in the right direction. You better mind the roads, though. Traffic thickens."

"What does fifty look like?" Dante asked.

"Uh ... looks like five and zero put together, I think."

"Ah," Saxton said. "I know what that looks like. Perfect."

They thanked Sputnik for his patience and promised never to enter the scrapyard again. The bull terrier took their promise to heart, but thanked Saxton in turn for giving meaning to Mars' name.

"She's a bit prouder to wear her tag and collar now," Sputnik said. "She just needs more time to make peace with everything else."

They soon found the freeway and travelled the ground adjacent to it. While they were walking, Saxton noticed that Dante had returned to the humble posture he maintained when they first met.

"You should hold your head up," he said with a frown.

"I'm a Tail," Dante argued.

"Well, I'm not a wolf and I'm not from your pack, so I honestly don't care."

Dante raised his head and slowly uncurled his tail. Fully upright, Saxton realized that the wolf was significantly larger than he thought he was— nearly six to eight times his own size. It became all too clear just how easily the wolf could do away with him if he wanted.

"Promises like the ones you made are hard to keep," he felt compelled to say. "Maybe you're not pack leader now, but one day, who knows."

Dante stared at him.

"You're one strange fox, Saxton. One strange fox."

They walked for days with little to eat, and on the sixth day of being on foot, Dante succumbed to a terrible dizziness that forced him to the ground. Saxton rushed to his side and carefully poked his forehead with the tip of his nose.

"Dante!" he exclaimed. "Are you all right?"

Dante blinked his eyes open, and when he looked up, he saw not one, but two foxes swaying side to side.

"Yeah," he replied, "yeah, I'm fine. But hold still, will you? You're making me sick."

"I'm not moving," Saxton said, quite befuddled. "You're clearly not well. Did the rain get to you?"

The wolf's empty stomach growled as if in response, and Saxton felt his own belly respond with a commiserative grumble. He lifted his nose to the air, and detected the bitter and sour smell of decay. "Hunting here is less than ideal. I smell carrion not far off. Think you can summon enough strength to walk a little further?"

"Yeah," he replied, though he did not want to admit he was very nearly dead on his feet. "But could I have some water? I think my tongue might just turn to dust."

Saxton moved his ears around like antennae, searching for the sound of moving water. His ears froze when they caught the very faint noise of water hitting pavement. "Wait here."

He trotted off in the direction his ears led him and, after a few minutes of crossing grass, rock, and two way streets, came upon a large concrete wall at the bottom of a manmade ravine. In the middle of the wall was a hole with four metal bars crossing over it, and water – salty and metallic smelling water – draining out.

Climbing down the ravine, Saxton pushed away the rumpled paper bags, aluminum cans and Styrofoam cups that had collected near the drainage. A cloud of flies hovered over the garbage, and the fox furiously shook his head to beat the gnats away from his sensitive ears. He lapped at the water settling upon the pavement, puckering his brow at the taste. It was not the best water he had ever had, but it seemed it would have to do. With his teeth, he picked one of the foam cups off the ground and dragged the cup along the runoff until it was half full.

Saxton returned to the parched wolf, and he gratefully drank the terrible water.

"Ugh!" Dante spat.

"I know. I'm sorry. At least it's spring now. We're bound to find some fresh river water eventually."

The wolf rose to his feet, feeling somewhat better. "I can smell the carrion. Let's go before someone else gets to it."

They picked up the pace, quickly discovering a mountain range made of empty food boxes, rotten fruit, maggot-infested meat, and other waste. In an instant, the smell of carrion had transformed into an overpowering scent that was difficult to describe. Near starving, however, the fox and wolf did not think twice about the filth, and jumped straight into one of the garbage piles. Startled, the crows who had already been feasting flew up into the air and cawed their discontent.

While Saxton devoured graying fried chicken in an oily paper bucket, Dante gorged on the remains inside several takeout boxes. They paid no mind to the ants that bit their lips and tongues as they ate, and they even swallowed several of the tenacious insects in their haste to silence hunger. By the time Saxton and Dante felt full, they also felt quite ill and heavy, and were sluggishly pulled into sleep.

Dante awoke hours later to the sound of Saxton rummaging around. Cans clanged and fell in the fox's wake, and the wolf watched with barely masked revulsion as he continued eating the rubbish. Carefully approaching him, Dante said, "We should go now. We're full enough to carry on."

But for whatever reason, Saxton didn't seem interested.

"Just a little longer," he said. "There are lots of things to scavenge, and we've only just begun!"

He poked his nose inside an opened can and scooped out green tuna. Dante shuddered. "Well, if you like this stuff, fine. I'm not eating any more of it, though."

The few hours that the wolf promised had somehow turned into two days. In that time, Saxton had swiftly grown lazy, disheveled, and irritable. By the third morning, there was a nagging voice in Dante's head that shouted at him that something was very wrong.

"Saxton," he began, "we can't stay here forever."

"I know. Just one more day, and then we're off."

"That's what you said *yesterday.*" He kicked a particularly offensive looking box of children's cereal down the hill. "How can you stand eating this? It's not real food."

Saxton shrugged. "If humans can eat this, so can we. It's easier than hunting, so why not capitalize on it?"

Dante opened his mouth, but realized he didn't know what to say. He remained silent and picked through the piles for bones and scraps that were somewhat acceptable.

On the fourth morning, Dante had had it.

He loomed over Saxton, who was still sleeping in a cardboard box, and picked him up by the scruff of his neck. Dropping the fox unceremoniously on the nearest trash heap, Dante stood firm and said, without faltering, "Get. Up."

Saxton rolled over and shut his eyes. "Mm … leave me alone. I'm resting."

"You've been resting and eating for three days!" Dante shouted. "It's time to get up!"

"Perhaps later."

"Perhaps now."

With that, he grabbed the fox's scruff with his teeth again and threw him into a thick puddle of mud. Saxton gasped and coughed as he resurfaced, struggling to pull himself out of the viscous soil and water.

"Have you lost your *mind?*" He looked down on his coat, which had been reduced to pitiful clumps of dirt and hair. "What are you doing?"

"Waking you up! Look around you! You want to live in this filth?"

Growling, Saxton would have bared his teeth if the hardening mud hadn't made it difficult to talk or move.

"Filth or not, this food is keeping us alive. We must do what is necessary to stay alive."

His words sent a chill down Dante's spine. In an effort to calm down, he approached him and helped him out of the mud.

"We are alive and we have a choice to make. If we – if you – stay here any longer, you will never leave. What would Quill say if he saw you now?"

Saxton looked down at himself once more, and this time was shocked to discover the feather that hung around his neck was every bit as sodden and foul smelling as he was. Suddenly embarrassed, Saxton found he could no longer look Dante in the eye without shrinking down in shame.

The wolf sighed. "If we get moving now, we might make it to the river before nightfall. You can wash up there, okay?"

Nodding, Saxton shook what soil he could off his fur and joined Dante's side. When he did not move further, however, Dante looked down on him to find downcast eyes.

"Please," he said softly, "lead the way."

It was near dusk by the time they reached the riverbed. Feeling quite grimy himself, Dante ran to the flowing water and enthusiastically jumped in. Saxton was never very fond of water, and remained perched at the river's edge where he washed his face, his tail, and his feather.

Watching him do a lousy job cleaning off, Dante swam up to the fox. "Here, let me get that feather off your neck."

He gently bit the twine—

… and pulled Saxton in.

Splash!

The fox rose to the surface, gasping, while the wolf broke down laughing.

"There you go!" Dante teased. "Squeaky clean now!"

"What are you doing?" Saxton sputtered, his thick red fur matting around his face. "Are you crazy?"

"Oh, come on, Saxton! You smelled worse than a five-day-old halibut left out in the sun."

"No, I didn't," he said indignantly as he paddled back to shore.

"Uh, yes you did. No vixen alive would've gone close to you. In fact, I bet all the vixens went running for the hills when you came along."

Reaching shore, Saxton heaved himself out and carefully patted his feather dry with his paws. The feather had lost much of its smooth, onyx barbs, and a pang of guilt hit Saxton squarely on the chest.

"Thank you," he said, "for getting me back to my senses."

Dante swam for land as well, shaking himself dry.

"Don't ever settle until you've fulfilled your word," he replied. "I'm only fulfilling mine."

Chapter Eighteen

Saxton did his best not to feel too disturbed by what had happened to him at the landfill. Dante tried to be supportive, explaining his behavior away as having been too long without food. The fox, however, sensed a deeper problem. He wasn't compelled to stay merely because of hunger. He had wanted to stay because it was easy, something any other fox would do.

After traveling for nearly a week, Saxton decided they needed to ask a local inhabitant for directions. They came upon a ranch in the middle of the night, and he reasoned this was as good a place as any to ask for help.

"You better keep your distance," Saxton whispered as they crawled beneath the thick bushes. "This is a sheep farm."

Dante brushed the leaves away from their faces with his paws, providing them a clearer view of the farm below the hill. "What? You don't think I can handle temptation?"

"I know you can handle temptation far better than I can," he replied, "but just seeing you will probably cause the herd to panic."

The wolf looked at the sheep, which, Dante had to admit, looked more than a touch appetizing. He tried to ignore the fact he was salivating. "I see your point. I'll howl if there's trouble coming."

"I'll be back soon." Another rustle of leaves, and Saxton silently slipped away. Dante watched as he treaded down the field's slope and leapt upon the top of the sheep pen. Saxton navigated the narrow wooden planks as though on a tightrope, and jumped onto the other side.

Most of the sheep were kneeling on the grass, sleeping. He didn't want to disturb then, so he whispered, "Excuse me, I—"

A ewe resting close to him opened her eyes. It took a moment before her eyes bulged from their sockets and she was on her hooves, baaing with fright.

"Exile! There's an Exile among us!"

All at once, the other ewes, rams, and lambs began shouting in unison:

"Exile! There's an Exile among us!"

Stunned by the noise, Saxton lowered his ears and shouted, "I am a *fox*, not an exile!"

"Foxes *are* Exiles!" Baaed a ram.

"Exiles!" Another ewe agreed. "Like the deceitful snakes, the arrogant owls, the greedy rats, and the wrathful wolves!"

"And the lazy goats, the conceited deer, and the gluttonous pigs— all fools!"

"But that's nearly everyone!" he exclaimed, aghast. "Where on earth do you get your silly ideas?"

"Silly ideas!" a sheep scoffed.

"How dare you insult us!" said another.

"How dare you insult our Keeper of the Green!"

"He hears our prayers and protects our wool, a greater protector you've never seen!"

"He raises the sun and lowers the moon; he grows the grass, and brings death at noon!"

"And those who don't believe in him are damned, damned, damned."

"Baa baa, to the Green Keeper!" the sheep sang. "Baa baa!"

He couldn't decide whether to feel angry or confused, and so Saxton finally asked, "Who's the Green Keeper?"

By the looks on the sheep's faces, he realized he should have bitten his tongue instead.

"He is the guardian of all that is good."

"The punisher and banisher of all that is evil."

"He has been watching over us since the beginning of time."

"And never will you see him because he is everywhere, always watching, always seeing."

"He knows if you are virtuous, and knows if you are depraved."

"And only if you are one of us will you ever be saved!"

"Baa baa to the Green Keeper! Baa baa!"

"I could never be a sheep!" The fox snarled. "I was not *born* a sheep! Maybe he knows if I am good or evil, but you fools certainly don't!"

But the sheep did not balk.

"The Keeper of the Green already knows all."

"And all foxes are thieves."

"Cheaters."

"Lonely and selfish creatures."

"Exiles!" the sheep baaed. "Exiles, they are all!"

Saxton huffed and gave up trying to reason with them. "Listen, I need your help for only a moment. My friend and I have been on foot for quite some time, and all we would like to know is—"

"Baa baa, be gone, Exile! Baa baa! Be gone!"

He gritted his teeth together, and tried once more. "I don't wish to harm any of you. I only—"

But again they turned him away.

"Baa baa, be gone, Exile! Baa baa! Be gone!"

The sheep's chorus was too much to bear. Saxton scrambled beneath the fence and scampered far and away until he could only hear their faint chanting. He looked behind him, swishing his tail and holding his nose up in the air in disgust.

"What brings you to our farm, Mr. Fox?" a female voice spoke up. "We have no chickens, so you may as well not waste your time here."

Turning around, Saxton stood face to face with a nanny goat who was resting by the open barn door. Relieved, he said quickly, "I was hoping to ask for directions. The sheep were not very helpful."

The goat smiled warmly and rose to her hooves. She looked at the corral, a hint of amusement sparkling in her rectangular pupils. "Yes, they are an entertaining bunch, aren't they?"

"Entertaining? A nightmare, to be honest. I couldn't get a word in edgewise. If I had a trout for every time they mentioned 'the Keeper of the Green—'"

"You've never heard of him?" the goat interrupted, and Saxton grew nervous.

"You believe in him too?"

"Yes," she replied, "but not in the way the sheep do. You needed directions?"

"St. Louis," Saxton supplied.

"Oh, you're very close, Mr. Fox," and at that Saxton was quite pleased. "Keep heading northeast. When you see a giant arch made of steel over the horizon, you'll know you're there."

"A giant arch?" He tried to imagine such a thing and couldn't.

"The humans made it," the goat explained, "or so Mr. and Mrs. Compton say. I don't doubt it. Only humans make such strange things at their leisure. If you're going there, you'd better keep your head down. The cars and people are louder, faster, and more dangerous than around here."

Saxton bowed, grateful for the help. "Thank you, Miss Goat. I should have visited you first."

The glisten in her eyes faded into something a little sad.

"They are ignorant and frightened and proud," she said somberly. "The only world they know is the fence that protects them. Everything outside it is wicked because it is different and unknown. What the sheep fail to understand, Mr. Fox, is that the Keeper of the Green loves all the creatures of the land. Even the wolf and the fox, who feed on his livestock, make sure the Green Keeper's burden is not too large to carry. He plays no favorites. He treasures all, even the most hated among us. We should all try to be more like him."

Saxton warmed to her words, but still felt dubious.

"The sheep seem to believe differently."

"The sheep believe what they want to believe," she replied. "It is easy to greet a mirror with a smile. It is hard to welcome a strange face, covered by scars, with open arms."

It had been a long time since the fox had heard words that made him think of Quill. Moved, he wished he had something to give the goat in return.

"I've heard that rats are called *Sewer Beggars*, and yet I know of a rat who lives on a train, who begs for nothing, and can read," Saxton said. "If it wasn't for him, my friend and I probably would not have made it this far."

"Then despite the struggles of his kind, that rat has been blessed with patience and cleverness. I am happy to hear it."

"Thank you again," he said, wishing he could stay and talk with her more. "It was a pleasure meeting you, Miss Goat."

"And I, you, Mr. Fox. The world is an exciting but imperfect place. Be wary of that one creature you might cross who is evil, but masquerading as good, instead of good, but struggling with evil."

He nodded and was about to leave when Dante's howl echoed into the night, and was followed by the chilling sound of screaming sheep. Saxton turned. Napowsa was at the sheep pen, tearing the wooden planks off and flinging them aside.

The sheep fell back, sticking close together and forming a giant cloud. Napowsa reached down and strangled one of the sheep with her teeth until it stopped making noise. Blood covered her face.

"Where's the *Lonely Thief*!" She growled. "I know he's here! Where is he?"

The sheep answered all at once, but cluttered together, not a word made sense. Napowsa roared again, shaking her head at the noise.

"Get as far inside the barn as you can!" Saxton ordered the goat. "Go!"

She was too scared to reply, but did as she was told. Saxton ran back to the sheep pen. Their faces squeezed out between the fence panels, their eyes large and their voices baaing and baaing.

"Stay calm!" Saxton shouted. "Stay calm and listen to me! Is there another way out of this thing? Another door?"

They continued to baa, and said nothing useful. Dante ran down the slope and joined his side.

"What're you doing? Let's get out of here!"

"I can't leave them!"

They heard barking in the distance, but rapidly growing close. They swung around and saw a collie racing for the corral.

"What's going on!" she shouted, and her eyes narrowed upon seeing Dante and Saxton.

"Bear!" Saxton hollered. "There's a bear!"

Just then, Napowsa rose on her hind legs and roared, drowning out the screams of the sheep only briefly. She was so big, she covered the stars. Part of a lamb's leg hung from her lower teeth.

"Good God," the collie breathed. Then she turned on her heels and raced for the farm house. "Master!" she barked. "Master! Master! Come out here! Master!"

Saxton watched her go, and then studied the fence. "She's getting help. Good. Dante, can you break this side of the pen down?"

"I can try."

He ran back several feet, and then sprinted forward, barreling the side of his body against the wooden planks over and over again until they splintered down the middle. The sheep spilled out like water out of a crumbling dam.

BANG! BANG!

Gunshots. Saxton's blood ran cold. He and Dante ducked as bullets whizzed passed them. One missed Napowsa, but the other grazed her shoulder, breaking skin and drawing blood.

The farmer kept her at bay with more bullets, while the collie ran around the field, gathering the sheep, but too many had gone astray.

"Come on," Saxton hissed. "We're going to help her!"

"Of course we are," Dante snorted, but didn't fight him.

They raced to the collie's side, following as she ran in a shrinking circle around the flock.

"Now what?" Saxton asked her, breath catching as he ran. She stared at him in shock.

"Now what? What do you mean, 'Now what?' I'm barely keeping them together!"

"We'll help get them to safety!" yelled the fox.

"Just tell us what to do!" added the wolf.

She hesitated, but seemed to understand she couldn't do this on her own, not tonight.

"Keep circling the flock! Nip at their heels if they try to get out! We've got fifty of them, and we lost two tonight. I've gotta account for forty-eight!"

"When we get all of them together, we should take them to the barn," Saxton suggested. "We can close the doors behind them. Keep them safe!"

"Yeah," the collie nodded. "I like it. You sure you're not a couple of mutts or somethin'?"

She jumped onto a sheep's back and hopped from the top of one to another, counting. Dante and Saxton continued circling, jumping back whenever a sheep tried to kick them in the face for their troubles.

"Okay! We're gonna force 'em forward and get 'em in!" The collie shouted as she leapt off a ram from the back of the flock. "Let's go! Move! Move! Move!"

Dante and Saxton flanked the sheep from either side, keeping the body of the herd intact. They pushed closer and closer toward barn, until at last the sheep stampeded in. Saxton and the collie pushed the barn doors shut with their noses.

They heaved a sigh of relief, but Napowsa and the farmer cut it short. *BANG! BANG!* Went the farmer's gun. He chased her away from his land, reloading his weapon as he went.

Napowsa barreled away, searching for safety, but her eyes lit on fire when they locked onto Saxton's as she ran.

"You can't hide, *Lonely Thief*! I'll keep running after you until you lose your breath and reach the forever dark!"

Her massive form left a black shadow sweeping across the grass, up the slope, and into the woods. Once she was out of sight, the farmer skid to a halt and slowly lowered his shotgun.

"You guys better go before Master sees you," the collie advised solemnly. She looked at them with kind eyes. "Thanks for the help."

They escaped the farm as stealthily as they could, taking care to avoid the direction in which Naposa had ran, but still wary of stumbling into her yet again.

"Dante," Saxton whispered, "is she going to haunt me for the rest of my life?"

They slowed their pace to a trot. The wolf looked at him, brow furrowed with worry, but posture steady and sure.

"I won't let her get to you."

Chapter Nineteen
SUMMER

They continued northeast, as the goat had advised, and took advantage of the night and its absence of people for safe traveling. Napowsa hadn't made another appearance in nearly six days, so Saxton gradually shook off the need to constantly look over his shoulder.

As the clouds cleared, revealing a bright full moon, the wolf felt compelled to stop in his tracks, sit on his haunches, and sing a most beautiful and haunting song.

Saxton watched in awe as Dante lifted his head to the stars, howling with such emotion that he felt his hairs prickle. There was great passion in Dante's voice, but also sorrow with the softest notes of hope. By the time the wolf was finished, the fox had a strange feeling of déjà vu.

"I don't know why," Saxton whispered, "but I feel as though I've heard that song before."

"You might have. Wolves always sing to the moon. She lights our path at night— reveals danger and guides us on our hunts. She takes care of us, you see, so it's only right that we thank her."

Saxton squinted at the silvery orb that hung above them like an ornament. "The sheep and the goats we … had an interesting time with … they believe in a guardian as well. Not in the moon, but something similar. I'm afraid I don't understand it as foxes aren't raised to believe in such things."

"And crows?"

He shook his head. "Quill always talked about how the birds praise the wind and skies. Not something I could really appreciate since I have no wings."

"Are you grateful for anything, then?"

He grew pensive, but eventually answered.

"Despite ... what happened ... I'm grateful we met. I wish things hadn't happened as they did, but maybe – I don't know – maybe it was meant to be; one part of my life ending and a new one beginning, I suppose.

"I'm also grateful for luck, as it always seems to find me when I most need it, and something else. I'm not sure what the word for it is. It's something I've always felt for my mother, my sister, and Quill, but wish I felt for my brother and father. It fills me with warmth no matter how cold the air is, and it pains me with intense longing if I dwell on it too long."

He glanced at Dante and realized that his rambling must have caused his friend to lose interest.

"I'm sorry. I must not make much sense at all."

They walked side by side in silence before Dante whispered, "No, there's a word for it, Saxton. I'm sure you've heard it before. It's called 'love.'"

They saw the infamous 'arch' the goat spoke of just as the sun began making its slow ascent up the sky. The city, which had just begun to come alive, was only sparsely filled with traffic. Nevertheless, Saxton cautiously navigated the streets, whether paved or cobbled, while Dante lowered his body to the ground in an effort to appear more like a stray dog and less like a wolf.

There were many buildings made of brick, and most of the areas with trees and grass had concrete paths slithering over them. While Dante didn't like the environment – it made him twitchy – Saxton was rather impressed. If they hadn't been pressed for time, he would have liked to explore a little longer.

One storefront they passed had strange, black and silver boxes containing brightly colored moving pictures behind its window. Another was filled with tables and upturned chairs, its wooden shelves lined with white mugs, and smelling of something roasted and bittersweet. And yet another had strange statues that looked frighteningly like human bodies without heads, wearing vibrant material around their shoulders.

But none of the stores' buildings compared to the alien-looking skyscrapers that loomed higher than the greatest trees. They made Dante feel unusually uneasy and small.

They continued through the city, following the sounds of train wheels, exhaust, and horns. Soon, they made it to the train yard where they found several freights preparing for departure. They located an NS train and quickly snuck inside one of the cars.

The ride was a long and uneventful one, and with no rats or other stowaways with whom to pass the time, Saxton and Dante grew restless. They could not wait for the next stop, when they could stretch their legs and find something to eat.

Every other afternoon, the train would stop to refuel or perform maintenance. Saxton and Dante made it a point to make their excursions outdoors quick and disciplined, but by the fourth stop the weather was particularly warm and pleasant. Delighted, they stayed out a touch longer, rolling in the lush fields and taking in the scent of flowers.

"We're in the dead of summer," Dante remarked. "That gives us about four moons to get to Exeter, before Quill's sister flies south. Hopefully winter won't come early."

"Relax, we're halfway there," Saxton grinned. "At this rate, I think we'll even have time to spare."

Dante was doubtful, but he clipped his thoughts before they could stumble out of his mouth. The fox was in a good mood today, and he didn't want to spoil it.

Not far away, Saxton could see a little township. The smells and sounds that emanated from it were very different from those of St. Louis. He could hear songs that were sleepy, but happy and full of life. He could smell meat laden with salt, fresh baked bread, and something bitter and bubbly he could not name; but there was something else, too, something feminine and bold and beautiful … something *wild*.

Intrigued, he couldn't help, but keep glancing at the village. He soon gave into his building curiosity and began to act upon it.

"Where're you going?" Dante asked.

"To town," he replied. "I think I can find food there—certainly, something more filling than these squirrels. I won't be long."

He was about to run off without a second thought, when the wolf grimaced.

"It's a bit far off." He peered at the train. "You sure you'll be back in time?"

"I'll be as quick as a lightning bolt," Saxton promised. "Howl away if you see the men preparing to leave."

"All right," Dante sighed, already regretting it. "But remember, 'quick as a lightning shot.'"

The fox smiled. "You'll never know I left."

Saxton sprinted across the field and, upon entering the town, was greeted by blossoming trees, clean streets, and tranquil people – people who were not in a hurry – settled on benches at the park or on chairs with a cup of something hot and creamy at the tables. There was a long line of small shops filled with knick knacks, sweets, loomed fabrics, and, to Saxton's pleasure, food.

He snuck into the nearest butcher's store, and eyed two generous slabs of meat sitting on display. He grabbed them and scampered out the door, where the mysterious smell that drew him into town stopped him in his tracks. Saxton shook his head free of it, and sped out of the village, running through bushes and brush.

He returned to Dante with minutes to spare. He held up the steaks he stole proudly.

"Look what I got," Saxton said.

Dante chuckled, greedily gobbling the beef. "Fine, fine ... I never should have—"

He broke off and stared at Saxton as if he had grown another tail. The fox cocked his head to the side. "What's wrong?"

"Your feather," he said breathlessly. "It's gone!"

Saxton looked down at his chest and felt the blood drain from his face. The piece of twine that had been wrapped around his neck was no longer there, and neither was Quill's feather.

Horrified, he glanced down the path he had taken back. "It must have fallen off! I need to go back and find it!"

Dante ran in front of his friend, blocking his path. "No! We'll miss the train!"

"It doesn't matter! Quill wanted to spend his last days in Exeter, what's the point if I don't bring him with me?"

He sidestepped the wolf and retraced his steps. Dante glanced back at the train.

"Do us both a favor and have engine trouble, will you?"

And with that he ran after the frantic fox, who was already a third of the way back to the village. When he reached him, Saxton had come to an abrupt halt, having recognized a group of bushes he ran through during his return.

"Look around the branches!" Saxton instructed. "It must have snagged somewhere."

The two of them bobbed their heads to and fro, sniffing about and poking their faces with bald twigs.

150

"I don't see it," said Dante. He glanced at the train waiting for them. The crew was already boarding.

"There it is!" Saxton shouted. Sure enough, the feather's twine had entangled around a particularly long branch. He gingerly pulled the twine with his teeth. Once the feather was freed, he slipped the rough cord around his neck.

No sooner did the feather settle safely atop his chest did the train's engine begin to *chug-chug, chug-chug* and release a high-pitched whistle.

Dante sprang forward. "Hurry! Let's go!"

They ran back to the tracks, but it was too late. The locomotive was already at full speed, and the caboose was too far for them to reach no matter how fast they ran. They slowed to a stop and watched as their ride abandoned them.

Saxton cleared his throat and nervously glanced at Dante, "Well, we've been long due for a stopover, I think."

"At least we know where the train tracks are," the wolf huffed.

He tried not to flinch in annoyance when Saxton pawed him on the shoulder. He looked down at him, and the fox was every bit as contrite as he should have been. It didn't make him feel any better.

"Listen," Saxton said, "everything happens for a reason, right? Well, maybe we were meant to stay here for a while. Explore, meet new strangers, all those things Quill talked about."

"You're disgustingly optimistic."

"And you're not optimistic enough."

"Look," Dante groused, "It's great that Quill believed in 'fate' and 'choice,' and whatever else makes you tick, but there's also a thing called 'making mistakes and owning them.'"

"I'm not saying I didn't," the fox said far too pleasantly. "I'm only saying we may as well make the most of things."

The wolf glanced at the village and shook his head. "I don't think I should get too close to this town, Saxton. It's too risky."

"You fared well enough in the city."

"Yeah, but we snuck around when most of the humans were asleep, remember? What humans don't see won't scare them. Right now, the sun's gonna be a problem, a big one."

"But you look like a dog when you're hunched down, right? No reason why you can't do that again here."

"Yeah, but in broad daylight? At least in St. Louis, I had night and shadows to help me out!"

"Then we'll avoid being in the light as much as possible. Look around you, Dante. There's not much to hunt in these fields, but there's plenty of food in the town. I can get food for us both there."

Though Saxton sounded reasonable enough, he couldn't shake the feeling they were courting danger much too closely, even for them.

"All right, but we can't stay here long. The longer we stay, the more likely a human's gonna notice me."

The fox gave him a toothy smile and led him to the village. He wondered how long it would take before his presence was deemed unwelcome.

Chapter Twenty

They entered town quietly and made use of the alleys and side streets to keep contact with humans at a minimum. A little girl walking sullenly beside her mother caught sight of the two strange 'dogs,' but before she could point and holler, her mother whisked her away with a tug at her wrist and pulled her inside a nearby shop.

Dante felt his insides clench as the occasional car drove past them on the street. It seemed to him that at any moment a man might approach them from behind, with a rifle or a shotgun at the ready, and there would be nowhere to run or hide because they were on man's land, not theirs.

But Saxton was enamored with the town. The humans appeared cheerful and friendly— characteristics he never dreamed possible in these peculiar creatures. He stole a glance to see if Dante was just as taken as he was, but instead found a heavy frown over the wolf's brow.

"Are you all right there, Dante? You look like you swallowed a bad grasshopper."

"I don't like cities, and now I know I don't like little towns either."

He cocked his head to the side. "But we've only just begun exploring it."

"I am not big on exploring, not when there are people everywhere."

"Keep fidgeting like that and those people will notice. Relax. Pretend you belong here."

"That's the problem: I don't."

Realizing the wolf was growing agitated with anxiety, Saxton led Dante around the nearest corner and behind a giant garbage bin. Dante's nostrils flared at the familiar and unwelcome stench of human refuse, but he gritted his teeth and bore the unpleasantness.

"Dante," Saxton said gently, "I understand you're out of your element here. But you have to believe me when I say there's nothing to eat elsewhere."

"Don't pretend to be wise!" he snapped. "If you— if you hadn't gotten curious in the first place, we wouldn't be in this situation!"

Saxton winced. "Yes, I know."

When he said nothing else, Dante sighed and gazed at the sky, wondering how he could admire someone who, at times, was so infuriating.

"You just can't help it, can you?"

"Help what?"

"Sticking your nose into everything."

He gave him a crooked smile. "Nothing ventured, nothing gained."

Dante looked at the crow's feather and remembered that nearly everything Saxton did, he did because of Quill. Most of the things he did were foolhardy, but they were also courageous and noble, and he would be lying if he didn't wish he had Saxton's confidence.

"You're not invincible, you know," he said at length. "You might be smarter than a snake bite, but you're impulsive too. If something happens to you and there's nothing I can do about it, I have to live with that. But if something happens to me, will you worry at all?"

His words brought Saxton up short. "Of course I will," he said, almost insulted. "That's a silly question."

The wolf said nothing.

Just then, across the street, they heard a loud clang outside one of the town bistros. Turning to the noise, they watched as a raccoon tumbled out of a trashcan and landed in a furry heap on the sidewalk before scuttling away. A man in a white apron stepped out of the restaurant with a large, oddly shaped stick in his hand, yelling.

"Get out of my garbage! Get out! Get out! Get out!"

The man swung the stick around, not using it to hit the raccoon so much as threaten him off the property. They watched as the raccoon

154

ran, dropping many of his gatherings – bread crusts, half-eaten fruit, and the like – and backtracked to pick them up again.

"Ah," Saxton said, "a local."

"Should we follow him?" Dante asked.

"Let's."

They glanced down either side of the street before trotting across. The raccoon was balancing an apple core on his nose, but immediately dropped everything once more upon seeing the wolf. The raccoon screeched, baring his teeth.

"I just escaped an angry man with a baseball bat!" He hissed. "You'll have to fight long and hard if you want to sink your teeth into me!"

"Please don't be alarmed," Saxton implored, walking in front of Dante and politely lowering his head. "We are interested in neither you nor your scavenges, although it looks like you could use an extra set of teeth."

Before the raccoon could protest, Dante gathered the chicken bones that still had scrap meat and ligaments on them.

"So," Dante mumbled through clenched teeth. "Where d'you live?"

The raccoon stared at them both, baffled, and held tightly onto a half-eaten sandwich. "Beg your pardon, but come again?"

Saxton smiled and explained his and Dante's predicament. When he finished, he picked up the fallen apple core and two slices of bread from the ground.

"Well!" the raccoon said, "if you didn't kill a rat, some dogs, or a sheep to get this far, I guess you two're owed a little hospitality."

The raccoon, who had introduced himself as Bandit, led Saxton and Dante away from the village toward a small area of woods just north of the town border. Not having spoken to anyone in a very long time, the raccoon grew gregarious and rather excited, detailing how he had come to live in Lattice, Pennsylvania, as the village was called.

"It's a nice area, really it is. Some of the humans like leaving food out in their backyards for the neighborhood raccoons and foxes. Of course, they don't appreciate it when we go through their garbage. Strange, aren't they? I don't see why they need to be protective of it if they're just gonna to throw it all out. Such a waste, really."

In a clearing of green, they approached what appeared to be a rustic cabin. The cabin stood along the edge of a grassy slope, and the back half of its structure was supported by large, wooden beams that kept it level and elevated. Dante set down the food he carried.

"Are there humans here?"

"Not this time of year. There are a few families that like to visit in the winter and summer. Otherwise, this place is pretty empty. As long as we don't make any trouble, they tend to leave us alone."

Dante eyed the scraps that each of them carried, and commented, "This is a lot of food for just one raccoon."

"Oh, it's not just for me, Mr. Wolf," Bandit assured as Dante picked up the food again. "It's also for my Clyde. He's taken ill, understand, and I've been running around town gathering supplies for the both of us. Barely anything to eat in the fields these days."

Bandit led Saxton and Dante down alongside the slope. Beneath the cabin, they could see a makeshift den. It was dry and spacious, and the ground was covered with dead leaves and brush, perfect for warmth.

"There's something I ought to tell you," Bandit said, blocking the entryway. "I'm afraid my companion is highly contagious. Mind his teeth and his claws. He likes to bite and scratch when he has a fit, so please do stay back. Watch your head getting in."

They crawled on their stomachs for about a yard before the distance between the ground and the cabin floor increased, and Dante could actually stand. Against one of the wooden beams was a bundle of leaves upon which a thin, listless raccoon lay.

"Clyde?" Bandit greeted, "we have guests."

"Guests?" Clyde's voice sounded like gravel. He lifted his head and forced his eyes a crack open to see the fox and wolf. Saxton suppressed the impulse to gasp while Dante tried not to look away. The corners of Clyde's mouth were frothing with saliva and his fur was mangy with self-inflicted bite marks.

"Welcome," said Clyde. "If you made it this far without making mincemeat out of my partner in crime, I'm guessing you folks are friendly."

Bandit deposited the food he had gathered at Clyde's feet. Saxton and Dante followed suit. Clyde sniffed at the offerings.

"Fancy anything?" Bandit asked. He crawled behind Clyde and added more leaves to support his back.

"No," he sighed. "Not today. I don't have an appetite."

"You haven't eaten in three days." Bandit gently reminded.

Clyde snarled, and Saxton and Dante took a step back. "I know, I know! I just want something to chew on."

"Well, your chewing stick is worse for wear. Some roots then?"

156

Talking seemed to make Clyde even more tired, so he gave a single nod more out of resignation than genuine interest.

"All right, then. I'll be just outside. Won't be a minute."

Saxton felt uneasy, but it was in a way that was markedly different from when he was being pursued by a hunter or predator.

"Perhaps we can come along?" he offered.

Bandit immediately recognized the wary tone in voice, but he took it in stride. "Sure, if you like."

Upon exiting the den and walking out of an earshot, Saxton couldn't help, but ask—

"What's wrong with him? He looks …"

"Yes, I know," the raccoon replied, his face hardening. "In a few more days … he'll be completely rabid."

Saxton froze, alarmed. Though he had never encountered a rabid creature before, Quill had once warned him to be wary of any animal with a peculiarly vacant look in its eye and that behaved out of sorts. 'It's a very tragic way to die,' Quill had said, 'very tragic. First you feel ill, like you've a touch of the flu, and then, little by little, you begin to lose your mind. I cannot decide which is worse: to not remember who you are and where you belong, or to have everyone avoid you in sheer fear.'

"I'm so sorry," he said.

Bandit didn't even blink. "As am I."

They spent the next few moments digging for roots in silence. When Saxton ventured several feet away, Dante cornered the raccoon.

"It's good of you to take care of him," he said privately. "I know not many would, given the risks. It must be difficult."

But the raccoon shook his head. "No. I love him, so caring for him is not difficult. What's difficult is seeing him suffer. Perhaps no one else can understand, but I will never leave his side, not even when he drives me up the wall." Bandit swallowed. "I'm going to lose him. There's nothing I can do about that. Every moment counts and it'd be a shame if I wasted any of it."

Dante glanced at Saxton who was struggling to pull a particularly stubborn yet succulent root out of the soil. When he finally succeeded, he gracelessly tumbled head-over-heels in the dirt. Dante laughed lightly, and Saxton heard him. He looked at the horrible state of his fur, and chuckled as well.

Seeing Saxton lighthearted for the first time in months, and realizing he could be happy despite how badly he had hurt him, the wolf decided: it was time to tell him everything.

Back in the den, Clyde gnawed at the roots. It served to relieve the tireless itch to chew away at his arms and legs, as well as protect everyone else from a sudden fit. Dante was famished, but felt guilty for eating the raccoon's spoils. Bandit cast aside his concerns with a flippant wave of the paw and said, "Don't stop. Please eat. It's not very often we have other creatures visit. Most of them are too afraid."

Saxton heard Dante's stomach growl. He had already eaten all the chicken scraps and bone marrow, but that was hardly a meal for a wolf his size. He broke his crust of bread in half and nudged it toward Dante with his nose. It wasn't much, but he hoped it would help.

After they finished eating, Dante helped Bandit clear out the den while Saxton kept Clyde company. They sat in awkward silence, and for a moment Saxton thought the raccoon had fallen asleep.

"Sometimes I wish he'd just pack up and leave, find someone else to bother," Clyde grumbled. "But then I think about how much I'd hate to be sick and tired and alone, and then I think about how much he makes each day bearable." He looked at Saxton, his eyes wide, a little crazed, but full of emotion. "I'm getting worse. My mind wanders and I can't remember what happened yesterday or the day before that, but deep down I know that kicking him out will kill him more than me, and I'm not about to break his heart." He squeezed his eyes shut, cursing his misfortune, and whispered, "It's too beautiful, you see? Too beautiful to break, and I just can't do it. So I'll keep him around, even if it hurts the both of us. I'm selfish that way."

"Staying with someone who wants to be with you in turn isn't selfish." Saxton said.

"I don't like seeing him so anxious."

"It's only because he cares, the same way you do about him."

Together they watched as Bandit fussed with the leaves, cached what little leftovers remained, and chatted with Dante as he went about his business of keeping everything in order. Saxton did not know why he hadn't noticed it before, but Bandit's posture was hunched over and he twitched in a nervous manner that said he was always harried. Yet despite his barely hidden fatigue, Bandit was somehow happy.

Saxton's eyes burned at the thought.

By nightfall, the raccoons were ready to retire. Bandit promised to help keep Dante from being recognized as a wolf, and Clyde mentioned that the train they needed wouldn't return for another three days. Until then, they would need someone very familiar with the town to safely navigate it.

They settled next to the entryway, giving the raccoons their privacy, and Saxton peered out from beneath the cabin to look at the stars. With few streets lights in the area, the specks of light that hung in the sky twinkled more brightly than they had seen in quite some time.

"Quill used to tell me this story about 'The Silver Crane and The Moon.' Have I told you that one yet?"

Dante shook his head.

"A long time ago, there was a crane with beautiful silver feathers," Saxton began, wishing he had Quill's special flare for storytelling. "The other cranes were jealous of her beauty and ignored her. She felt so lonely, she befriended the moon. The feathers she dropped became the stars in the sky. Now they shine together." He thoughtfully swayed his tail from side to side. "Bandit and Clyde are lucky to have one another— like Sputnik and Mars. We've met a lot of interesting creatures, haven't we? But it makes me wonder if anyone will remember our story, about a fox and a wolf that didn't quite fit anywhere except elsewhere."

Dante opened his mouth to speak, but found the words would not come out. He snapped his jaws shut, and the faint clack of his teeth coming together like scissors caught Saxton's attention. He scrutinized the way Dante clawed absently at the soil, the way his tail twitched with tension.

"You wanted to know about my face," Dante started, and Saxton looked at him with surprise. "You wanted to know about my family. Are you still curious?"

The way he spoke sent a chill down Saxton's spine, but he nodded. The wolf took a deep breath and, having already rehearsed in his mind how he'd like to begin his story, began speaking as though he was talking about someone else.

"Last winter, before we met, there was an ice storm so bad it killed several members of my pack; my aunt, two of my uncles, and my grandfather ... they're all gone. But what was worse was that the cold didn't kill them quickly, no. No, it took its time." Dante swallowed thickly as the images he tried so hard to bury in the back of his mind –images that left the taste of ash on his tongue – resurfaced with a vengeance. "We were on our way back from a failed hunt, a hunt I had ruined, when the flurry hit. It was so hard to see, we didn't realize we were walking over thin ice. When the ice broke, most of us managed to escape the freezing water. Me, though ..." he laughed cruelly at himself, "I was impossible. If I couldn't even help my family bring down an elk, what were the chances I'd be able to save myself from an icy river?

"Uncle Fritz saw me struggling. I was close to drowning when he grabbed me by the scruff of my neck and hauled me to solid ground with his teeth. He was always nice to me, Uncle Fritz; never gave me a hard time like my brothers. But in saving me, the water around his body began to freeze and he couldn't get out. Uncle Aspen and Aunt Dakota tried to help him but only managed to get trapped themselves. And Grandpa, well, Grandpa was old. He didn't have a chance.

"It was too dangerous to help any of them, so my father ordered us to wait out the storm. The water hardened pretty quickly, and by the time the storm died, we couldn't break any of them free." He gritted his teeth and screwed his right eye shut. "Their heads were sticking out of the ice. Their *heads*, Saxton. And they were still alive, howling and whimpering in pain. There was nothing we could do. We had no choice but to leave them there to die."

Saxton felt bile rise to this throat, and he remembered the smell of gun powder, dogs, and men. His ears rang as he remembered the shells zipping over his head. His heart pounded against his chest like a little bird in a cage. He had chosen to be a fool that day, and nearly died for it.

"Every time we went on a hunt, we'd pass the river and see their heads staring at us … only their eyes had gone pitch black and their voices had disappeared. Yet, sometimes, when the night was darkest, you could still hear them howl."

Dante choked back a sob, and finally shed tears.

"Rush said the whole disaster was my fault. If I hadn't tripped over my own feet during the hunt, we would've had food and not returned the way we came in failure. I wouldn't have fallen through the ice, Uncle Fritz wouldn't have gone back for me, and everyone else would still be alive."

Saxton watched Dante as he tore the words, one by one, from his own throat. He wanted to tell him to stop if he did not wish to continue, but saw that Dante needed him to listen even if it pained him to speak.

"My sister, Timber," he went on, "told him he was speaking out of turn, but I believed him. How could I not? We had nothing to eat for days and we lost part of our family. I couldn't pretend to be a member of the pack if I couldn't do my part. I had to help them survive. I had to earn my place.

"So I went off on my own in search of caribou. I couldn't believe my luck when I actually found one all by itself. This was it, I thought, this was my chance to redeem myself— to show my family I wasn't deadweight." Dante snorted. "I don't know if I was desperate or

160

delusional thinking I could kill a caribou on my own. Without thinking twice, I chased him down. I got close, so close, Saxton! I scratched him up pretty bad on the hindquarters, but he always managed to pull ahead. I didn't want him to get away, so I tried to pull him to the ground. It was in that moment, the moment I thought I had finally done something right, that he kicked me in the face.

"But I held on, and we tumbled and rolled in the snow. Something ripped, and then there was loud ringing. It lasted for a few moments before everything around me became blurry and the air grew muted. I tried to stand, but the ground was shifting beneath my feet— like I was hanging onto a log adrift in a powerful river. I stared at the snow, focused on it to get my bearings. When I could finally see again, there was blood everywhere. I thought I did it. I thought I took him down. But when I looked ahead of me, the caribou was gone. He'd escaped. The blood on the snow, it was mine.

"What an embarrassment. I was forced to return to my family with my tail between my legs. That night, the pain overcame me, and it was obvious I was officially useless to the pack. The kick from the caribou gouged my left eye, and the fall tore off most of my left ear. It took me weeks before I could balance and walk right again. My brothers and sister brought me scraps of food just like Grandma. She's so old she could barely chew! I could tell they resented it, but my father never let on he was disappointed or angry. In fact, I've never seen him so sad.

"I couldn't take how he would look at me. Always worried. Always pitying. At night I heard him scolding Rush to treat me with respect. Rush said I was a burden, that I was slowing them down and costing them their lives— their survival. But Father said I was still a member of the family, said I should be loved and taken care of like anyone else. Father meant well, but ... Rush was right. So I left."

When Dante finished his story, he couldn't decide if he felt better or worse. He looked at Saxton, not sure what to expect. He received only a question.

"Why are you telling me this now?"

Dante grimaced. He had already been entirely truthful tonight. There was no point in stopping now. "Because one day, it might be too late. One day, I'll lose the chance to be forgiven."

Saxton stroked Quill's weatherworn feather with one paw.

"Oh, my friend," he whispered sadly, "put down the weight you carry."

Chapter Twenty-One

"I have a friend in town," Clyde said gruffly, his eyes struggling to focus but failing. "She's a tough one, but she'll do good by you. She's a stray cat named 'Tootsie.' She's a calico, so you'll recognize her by her spots and odd colored eyes." Without warning, Clyde's eyes went wild. He frothed more profusely at the mouth and began clawing at the air. Bandit stood between him and his guests, blocking the fox and wolf from possible harm. When Clyde's fit subsided, he continued, "Blue and yellow, they are, blue and yellow. She knows the town like the back of her paw and she ain't hard to find. Catch her fish or something just as tasty, and she'll pay you attention."

"What about me?" Dante asked. "You mentioned there might be a way to get through town without causing problems?"

"Ah," Bandit said, "I have just the thing." He ran off to a corner of the den and unearthed a collection of shiny objects from the soil. "When I'm in town, I like to pick up a few things to spruce up the home." He lifted what appeared to be a leather belt that had a circular piece of metal hanging from it. "This is a dog collar," Bandit explained. "The tag's a bit rusted, but from afar, a human can't tell the difference. Put it on, and I'm certain you'll be left alone— you won't even need to try and make yourself look smaller! Humans are fairly simple when it comes to things like this. If you put a regular Joe in a long white coat, everyone'll think he's the smartest guy in the room!"

Dante lowered his head so Bandit could reach his neck. Bandit looped the collar around him and fastened the buckle. The wolf pawed at the collar with his hind leg.

"It's tight," he grumbled, "and uncomfortable."

"Yes, you are quite a bit larger than your domesticated cousins," Bandit acknowledged. "I'm afraid that's all I have."

Dante shook his neck to release some hairs that were painfully snagged beneath the collar. "I'll get used to it. Thanks, Bandit."

They nodded and said their goodbyes to the two raccoons. Following Clyde's instructions, Saxton snuck into a fish market and stole a modest trout from a crate filled with ice. He was about to depart when it dawned on him that Dante must still be hungry after last night's meager meal. It wouldn't do to have the wolf attack and eat their guide in a moment of sheer desperation. He turned around and plucked two smaller trout from the crate, dragged them across the floor, and squeezed out the back door. After Dante finished eating his share of the fish in the adjacent alley, Saxton took the third fish and began searching for Tootsie.

Clyde was right. It did not take long for them to find a white cat covered with orange and black markings sunbathing on an awning above a closed store. Saxton announced their presence with a high-pitched yip.

The cat lazily opened one eye, the blue one, and then the other. "Well, well, well," Tootsie purred. "Look what the cat dragged in: a dapper fox and a ..." Tootsie paused, one of her brows quirking at the sight of Dante's dog collar. "... a housetrained *wolf*. Boy oh boy, the world gets stranger every day, don't it? Do ya bite?"

"If you get me angry enough." Dante growled. The cat laughed.

She stretched with languid grace, and then jumped from the awning onto a postbox, and from the postbox to the ground. Circling them both, she sniffed at the trout Saxton held clenched between his teeth. She seemed to know why they had come to see her. "Good old Clyde. How is he these days?"

"Not well," Saxton answered, having lowered the fish to the ground. "I'm impressed he remembered you."

She smiled. Dante did not know if it was her sharp fangs, but when she grinned like that, it seemed more cruel than friendly.

"When I first met him, he was still a youngster. Neighborhood dog almost got to him, but I happened to be on one of my midnight strolls. Hard to forget your savior, you know?"

She spoke with a casual arrogance that reminded Dante of Scratch. Saxton, however, noticed that the end of her tail was missing, possibly having been bitten off by the dog she had mentioned.

Tootsie glanced at a nearby dark alley and released a long, ear-splitting yowl. Out of the shadows, a second cat appeared. She had blue-gray fur that was matted with dirt and fleas, and she was so terribly thin Dante and Saxton could see her ribs. She bowed her head as she approached Tootsie, who pawed the fish lying before Saxton's feet.

"Take this to the colony," Tootsie commanded. "I'll see you and the others when the sun sets."

The cat nodded, but glanced warily at the fox and wolf. "Out-of-towners?" The cat hissed. "They're bigger than the raccoons or the opossums. You sure you can handle them on your own?"

"You have your orders. Now scat!"

Not wasting a second more, the cat took the fish and disappeared into the alley. Tootsie gestured for Saxton and Dante to follow her off the sidewalk with a tilt of her head.

"So, you came for a crash course on the ins and outs of Lattice, hm? Well, Bandit and Clyde referred you to the perfect teacher. Follow me," she instructed. "Don't look at anyone, don't touch anyone, and don't make a sound if you can help it."

She led them to a side street that was darkened by a row of brick buildings facing east. Judging by the balconies holding potted flowers or air drying sheets, Saxton guessed that different groups of human families actually lived in the same housing.

"Be mindful of the sun and the way it casts shadows. In broad daylight, you want to stay off the main streets and sidewalks and stay on the streets that are between buildings or houses. No buildings and no houses mean no shadows and no shadows means no coverage, you understand?"

"Even if the buildings and houses are full of people?" Saxton questioned.

Tootsie rolled her eyes. "Kids got school. Mommy and Daddy have work. Homes are usually empty from nine to five." When it was obvious that neither Saxton nor Dante understood what 'nine to five' meant, she explained, "From sun up to sun down, people abandon their little nests. Believe it or not, boys, when the sun's out you're safest near where they live. Where they work, well, that's a different ball game."

She showed them her favorite alleys and hideaways, and later the local restaurants. "You probably figured this out already, but if you need to get food, get it through the backdoor. If the backdoor's locked, slip in a window. Don't ever use the front door. You'll get your nails clipped."

Saxton flinched. He had used the front door of the meat market.

"There are a few places that are safe to pass by," she went on. "In fact, some of the humans leave out leftovers for the girls and me. I recommend Antonio & Emil's. Great pasta, but I reckon you two'd be more into the meatballs. They're the size of baseballs, I tell you. Really good eatin'. Now, McCarthy's Fish 'N' Chips gets fresh deliveries on Mondays. That means they throw out all the old stuff on Sundays. Since almost everyone is visiting the church around eleven in the morning, that's the best time to raid their dumpsters."

Tootsie peered at Dante. She eyed him up and down, and then sighed. "You're a different story, though. Fat chance you'll get inside anywhere, Mr. Big Bad Wolf."

Dante clenched his teeth together. He seemed ready to pounce on the cat and make a fast snack out of her.

"He might be a wolf and he might be big," Saxton argued, placing himself between the two animals, "but I assure you he's hardly of poor character."

The cat let out a laugh.

"Oh, I'm pulling your tails, sweethearts! Have a sense of humor," she purred. "Point is, your friend's out of luck around here. Stick out of sight and out of the human's minds. If he wants to eat, he'll have to wait for lights out before he can raid the trash."

"*Trash?*" The wolf repeated. "You're kidding me."

"I'll get real food for the both of us," Saxton assured.

"That right, Foxy? Well, good for you. This world we live in, it's a rough one for sure. Every day the air gets a little worse than yesterday, and every day everyone gets a little more desperate to survive." She stopped a few yards away from a particularly lavish house with a carefully manicured lawn and garden. "Look at that window over there. See that cat? All white and clean with his stupid little nose sunken halfway in his face? Well, he's one of the lucky ones who've got things made. Two square meals a day, a master to groom his fluffy hair, and a hoard of squeaky toys I bet he doesn't even know what to do with. If you don't have luck like his, then you gotta make your own luck, and you do that by watching out for you and your own."

She gazed at the sky, which had become orange and fuchsia. The sun was well on its way to retiring for the evening. "I'll show you what I mean."

Tootsie led them to another area of town. The neighborhood was in slight disrepair, and there were a few store fronts that were clearly out of business or had seen more prosperous days. Through a broken window, they entered an abandoned clock shop. Stray cats lay everywhere – on the counter, inside the empty cash register, on the shelves and grandfather clocks – with their ears flicking dust away or their tails coiling and uncoiling lazily.

"Welcome to our home," Tootsie said. "It isn't much, but it's ours, at least for the time being. There's been talk around town that the humans are gonna raze this place."

"There are so many of you," Saxton observed, wondering if there were even more cats hidden away in nooks and crannies he hadn't found yet.

"It's been a pretty hard year. About two years ago, there were only ten of us. This year, a good number of the colony used to have masters and a decent roof over their heads. But when the masters lost their jobs, cat food and cat litter were the first expenses to go out the door, which basically meant the cat."

"Anyone's welcome to stay?" Dante asked.

"Sure, as long as they follow the rules."

The blue-gray cat they had seen earlier approached them with a tiny piece of trout between her teeth. She set the morsel before Tootsie and said, "Here's your share, Toots."

Dante couldn't stop himself from gasping. The fish they had stolen earlier today was almost half as big as Saxton himself. Now what remained of it could hardly feed even a finicky weasel. But Tootsie made no complaint and delicately nibbled away at her humble dinner.

"We should have gotten you more," Saxton said apologetically. Tootsie shrugged.

"We accept donations, not pity. Everyone here brings in their fair share, and together we divide everything among us. Territory, shelter, food, water— you name it. No one owns any of it but everyone has it. This way of living is the only reason we've managed to survive. Alone, most of us would be as good as dead."

Saxton and Dante stared at the cats around them. Most of the felines were thin and sickly. Even Dante, who was always the last to eat in his pack, knew whatever food he earned was fair – even generous – for what he contributed. Tootsie, however, was clearly the leader of her colony, but did not earn any more food than the others.

"How can you live like this?" he objected in hushed tones. "If everyone's hungry, someday you'll tear each other apart."

"Look around you, Dante," she said patiently. "When everyone's just gettin' by, there's no one to get angry at. But if someone's got more than everyone else, well … that's when the nails and teeth come out."

Saxton frowned. "That sounds terribly unfair. I can't imagine a life without choice or keeping what's yours."

The cat lapped the last of her fish and licked her paws. "Then you've never been poor, Foxy. You've never been poor."

Chapter Twenty-Two

That night, Tootsie sent five of her cats out on patrol while the others remained behind to care for the kittens. When all the clocks in the shop struck eight, Saxton's ears twitched. In the distance, he could just barely hear the sound of strings being plucked, deep voices singing, and feet stomping in rhythm against a sticky wooden floor. There was also that smell again: alluring, spicy, and simply irresistible.

Tootsie noticed something had caught the fox's interest. She strained her ears before meowing in understanding.

"That's music," Tootsie said. "Human music. Wanna see it?"

"Is it safe?" Dante asked.

"Most of the people at the pub are probably as drunk as sailors by now. By the time we get there, they'll think you're an overgrown husky if you wag your tail like an idiot and smile at everyone." She jumped off the cashier's counter. "Come on, kids. If you're stuck here, you might as well have a bit of fun."

They walked several blocks along the smoothly paved streets, and with each step the music grew louder and livelier. The 'pub,' as Tootsie had called it, had a sign that hung just above the door and featured a bull's head. Inside, it was filled to the brim with half-exhausted but merry men and women smelling of hops and fermented grain. Saxton and Tootsie slinked in between and around the forest of legs, while Dante nudged his way through the tangle of people. A few of the exceptionally intoxicated men even lowered their hands to ruffle the back of his neck. It took all of his self-control to resist biting those

168

clumsy hands and smile and bat his tail instead, as Tootsie had commanded.

Hopping onto an empty stool, Tootsie pawed two partially eaten burgers from a pair of abandoned plates and threw them onto the floor for Saxton and Dante to eat. She then jumped down and joined them, observing the hubbub.

"What are they doing?" Saxton asked.

"They're celebrating the end of the day, Foxy. Like me, they've gotta work day in and day out to put food on the table and take care of their families. Small joys like drink, company, and music keep their spirits up, especially when it's gettin' harder and harder to make ends meet."

"What changed?" Dante asked.

"I don't know," said the cat. "But if I had to guess, some people got greedy, and others had to pay for it ..."

Just then, a young man with an unruly beard jumped upon the bar counter with a violin in his hand. Tapping his right foot against the counter surface, the man set the beat for the next tune and his audience clapped along with enthusiasm.

Down the road and up the path
Here comes a fork, now do your math
North and South, and East and West
Chin up, boy. Do your best!

Despite his gruff appearance, the young man's voice was light and airy. Even Dante bobbed his head with the song's lyrics, and was more than tempted to offer a howl.

Time and time and time again
I walk until I reach the end
But no matter how far I go
I always come right back to you

Right back to you
Right back to you

So you take my hat and hang it high
Gimme a slice of them apple pie
Stoke the fire all hot and nice
Then sit with me for good moonshine

We look at stars all bright at night
Wonderin' if it'll all be all right
I look at you, you look at me
Who'd'a thought this life would be

In front of the bar, the people began to form a small circle around something on the floor. Whatever it was, they cheered it on and laughed, utterly delighted. Saxton squeezed through the crowd to see what everyone was looking at. He all but lost his breath when he saw a beautiful vixen with silver fur dancing in the center of the floor as if she was human.

Time and time and time again
I walk until I reach the end
But no matter how far I go
I always come right back to you

Right back to you
Right back to you

She moved her little feet backwards and forwards, side to side in time with the music. Some of the patrons were so pleased with her delicate performance that they threw generous pieces of bread and sausage on the floor. As she spun around, Saxton smelled it: the wild and bold scent, spicy and feminine and alluring. It was *her.*

Every now and then,
Sometimes life gets a little crooked
I'd scratch my head, all confused
Never thought I'd be so lost— did you?

Then I'd backtrack.
Get my bearings straight.
Sometimes home was never where you thought it was.
Sometimes home moves around.
Like a silly ol' bumblebee.

Who the hell needs a compass?
When all I need to find my way is you

The silver vixen turned her head – sensing she was being watched very intently – and met Saxton's intent gaze with her stormy yellow eyes. Tootsie came up from behind Saxton and smirked.

Time and time and time again
I walk until I reach the end
But no matter how far I go
I always come right back to you

Right back to you
Right back to you

The vixen gave Saxton a quick smile before turning herself in a graceful circle, swishing her tail about as if it was a luxurious scarf.

Who needs a compass when I've got you?

"Who … is *that?*" Saxton whispered.
"*That*," Tootsie answered, "is Two-Step."

Chapter Twenty-Three

"Hi, Toots," Two-Step greeted. Her voice was soft like velvet. "Out to paint the town red?"

"Never too old for mischief," the cat joked back. "Two-Step, this is Saxton. Bandit and Clyde sent him and his buddy over there my way."

"Well, you certainly are a handsome one," Two-Step said without a trace of shyness. She took a second to identify Saxton's friend across the pub and did her best to react coolly. She had never seen a wolf up close before, and all she had ever heard of them was from fairy tales and fables. Nevertheless, she put on a courageous smile, and in that moment Saxton knew he was done for.

"Your friend over there looks a little worse for wear," she said, leaning closer to whisper into his ear. "I take it he's not used to noise and people?"

"I'm not either," Saxton admitted. "But I—"

"Was curious," Two-Step finished with an impish grin. "Yeah, curiosity is how I wound up here myself."

"Lucky for you, you're cute and friendly," Tootsie added. "She's pretty much the town celebrity."

Saxton's brow wrinkled. "Celebrity?"

"Oh, Tootsie, stop," she replied. "Don't listen to her. I'm just an offbeat fox. Never found living in a hole in the ground or running for my life all that appealing."

"So one day, she decides to dance for a living," Tootsie explained. "Humans love it when we do silly tricks like that, who the heck knows why. I remember Rusty tried to talk you out of it."

"I'd rather not talk about him," Two-Step said sharply, and then she turned to Saxton. "So, how long are you here for?"

Dante watched impatiently as his friend fumbled with niceties and the female fox humored him with a giggle or two. He rose off his haunches, briskly dodging a hand before it could pat the top of his head. He approached Saxton and announced, "I can't stay here much longer. I'm going."

But the fox was too distracted to realize Dante wanted him to call it a night as well. He merely nodded and followed Two-Step closer toward the pub's musicians. Rubbing her side against one of Dante's front legs, Tootsie yawned.

"Let's go, big boy. Your friend's gonna be a bit preoccupied tonight."

He followed Tootsie out the door and snorted, "He's got the focus of a pup."

The cat laughed, and for the first time, the wolf actually appreciated it. "Why's that?"

"That crow feather around his neck? We're supposed to take it to New Hampshire. At this rate, I'm not sure it will happen."

"He'll come around," Tootsie said gently. "Females have this magical effect this time of year. You're no more immune than Foxy is."

"And what about your magic?" Dante challenged, but the cat only shook her head.

"Males are a load of trouble and then some. There's nothin' fun about bein' a single mom."

"Funny you should say that. When we were in Missouri, we met a pair of scrapyard dogs who couldn't have any pups. Couldn't tell you how badly they wanted them."

"Got fixed, right?"

Dante bowed his head. "Yeah, they were."

Once outside, the music died down and soon the only noise they could hear was the sound of their nails clacking along the pavement.

"I can understand that, I guess. I mean, if your mate's gonna stick around, why not have a couple of little ones to keep you on your toes?" Her smile became a little sad then, but she tried not to show it. "There are too many felines in my life right now and not enough

173

resources to even think about having kittens of my own. Maybe someday, if things ever get better ..."

In the pub, Saxton and Two-Step nestled against a corner and watched as the humans milled about and occasionally tossed them scraps. Two-Step nodded toward the young man with the beard who had been dancing on the bar.

"That's Paul, Paul Schilling. I met him about three years ago. He was fifteen years-old then, now he's studying at the University. When he visits, we sometimes get together for a couple of songs."

"How did you meet him?"

"In his backyard. Paul was raking leaves and whistling a cute little tune. I took one look at him and knew he wouldn't hurt me. I can't explain how, I just knew. So I walked up to him and lay down, watched him do his thing. When he finally noticed I was there, he froze like a deer in the headlights. Didn't cross my mind he'd think *I* was a threat, so I did the only thing I knew to calm a stranger down: I yawned. He laughed and eased up then. I've been visiting his backyard ever since. He must've told the neighbors about me. When I make my rounds around the block, they usually leave me something to eat on their porches or in their yards.

"I love people," Two-Step went on, her eyes dreamy. "They're so interesting. They care about things, y'know? Complicated things like music and art and love. Mother and Father never quite forgave me for ditching the forest in exchange for this place."

Saxton watched the vixen with wonder, but then he remembered the day his life was flipped upside down.

"The first time I met humans, they pointed a gun at my face."

She looked at him and didn't know what to say to that, and so she laid her head upon the floor and perked up her ears to give Saxton her full attention.

"I was only a kit," he continued. "I never really thought of humans as anything other than another animal to avoid. But they did something strange ... something I still don't understand."

"What did they do?"

The corner of his mouth twitched. He never gave it much thought until now. "They let me go."

Two-Step blinked in surprise, but then smiled knowingly. "You must have done something to impress them," she said. "Humans can be heartless, but they're not all like that. Some of them can be quite kind when they choose to be."

"They said they would come after me another time. I don't think they let me go out of benevolence so much as sport."

"Your friend the wolf," Two-Step interjected, suddenly changing the topic. "How'd you meet?"

"He tried to eat me."

"Really? Did he decide to let you go?"

"No," he said. "I did."

He fell silent and didn't go into the details of the story. Perhaps he didn't need to as Two-Step seemed to understand.

"Whatever happened," she said, "you saw something in him and gave him a chance. Like Paul with me. Like the hunters with you."

'Like Quill with me,' Saxton thought. He nearly jumped when he felt Two-Step move closer to lean against his side. Her tail swished back and forth before curling around them.

"Paul believes that a man is defined by his actions, not his name or anything else, not even the most basic nature he was born with." She paused. "What do you believe in, Saxton?"

The pub was full to bursting well into early morning. Saxton and Two-Step made a nimble beeline for the exit, each of them taking one last look at the people and their music. The vixen led Saxton around town, showing him the houses that were friendly to foxes and the houses that were not. At last, she stopped before a small rectangular window that led to a basement.

Two-Step pushed the window open with her nose and entered. Saxton followed suit and took in the environment around them. Directly beneath the window were stacks of cardboard boxes which they used like a short flight of stairs to reach the cement floor. Old furniture stood around them here and there, making the basement an odd sort of forest composed of chair and table legs where tree trunks should have been. Flush against one of the walls were two square contraptions, one of which had a window on its side while the other did not. Beside one of the machines was a small basket filled with sheets.

"You live here?"

"Believe it or not, the basement is pretty warm. The family keeps their washer and dryer down here. Along with the radiator, I get lots of heat."

"Do the humans know?"

"Yes, but I try to stay out of sight." She studied the uneasy look in his eyes. "I keep the rodents and bugs at bay, so I'm basically free pest control. They leave dog food every now and then, though, usually when winter comes."

Two-Step sauntered to the basket and carefully lifted one of the sheets from the bundle with her teeth. A diminutive male kit with sandy fur popped his head out.

"Mommy?"

His tiny voice was so sweet and helpless; it vaguely reminded Saxton of his sister. Two-Step turned to him, her face a touch nervous.

"This is Boots ... my son."

Chapter Twenty-Four

It was morning, and Saxton had not yet returned. Dante was hardly surprised, but he paced the dusty floorboards of the abandoned clock shop with mild irritation. The cats observed his anxiety, bored.

"Where is he?" he growled.

"Probably, enjoying a good lie in with the vixen," one of the cats purred. "Relax, he'll come around. Train's not comin' 'til tomorrow anyway."

"But if he gets too comfortable, he'll stop caring. He'll just stick around and forget everything we've been through just to get here."

Tootsie stretched out of her cubby hole and greeted her fellow cats good morning. She walked up to Dante, who was so wound up in his thoughts he didn't notice her take a seat before him. "He's not you, you know. If he wants to settle, he can. He can do whatever he wants."

"There are things that are more important than what you want, like honor and upholding your promises."

She stroked Dante's right foreleg with one of her paws. "Could you follow me for a moment?"

She led him away from the members of her colony, and to a more secluded corner of the store. After looking around them to make sure no one was listening, Tootsie whispered, "Not everyone values honor or promises the way you or I do. None of my cats will tell you this, but we've seen plenty of our members leave because they didn't like the rules. And you know what? I didn't stop them. It's not up to me to tell them how to live. I can only offer an opinion, at least, and leadership, at most. You have to remember he's a fox, Dante. Foxes don't have the need to obey rules and respect authority wired into them like wolves do. There's nothin' you can do to change that."

"He's different," he said with conviction.

"Yeah, I don't doubt that. But let me put it this way: he's only a fox and you're only a wolf. And me? I'm just a stinky old cat. We might have big ideas in our heads, but when it comes down to it, we need food, water, and a little bit of companionship like everyone else. Your friend, he's in his prime. So are you. He wants, probably *needs*, a mate. You want to deprive him of that chance?"

With a huff, Dante shook his head and looked out one of the dirty windows. "It's like you said: we need our own kind. Maybe that's the problem. Maybe that's my problem."

He walked up to the large hole in the window and crawled through it. Tootsie followed him out.

"Where you goin', big guy?"

"For a walk. I need to think."

Saxton woke with Two-Step's soft head beneath his chin. Boots was curled up between his mother's paws, breathing lightly. He watched them in silence, wondering if his father once felt the way he felt now: content, surprised, and a bit overwhelmed. He had had no idea what to do when Two-Step had introduced him to her kit, but when Boots had stumbled out of the basket in an effort to greet him, instinct had taken over, Saxton picking him up by the scruff of his neck and gently sitting him upright. Two-Step had been pleased.

He shifted around and tried to ignore the point of Quill's feather poking against his ribs. He looked down at it with annoyance and, without thinking, lifted the twine around his neck up and over his head. The feather floated to the floor, where it came to rest in a pile of dirty laundry.

Two-Step yawned beneath him. Her eyes blinked open and she licked Saxton's cheek.

"Did you sleep well?" She asked.

"Very. In fact, I haven't slept so well in a long time."

They watched as the sun began to creep its way through the basement window. It was tempting to ignore the brilliant light in favor of remaining in bed.

Boots, however, had other ideas. He tugged at Saxton's tail, jolting him upright with a yip!

178

"Boots!" Two-Step chided, though there was mirth in her voice. "That's rude!"

"But I'm hungry, Mommy. What's for breakfast?"

Two-Step glanced at Saxton, who was smoothing his tail with his paw. "Well, if Saxton is up to it, maybe I can pick something up from the bakery. What do you think, Saxton?"

"Sounds good to me." He grunted when the little kit climbed over his shoulders.

"Can I come? I wanna go out."

Two-Step peered at Saxton again, and he read the question in her eyes. He smiled at Boots and licked his forehead. He squirmed beneath his touch. "It's a beautiful morning." he said. "Sure. Why not?"

The wolf wandered through the outskirts of town until the land shifted from tamed to wild. He caught a scent in the air. It was a strong, wintery smell that inspired awe as well as fear. The owner of the smell was directly behind him. Dante did not need to turn around to know who it was.

"Timber."

He said the name in almost a whisper. She approached him with carefully placed steps.

"Dante. My, you've gotten thin."

From the corner of his eye, Dante watched as his sister came around to meet him, face-to-face. She had grown much larger since he had last seen her, but she was still violently beautiful. Her fur was a chestnut brown that grew lighter in shade as the hair approached her legs. Her eyes, big and shrewd, were hues of yellow or green, depending on the light. Timber stood tall, shoulders straight and head perfectly poised. No one in Dante's pack had any doubt that she would one day become leader.

"How did you find me?" he asked. It surprised him that after so many months of travel, he had still been found.

"It wasn't easy," Timber replied. "Your scent went cold after North Dakota. I almost gave up, but luckily the local crows were helpful. They said you and a fox were heading east. I went in that direction until your scent returned several miles back."

"What are you doing here?"

She frowned at him for a moment.

"Honestly, Dante, don't you think that's a question I should be asking you?" She paused, her eyes softening. "Mother and Father sent me to search for you, of course. You won't believe how much Father's been pacing, worrying about you. I was beginning to fear he might turn our territory into a valley."

"He doesn't need to worry about me anymore," he returned. "I'm doing just fine on my own."

"Oh? What happened to your neck then?" she asked.

He had forgotten about the scars the barbed wires left him. He tried not to swallow, but did so anyway.

"I had a bit of trouble. I got out of it, so it's fine."

"The fox helped you, didn't he?" Timber was sharp, sometimes too sharp. He loved her, but hated her scrutiny. "Interesting for his kind. I've never seen it before."

Dante gritted his teeth. "What do you want?"

She looked as though she was about to say 'Isn't it obvious?' but thought the better of it. "For you to come home." With a pause, she lowered her head. "We miss you, Dante. We need you."

Snorting, Dante rolled his eye and looked away. "Please. The pack is better off without me. Everyone knows that."

"That's a matter of opinion," Timber retorted. "The pack has been awfully serious as of late—"

"I don't want to be missed because I'm the butt of everyone's jokes!" he snarled.

"Ah, so is that the real reason you left? Dante, if you think you were doing your family a favor running off, think again." Her tone sharpened in a way that always put him on edge. It was ridiculous, really. He had a full six inches in height over her. "You're *not* a joke," Timber said eventually. "But you were very good at making us laugh. Even Rush's been a bit somber these days. That's very strange for him."

The thought of his brother did not make Dante any happier. He didn't know what to say. It had been more than half a year since he had seen his family, and for whatever reason, he found that he both missed them and wished to forget them.

"Won't you come home?" She was always persistent. "You're family. We never abandon family, no matter how difficult it gets."

At that, he turned on her, baring his teeth. Surprised, Timber took a step back.

"That's a lie! We abandoned Fritz, Aspen, Dakota, and Grandpa!"

Timber stared at him, disturbed by his outburst, and forced her forehead against his. Thinking of what Saxton would say to this, Dante refused to yield. He could see the barely masked alarm in Timber's face when she felt the pressure of his pushing, however gently, back.

180

"They sacrificed their lives for us … for you," she hissed. "We won't ever forget that, and neither should you."

"I will never forget," he growled. "They should never have needed to make that sacrifice in the first place. They should be alive. *I'm* the one who should be dead."

She relented, pulling away. "Stop punishing yourself. It's false heroics. If you want to be forgiven, start by forgiving yourself."

Her words, instead of angering him further, succeeded in cooling the boil he felt in his veins.

"Saxton said something similar …" he said, chastened.

The corner of Timber's lip curled over her right fang. She was clearly put out. "The fox again?"

"His name is Saxton. He's not perfect, but he's got a good heart. It's like you said, he saved my life. You should respect that."

Timber felt a strange pang of jealousy, but before she could feed her own outrage any further, Dante pulled her from her thoughts.

"I can't go back. Not yet. I have a promise to keep."

Dante didn't say anything more. Whatever the promise was, it was too personal to share with even her. After years of standing up for him, Timber wondered how she had failed to acquire this kind of faithfulness. She found herself growing upset again, and so she chose to speak reasonably before her emotions got the better of her.

"Then you'd best fulfill it. Once you have, we'll be waiting for you. Head north. The entire pack has migrated from Saskatchewan to Quebec."

"Why?"

"I told you, we're family. I'm on a mission to retrieve you, and should I fail … someone can continue where I left off." She sighed, allowing herself to look as tired as she felt. "You don't just keep our spirits up. You keep us honorable. You hold onto your honor more fiercely than anyone else in the pack. Rush always envied that. It really is no wonder he enjoyed bringing you down whenever he could."

Dante's chest tightened. "I didn't know that."

His sister began walking away. She looked back for only a moment, giving him just enough time to see the reserved affection in her smile and voice. "We're waiting, Dante. Try not to take too long."

Saxton followed Two-Step along the streets, keeping an eye on her son, who tramped along between them. Before long, a warm, sweet aroma embraced their senses, and they all began to salivate. They went around to the back of the bakery, where Two-Step scratched the backdoor three times. A minute later, they heard footsteps. The door creaked open to reveal a stout woman with gray hair and cheerful crow's feet at the corners of her eyes. Two-Step backed away to a safe distance. Boots and Saxton followed her example.

"Two-Step!" she greeted. "Good morning! My, oh my, your little one has grown!" Her eyes drifted from the two familiar foxes to the third she had never seen before. Though the moment was brief, a hint of nervousness filled her eyes. She rallied, however, and forced herself to smile. "And who's this? A new boyfriend?"

Saxton didn't know what the woman meant by that word, but he knew she was referring to him. He cautiously stepped forward, placing himself between the woman and Two-Step and Boots. Two-Step came beside him and rubbed her shoulders against his. The woman laughed.

"Well, I guess I'm right, then. Wait here. I'll be back."

She abandoned the door only to return moments later with a basket of bread and eggs. Reaching into the basket, she gently pitched three rolls into the alley. As Two-Step and Boots ran after the bread, Saxton darted behind a crate, startled. He peaked from behind the box and watched as the woman reached into the basket again. She grabbed the eggs and, one by one, rolled them toward the foxes.

"There now," she said. "Enjoy!"

She returned to the bakery and shut the door behind her. Boots skipped to Saxton with a roll of bread in his mouth.

"'Ere's ors!" he said with a muffled voice. Saxton took his share, and Two-Step brought him his egg.

"Do you always eat like this?" Saxton asked, worried by the thought that Boots may never learn to hunt.

"Most of the time," Two-Step replied, and there was something in her tone that told him she didn't like being accused. "It's easier than hunting."

"But what if no one can feed you? What if you approach someone who is afraid of you?"

"You certainly had no problems with the humans last night," Two-Step scoffed.

Uncomfortable, Boots pretended to not pay attention to the two adults on the verge of arguing. He busied himself with an empty glass bottle that made pretty noises whenever he pushed it.

"I ..." He didn't want to start a fight, so Saxton tried something else. "I know. I should have been more cautious, but Tootsie said it would be all right since everyone was drunk." He cleared his throat. "Anyway, I was distracted by a certain vixen with pretty silver hair ..."

182

Two-Step wasn't the type to be embarrassed, if flattered or otherwise. She gave him a sly grin. "You're changing the subject."

He noticed Boots roll his eyes and sigh.

"Yes, well … my point is, it's important to know how to hunt. I'm thinking of not just you, but your son."

Boots looked up at him, then at his mother. Two-Step scowled. "Do you have a problem with the way I live?"

"No, of course not, but if worse comes to worst, I'd like you to be prepared, that's all."

Studying him, Two-Step accepted his words at face value. "Okay, Saxton. I get what you're saying. But if you want my son to learn how to hunt, I'm gonna need your help. There's only one of me."

Saxton hesitated. They had only known one another for several hours, and the thought of choosing her as his mate now made him feel rather skittish. But he swallowed his fear down, held onto his nerves, and said, "When we came into this town, I found this wonderful smell. It drew me in, hypnotized me, and we missed our train. Maybe that was meant to happen, so I could meet you."

Two-Step held her breath. Her eyes brimmed with hope, but were tempered with doubt. "What are you saying, Saxton?"

"I'm saying … I'm saying I know we just met, but I think you're beautiful and smart and tough. I'm nervous about all this – it's new to me – but that's all right isn't it?"

She smiled a little, chuckling. "You're such an idealist. I'm not perfect, y'know."

"I know, but neither am I."

The curl in her lips straightened a bit. She nodded to her kit. "What about Boots?"

"I was adopted," he said. "If I can be a crow's son, Boots can certainly be mine, if he wants to be."

Two-Step turned to her little one. "Boots?"

"You'll really teach me to hunt? You'll stay with Mommy and take care of us? Like a real daddy?"

The little kit was so eager, he was shaking with excitement. His bright smile and big eyes made something twist in Saxton's chest. He suddenly, inexplicably, felt very protective.

"Yes."

Dante debated returning to the cat colony. The cats were, if not friendly, courteous enough, but the smell of cat dander was oppressive, and he would rather meander about the countryside where the air was crisp. He then considered looking for Saxton, but rebelled at the notion that he was at the fox's beck and call. They were friends, he thought. It was a fragile friendship, but a friendship all the same. He wondered, if their situations were reversed, if Saxton would tolerate giving up the forest and eating far too little. He hoped he would, but he was not sure.

He stopped at a brook for a drink and saw his reflection. Timber was right, he had grown thin. He did his best to ignore the creeping nausea that would, at times, assail him with such force he thought he might retch.

As he took a turn down a natural foot path, his ear twitched at the sound of livestock jostling against one another— a herding dog barking and nipping at their ankles. Dante followed the noise, and came upon a plot of land where a flock of sheep grazed.

He licked his teeth and realized he was growing dizzy with hunger. He prowled toward the heard. There was a bark and Dante jumped. Glancing around, he sighed with relief when he saw the dog was merely rounding three sheep that had strayed too far away. He hadn't noticed him.

It was then that it occurred to him that he was walking into dangerous territory. He took a step back and almost turned around altogether, but his stomach seized him once more with hunger.

'Maybe they won't miss one,' Dante thought. He lowered his body to the ground, blending in with the tall grass. He tried to recall Saxton's hunting techniques during their journey, and knew that his size was against him.

The sheep flowed en masse, like a wave of clouds, heading toward the corral. It would be prudent to take one of the sheep bringing up the rear.

Dante focused on a particularly fat lamb lagging behind, struggling to squeeze in between its herd companions to find its mother. It only succeeded in being kicked back and scolded.

He crept toward the little thing, and grabbed it with his teeth.

There was a struggle, but it didn't last long. One bite, one swallow, and the dizziness Dante felt vanished bit by bit. It was not to last, however, as the herd proceeded to scream and stampede in a panic.

The herding dog swung around and ran toward the chaos.

"Stay calm! Stay calm!" he barked. "What's happened?"

"Wolf!" A sheep bleated. "Wolf in field! Wolf!"

"Remove the Exile!" Another baaed. "Remove him!"

The dog weaved through the sheep until the smell of fresh blood began permeating the air. He found the wolf still eating.

The wolf looked at him, his one eye wide and feral. He leapt at the wolf with gnashing teeth.

The wolf held onto the ground as the dog pulled on the skin at his back, vainly attempting to pull him away from the dead lamb. Merely annoyed, the wolf rolled over, throwing the dog off his back. He bared his fangs, nearly five times the size of the dog's, and growled.

BANG!

A bullet zipped past him, but grazed his cheek, drawing blood and knocking him over.

His eyes came into focus. He remembered Mother and Father, Timber and Rush. He remembered heads in a frozen river. He remembered a crow, a feather.

He remembered Saxton.

Dante's tail curled slightly between his legs. The herding dog snarled at him and said, "Master will be here soon. You made a big mistake, coming here. I thought your kind knew better."

He turned to run away, but the dog ran after him and blocked his path.

"Please," Dante begged, "let me go."

"You killed one of my charges! I'm no fool! You will be back again and again until there are no more!"

There was a click of metal behind him, but Dante did not turn.

He knew there was a black tunnel, the barrel of a gun, waiting there.

Chapter Twenty-Five

Boots proved to be a quick study, and Saxton's heart thrummed with pleasure and pride when the little kit caught a squirrel all on his own after only five tries. He wondered if being a parent felt like this every day: worried the little one would grow discouraged, protective when there was a stumble or fall, and proud with every lesson learned. It had only been one afternoon, and already he could see himself as a father.

He thought, just briefly, about Napowsa. Thoughts of her were usually set aside along with his guilt, but this time he couldn't ignore her. Eight seasons was a long time for a cub to stay with his mother, and so many memories could be made in that time. He tried to imagine what Two-Step would do if Boots died. It made him shudder.

It was near dusk when Saxton finally returned to the cat colony. When he arrived at the abandoned shop, his nose twitched at the absence of Dante's scent. He found Tootsie lounging atop a strange, metal box with numbers and peculiar words on its surface. A tiny bell rang whenever Tootsie shifted her weight or batted her tail.

"Ah," she said, "the prodigal fox returns."

"Where's Dante?"

"He's been gone since this mornin,' Foxy. Didn't tell me where he was headed."

"And you didn't think to ask?"

She peered at him with displeasure. "If memory serves, you didn't think to come back sooner."

Saxton flinched. "You're right, I'm sorry. Did you at least see which direction he went? I have something important to tell him, and I don't think it can wait."

"And what's that?

"Well," he replied, hoping he sounded more excited than nervous, "I know it's fast, but I think I want to start a family ... with Two-Step."

Tootsie studied him, one brow eloquently raised.

"You weren't kidding around. That is fast. Can't say I'm not happy for the vixen, but what about Dante?"

The fox deflated, but remained honest. "He says he owes me a debt. I don't believe he does anymore and ... I don't know. I've nearly gotten the both of us killed more times than I care to think about. Maybe this whole ... *thing* I've gotten us into isn't worth all the trouble. I'm happy here. I'm hoping he'll understand."

Ears flattening, Tootsie hopped onto the floor. She was already a rather nasty, feisty, looking cat, but when she was the least bit annoyed, she looked fearsome.

"Y'know, Foxy, Dante and I had a little chat this morning about you. He looks up to you, y'know that? Thinks of you as a *friend*. I told him you can do whatever the heck you wanted with your life, but I never thought you'd just shrug him off like a ratty old sweater."

"That not true," he protested, but his voice was uncertain.

"No? So what happened to your feather?"

Saxton looked down at his bare chest and withered, jaw snapping shut.

"I'm not gonna tell you what to do," Tootsie went on, "but I will tell you what I think: that wolf of yours? You'll never make another friend like him. That's the truth."

She swung her tail around, exposing the missing tip.

"You say you're not like other foxes, that you're not a *Lonely Thief*. Dante believed it. Still believes it. So are you gonna prove him wrong, or are you gonna fight for him the way he fights for you?"

Chapter Twenty-Six

When Dante opened his eyes, a bright, unnatural light beat upon his head. He felt slightly ill and disoriented, and the white tiles and sterile smells told him he was not where he should be.

Panic overtook him and he tried to run, only to find that his legs were bound by leather straps onto a metal table. He tried to howl for help, but his jaws were muzzled. His good eye frantically darted around. There were people surrounding him, three of whom wore odd little sheets covering half of their faces.

"Doctor Lee, he's awake," one of them said.

"So he is," a graying man in a white coat replied. "He's a tough one isn't he? Thought that bullet would've kept him down longer."

"Should we dose him with more tranquilizers?"

"No, let's hold off until we've got him tagged and rolled into the sanctuary."

Dante's mind raced. When one of the masked humans approached him with scissors, he struggled against his binds.

"Whoa! Hold still, big guy! Just want to get this sucker off."

The man held him down by the throat. There was a snap, and he pulled the dog collar off him.

"Weird. Is he a halfie like Old Sol?"

"With his size? No, I don't think so. He's pure wolf."

"How'd he get that on then?"

A female human, also with her face half covered, sighed. "Guys, come on. Who cares? Just get that tracker on him so we can call it a day. My son's got a game this afternoon, and I'm not gonna miss it."

At her direction, they held Dante still while she fastened a bigger collar with a peculiar black device attached near the buckle.

"Done and done. Welcome home, buddy."

Doctor Lee and the other humans rolled the table he laid on down a hall and out two doors that led to an enormous field. Men wearing brown uniforms stood at the ready, bearing guns and bullets shaped like needles. Dante searched for an escape, but could not find an opening in the cabled fence that surrounded the area. The fence seemed to disappear into the trees and mountains.

The table was lowered to the ground. He whimpered when he felt a needle pierce his abdomen. He drifted to sleep as the humans removed the muzzle from his mouth and the straps from his legs. When he breathed in, he couldn't believe it.

He smelled wolves.

Dante opened his eyes to the sound of screaming.

"*No!* No, please, I beg of you! Don't kill them! Don't kill my young! Please!"

A female wolf prostrated herself before a disfigured creature so gruesome Dante could hardly recognize it as one of his kind. More than half of its fur had been ripped clean off its body, and what little hair remained grew only in haphazard patches. Its exposed skin was an angry red, and its muscles and veins undulated beneath its movements, pulsating. Dante tried to stand, his injured shoulder complaining at being used. He turned to look at it, and found it had been tightly wrapped with human bandages.

"I obey only Jezebel," the creature growled, leaning more of his weight against the two wailing pups trapped beneath his feet. "Where is the third?"

As her young cried, the mother wolf closed her eyes and dug her heels into the ground. "I don't know."

The creature's lips twisted. "You're a terrible liar. I'll ask again: where's the third?"

She looked at him in defiance, her eyes full of anger. "I'll never tell you— you disgusting *Mongrel*."

The Mongrel snarled and abandoned the pups beneath his feet. He leapt at the female and would have taken her down, but something powerful shoved him aside. The Mongrel tumbled onto the ground, dazed.

"Are you all right?" Dante asked the mother.

But she was so frightened for her young she did not waste time thanking him. Instead she took her two pups and bolted for the thicket. Dante moved to go after her, when a set of teeth tore into his back. Yowling, he bucked his legs, but the Mongrel refused to let go.

Dante slammed them both onto the ground, and they landed on their sides. Stunned from the blow, the Mongrel released him. Dante stood again, but wobbled on his feet, still woozy from whatever the humans had injected him with. When he found his bearings, he showed his teeth and pulled back his ears. The Mongrel did the same.

"Who do you think you are newcomer?" The Mongrel seethed. "You shouldn't have intervened!"

"Any wolf worthy of his pack would fight for the lives of the young," he barked.

The Mongrel laughed. It was an eerie, hollow sound, filled with resentment and hate. "But I don't have a pack, *Brother* Wolf, and by the looks of it, neither do you."

They circled one another, neither taking their eyes off the other. The tableau would have resembled a mirror if one side were not so brutal, while the other, so kind.

"I still have my honor," Dante rejoined. "Looks like you've forgotten yours."

The Mongrel lowered his voice. It was all the more deadly for it. "Maybe if I were a full wolf I'd give a damn."

They fought. There were flashes of teeth and nails, the metallic taste of blood, and sometimes a bit of sharp pain. Without fur to protect him, the Mongrel bled more easily than Dante with every wound received. Dante restrained himself, not wanting to be too vicious, but the Mongrel had no such reservations.

"Enough!"

The teeth clamped over Dante's front right ankle suddenly released. The Mongrel sat and bowed his head for the beautiful white wolf that stood before them. The white wolf assessed the Mongrel first. He was bleeding from head to toe, but he remained perfectly still. It was as though he felt nothing.

"You should call for your human," the white wolf said. "She will see to those wounds"

"Yes, Jezebel."

"You're dismissed, Solomon."

190

The Mongrel nodded once and left without sparing Dante a glance. Once he was gone, Jezebel approached Dante, her frosty eyes attempting warmth.

"I see you are new to the preserve. When did you arrive?"

There was something about the way she carried herself that made Dante shiver. The feeling reminded him vaguely of his sister, but held none of the familiarity.

"I don't know," he answered. "I woke up not long ago. To be honest, I thought I was either dead or dying."

She smiled. "Yes, the humans tend to lean too heavily on those tranquilizers. You should feel more like yourself in a few hours' time. I take it you haven't met my pack yet?"

"No," he hesitated, "just— just that ..."

"Mongrel?" Jezebel finished for him. "Sol's, shall we say, rough around the edges, but he serves me well. I'm sorry for the hostile greeting."

"I'm not worried about the greeting. I'm worried about the fact he tried to kill a mother's pups!"

Jezebel's brows knit together. "Did you see this?"

"Yes! He was about to attack the mother, but I managed to stop him."

She fell silent for a moment. "I shall have to speak with him. What is your name, Brother Wolf?"

"Dante."

"Come along, Dante. I will introduce you to the others."

She led him west across the field, away from where the mother wolf had run off. They entered a clutch of trees which gave way to a circular clearing with an enormous boulder situated at its center. The pack was circled around it. The pack was of a good size, possibly two times that of Dante's own. As they walked past, the wolves touched their noses to the ground.

Jezebel hopped onto the boulder, and Dante knew at once he was not to follow her. Instead, he remained at the side of the stone.

She raised her head to the sky and howled. More pack members emerged from the shadows, joining the others around the rock.

"It is a good evening, my pack. The humans have brought to us a new member, Dante."

The wolves batted their tails and stomped their feet on the ground, panting in excitement. Jezebel looked around her, pleased.

"From where do you come, Dante?"

"North, across the border."

"And how did you come to be here?"

"I ..." He paused, embarrassed. "... I was hungry." The wolves whimpered in sympathy. "I killed a lamb that belonged to a farmer. It was ... stupid of me. The farmer would have shot me dead if not for ..." his mind raced as he suddenly remembered a young man with a beard, riding on a bicycle with a violin strapped onto his back. He had jumped off his bike, leapt over the fence, and pulled the rifle upward as it fired. "... if not for Paul ..."

"Hunger is a powerful motivator," Jezebel said, not unkindly. "But you are safe here, and there is always room for one more in my pack. Brothers and Sisters, let us welcome Dante, our newest member, our newest soldier!"

The wolves howled, one after another, until the forest sounded as though it was full of ghosts.

That night, Jezebel's wolves returned from their hunt with the limbs and ribs of a moose between their teeth. Jezebel permitted her mate, Cassius, and her sturdiest pack members, Trigger, Pistol, and Whiplash to eat first. Dante observed these wolves with mild apprehension. They were a muscular lot, each of them baring faded scars from skirmishes past. But what struck him most was their unbridled aggression, even in eating. No low-ranking wolf dared to sneak a bite.

As they feasted, Jezebel looked at Dante and invited him to eat next to her.

"I couldn't," he said.

"You are my guest," she insisted. "And any wolf strong enough to take on the Mongrel is a strong wolf indeed. If you are to be one of mine, you must be healthy for the next hunt."

Reluctant to upset the others, he took a small tear off the moose leg. When Jezebel smiled at him, Dante took a larger share to satisfy his fill. The meat was tough, and the lower-ranked members jostled about for space once Jezebel permitted them to join, but never did he feel so welcome.

Chapter Twenty-Seven

Saxton waited three days for Dante to eventually return. When he did not, the fox left the cat colony, feeling abandoned and wounded. It crossed his mind that this must have been what Dante felt like before he left. The thought chastened Saxton, but did not stop him from feeling a sharp sense of loss.

His first impulse was to return to Two-Step, to listen to her sweet words and bury his guilt under nuzzles and soft licks. But the more he thought about the vixen, the more he realized he had traded a friend of nearly a year for a mate of hardly a week.

That, he thought, was hardly fair.

And so, he began his search.

After investigating the countryside and coming up fruitless, Saxton decided to pay Bandit and Clyde a visit. He cautiously hoped Dante had dropped in on them earlier today and if not, was at least seen by Bandit around town. He came to a halt. Bandit was sitting outside his den, holding a gnawed root between his paws.

"Bandit?"

The raccoon looked up. His eyes were red, bloodshot. He looked as though all the wind behind his sails had deserted him, and he was now hopelessly adrift.

"The light of my life has been snuffed out."

Saxton looked away, while Bandit returned his gaze to Clyde's chewing root.

"What do I do now?"

The fox stepped closer. Bandit was a soft ball of anguished heat. It was clear he had been crying all day.

Saxton wanted to say something to the raccoon, something comforting. But he found he had no words, so he sat with Bandit until nightfall. He only left once Bandit found the strength to put down the root and say goodbye to the place he once called home.

He went to Two-Step with acid in his stomach.

"I've been left behind once already!" She hissed, her eyes sparkling like a lightning storm off the harbor. "You think I'm dumb enough to let that happen to me and my little kit again? How dare you. You made a promise, not just to me, but to Boots!"

Saxton watched as the kit in question crawled beneath a bed sheet, covering his ears and his head, and whimpered. They had been arguing for a good five minutes in the basement, and the little one braved the distress of seeing his mother lose her composure. He looked back at Two-Step, who was a stone's throw away from being murderous. Quill once said there was a human expression that went as so: 'Hell hath no fury like a woman scorned.' Saxton did not know the truth of those words applied to vixens as well.

"I am not abandoning you, Two-Step. Nor am I abandoning my friend either."

"Your *friend*," the silver fox snorted derisively, "left you! He's a wolf. He can't live in a place like this."

"I know. I should have realized that, but I was too stubborn to care. I've spent hours searching for him and have failed to find him. He could be in trouble—"

"*Trouble?* A wolf his size should be more than able to take care of himself."

"A bullet can take down a creature of any size, Two-Step."

She huffed back at him.

"I thought you were one of a kind."

"I am."

Her eyes blazed. "Then prove it."

Saxton walked to the laundry basket and retrieved Quill's feather from the ground. He slipped on the twine with one movement, and then made for the window. Two-Step watched him in disbelief.

"What are you doing?"

He stopped at the top box and looked down on her.

"Proving it."

Saxton picked up Dante's scent near the sheep corral. It was faint, but there. It unsettled him that he found it within a farmer's territory. He sniffed at the patch of grass that was laden with dried blood. He sighed, relieved to find that very little of it belonged to Dante.

Around that area he also smelled dog, a koolie perhaps, and two men. One man's scent was older, saltier, and acrid with anger. The other's was younger and earthy. It was hot with tension, but defiant. Looking down on the soil, Saxton saw a pattern of footprints dancing around one another, as if in a struggle. The wolf prints farther away were distorted. It looked as though Dante had taken a fall.

"Five seconds, fox. Five seconds and you're gone. Five …"

"Wait!" Saxton protested, turning around to face the herding dog. "I intend to leave, but I have a few questions!"

He paid him no heed and continued counting.

"Four ..."

"There was wolf here. Is he dead or live?"

"Three …"

"Is he dead or alive?"

"Two …"

"Answer me!"

He didn't. Instead he howled for his master and lunged forward in an attempt to bring him down. Saxton dodged, ran through the wooden fence and off the premises. The dog chased him as far as he could, and remained barking until the silhouette of a man came running in the distance. Saxton ducked behind a tree and watched through the tall grass as the farmer approached the fence, gun in hand, and surveyed the area. A few minutes passed before the man lowered his gun and returned to work. His dog followed him, pleased with himself.

Saxton emerged once they disappeared from sight. It was then that he noticed wolf hairs sticking in the mud along the dirt road. He followed the hairs until they suddenly disappeared before a pair of large tire tracks. He raised his nose into the air, and smelled that Dante had been taken north.

He followed the tire tracks until he came upon a paved intersection. The tracks and Dante's scent now gone, he sat on the ground not knowing which way to turn. And so he remained there, hoping that a sparrow or squirrel had seen a vehicle carrying a wolf. He was disappointed to find that the squirrels were an anxious bunch that fled the moment he opened his mouth, and the sparrows were not all that bright.

His patience was rewarded when the sun set and a cloud of big brown bats emerged for the cool evening. One of the bats flew just above Saxton's head, making a fast meal out of an unfortunate moth.

"Miss Bat!" The fox yelled. "Would you be so kind as to spare me a moment?"

The bat turned around in the air and landed in a nearby tree. She wrapped her wings around her body like a cloak and hung upside down.

"Well? Speak up! The hunt just started, and I'll be hungry tonight if you don't hurry!"

"I'm in search of a friend. Do you know of any place that humans might take wolves?"

"There's a wolf preserve to the east." She pointed the general direction with one wing.

"A preserve?"

The bat rotated her head and sneered. "If he's there, your friend's alive. If he's not, your friend's a rug on a man's cabin floor."

With that, she beat her wings and vanished, leaving a rain of leaves in her wake. Saxton glanced at the setting sun and took the road heading in the opposite direction. He ran at a moderate pace for a few miles, but still had not seen the wolf preserve the bat had spoken of.

"You missed a left turn a few roads back," a familiar voice spoke.

He stopped to find Two-Step coming out of the bushes.

"If you're gonna do this," she went on, "you might as well go in the right direction. Follow me."

She led the way, and he stared at her.

"How long have you been following me?"

"Long enough to know you're not as smart as you think you are. Now, hurry up before I change my mind."

Saxton smiled in spite of himself. They backtracked in silence until they turned onto the road he should have taken earlier. "You seem calm," he managed to say.

"I had time to cool off and think things over," she replied. "You know, I've been gettin' along fine without you or anyone else for years. That won't change whether or not you stay with me."

"You were very angry." he couldn't help saying.

"I still am. I don't like being teased. I don't like thinking something good is on its way only to have it get up and leave." Two-Step growled. "And don't get me started on hurting my little kit."

"I'm sorry."

"Good. You should be."

196

Not far off stood a large, single story building. It was a rather humble structure compared to the houses at the center of Lattice, but it appeared to be strong and sufficient nonetheless.

Behind the building was a fence that was so expansive, Saxton could not tell if it ever ended.

"What kind of backyard is this?" he asked.

"It's not a backyard, not one for humans anyway. The land you see, it's all for the wolves." She took a step back. "This is as far as I'm going to take you. You're on your own from here on out."

Saxton nodded. "Thank you. You didn't have to help me. I know you're against this."

"Yeah, well, that doesn't mean I'm against you."

When she said things like that, it made his heart pound. He swallowed and didn't bother trying to hide it.

"I'll come back," he said.

Two-Step smiled for a second, as though she couldn't help herself, but then her lips tightened. "Don't ask me to wait, Saxton, because I won't."

"Whether or not you do makes no difference to me," he said, unflinching. "I'm coming back. And if you do find someone, well, maybe we can still be friends."

Two-Step shook her head, exasperated.

"You sure are stubborn. You're gonna be a tough one to kill." To his surprise, she licked him across his nose. "Do me a favor: try to stay in one piece."

Chapter Twenty-Eight

When dawn rose, Dante was awoken for the first hunt of the day by one of his neighbors. He had been excused from the previous hunts as a new member in need of recovering his strength, but now that three days had passed, he had no excuse to avoid the proceedings. They trekked northbound and scaled a mountainside until they reached a cliff that overlooked a valley. There, they met another group of wolves already waiting. For a moment, Dante was taken aback by the number of them that appeared for the hunt. He did not recall seeing as many wolves at the welcoming feast, nor did he see them among the pack members that brought him food for the first three days since his arrival. Many of them, he noted, were wary and thin.

Dante's good eye locked with green ones, and he instinctively looked away before the other wolf acknowledged him. He gathered she must have been female, and a pretty one at that.

"Is everyone here?" Cassius asked. He was a large, black wolf with irises so dark; he looked to be more shadow than animal. To his right stood the Mongrel, and the scratches Dante had inflicted upon him were cleaned and patched with human bandaging.

The Mongrel surveyed the group. He gave Cassius one nod.

"My pack," Cassius began, "Sniper has informed me that there is a herd of elk heading northeast, across the riverbank." He nodded to Sniper, who stood to his left. "We will wait for them on the other side of the river, and take down three from there."

Cassius walked around the pack, assessing his hunters. Using the length of his body, he forced the pack apart and into three smaller groups. "Trigger, you lead hunting band one; Pistol, two; Whiplash, three. Let's go."

Trigger stared at Dante, his hackles raised and his throat rumbling. Dante took a step back, which seemed to please him.

"So the newcomer is in my band, hm? Well, you might have some fight in you, but let's see how good you are on your feet. Mark my words, Brother: if you trip us up, I won't let you forget it."

Dante didn't deign to reply, and followed the pack down the other side of the mountain. When they were halfway near ground level, he felt a nudge against his side. It was the female, the gold and tanned wolf with green eyes, whom he had seen earlier.

"Don't let Trigger get to you," she whispered. "No matter how hard you try, he's impossible to please."

It wouldn't do to disparage an upper ranked wolf, so Dante said, "Difficult leaders often make good ones— like Cassius."

The female stopped herself from barking a laugh. "Yeah. Sure. Did you enjoy the welcoming feast?"

He looked at her fully this time. Her build was rather small, and she looked rather tired and malnourished. "Yeah, I did. Didn't you?"

"Most of us Tails weren't invited," she replied hotly.

That did not make sense. He had seen lower ranked wolves at the welcoming feast, though in fewer numbers.

"Why not?"

"Look at me. Do I look mean and tough to you?"

"Tough, maybe. But mean—"

"You have to fight tooth and nail to be at the top. You don't, and you trickle to the bottom and beg."

"I ..." He stopped himself before he said too much. "In my previous pack, none of us had to beg."

"No?" She smirked. "How many were you?"

"Seven strong. All family."

Her smirk broadened, but there wasn't humor there. "Ah, there you have it. This pack is thirty strong and still growing."

"*Thirty?*"

"Thirty," she repeated. "You can only have two in the position of Head, a pair of Fangs, a pair of Eyes, and Four to six legs. The rest are all Tails."

Dante fell silent, his heart quickening as he remembered the wolf mother's cries for her young.

"And how many have been killed?"

She gave him a look. It wasn't surprised.

"I can't say."

Saxton approached the fence and studied it from post to post. Instead of barbed wires or chain-links in between each wooden pole, there were cables that looked soft enough to chew through. He gingerly stepped forward, opened his mouth, and bit down. Lightning ran through him from nose to tail. Yelping, Saxton fell backwards. His mouth tasted like ash, his heart was in his ears, and his toes were vibrating. Above him, someone laughed.

"Not very bright, are you?" It was a squirrel. "Touch that again and you'll get cooked!"

"Thank you, I'll keep that in mind," the fox said dryly. He looked at the cable he bit; he had exposed a bundle of wires woven within. Examining them closer, but staying a safe distance away, he could feel that the wires were very hot. A small spark popped from them, and the tiny flame was carried by the wind before disappearing.

Not inclined to be shocked again, he began digging at the foot of the enclosure. By noon, he was irritated to find that it extended underground more than four feet. He was exhausted and covered in mud, but he refused to give up so easily and attempted a second tunnel several feet away. He doubted his efforts would yield different results, but the exercise would give him time to think of another plan.

Dante's scent was in the air, mingled with that of his brothers and sisters, not of kin, but of kind. A fist of anxiety wrapped around his throat. He had come this far, and he frankly did not know what to do if Dante decided he wanted to stay here.

'Well,' he thought, 'it's a taste of my own medicine.'

They waited on one side of the riverbank until the sun was well on its way to the top of its arc. Hidden within tall grasses and underbrush, the three hunting bands positioned themselves at three different angles to surround the elk. They watched the elk sloshing their way toward them, and adrenaline roiled in their blood.

Dante shifted his weight from side to side. He could take down a little lamb with nowhere to go, but a full-grown elk in the wild was another story. His head pounded, and his left eye – or rather, where his left eye had been – began to ache. He remembered the caribou and the

200

snow. He remembered the shame and the blood. He remembered feeling lost and alone, wanted by no one.

He felt ill.

The elk were moving closer. He tried to calm himself. His feet were shaking. He could hear his peers whispering and laughing. He wished they would stop gawking at him. They had the same skeptical look Oakley, Rush, and sometimes Timber had before a hunt. 'All honor, plenty of fight, but no coordination,' Rush had said. There were times he wished his brother was someone else.

Dante thought of Saxton and the first buck he caught because of him. What would he say now? 'Come now, Dante,' he imagined; his voice would be kind, but a touch superior. 'Stand straight and uncurl that tail from between your legs. Now, look for the weakest of the herd. It will save you time and energy, and you'll be less likely to get hurt. You could be a pack leader one day, so hold up your head and put down the weight you carry.'

He let out a breath, his chest hurting less.

Howooooooo!

Trigger, Pistol, and Whiplash raised their heads in song, and their bands emerged from the grass as one. The elk grunted and groaned, and a fair number dared to fight back with their antlers and hooves. The vast majority bringing up the rear immediately retreated. Dirt flew around, the land turning into a battlefield, and even with only one eye, Dante thought he had never seen more clearly than now.

Trigger sprinted for an elk large enough to kill him in one blow. It was too dangerous a target, so Dante found another elk, also large, but slightly lame on one leg. He went after it, not quite sure where his fear had gone, and leapt upon its back. The elk bucked violently, but Dante held on with his teeth and deeply embedded claws.

"Get off me!" The elk screamed. "Get off me or I will crush your ribs!"

Dante twisted the flesh between his teeth, and the elk moaned, toppling to his side. The wolves assisting Trigger were kicked and wounded, and some were even gored by the elk they surrounded. When they saw Dante bring down an elk on his own, they much too quickly abandoned Trigger to help Dante finish his hunt.

Unable to kill the elk on his own, Trigger angrily let go of its hind leg. The elk nearly impaled him, but he dodged the swinging antlers and ran a safe distance away. He watched, seething, as his band pinned Dante's elk to the ground while Dante delivered the killing bite.

The chaos of the hunt simmered with most of the herd no longer in sight. Dante looked around him, contented to see that they had been successful in taking down three elk as planned.

Jezebel and Cassius approached them, walking side-by-side. Though Cassius was clearly a fighter, Jezebel was something else entirely. She stepped lightly over the soil. Her face was calm and her eyes revealed nothing. Dante only felt ice.

"Well done, my pack," she said softly. "My strongest fighters, you may eat first. That includes you, Dante. I saw what you did here today."

Dante watched as Cassius, Trigger, Pistol, Whiplash, the Mongrel, and four others began to eat alongside Jezebel.

"What about the others?"

"They'll get their share when the strongest are through."

He glanced at the waiting wolves and saw a pair of green eyes among them. It occurred to him he hadn't even asked for her name.

Not wanting to disrespect Jezebel, Dante ate until his hunger was placated. He licked his lips, but was stunned that the higher ranks were still eating, and did not look to be finishing any time soon.

Dante forced his mouth shut, thinking how Saxton would advise him against saying anything foolish.

Jezebel was eying him and said, "Dante, do not forget to take a limb with you for caching."

He did as he was told, and remained silent.

The meat was down to skin, innards, and the less favorable muscles when the higher ranks abandoned the carcasses at last. Jezebel looked at the others, her Tails, and nodded graciously.

"You may begin."

The wolves descended upon the remains with an enthusiasm Dante could only compare to vultures. When all that remained were bone fragments, they abandoned the site and returned to their home territory. Dante carried the leg he had taken. He did not fail to hear the sounds of his neighbors' complaining stomachs as they trekked up the mountain. It was not so long ago when he'd been that hungry himself.

It was sunset by the time they were home, and Jezebel commanded all to rest until their nightfall hunt. As the wolves dispersed, Dante sought out the female he had spoken to, and laid the elk leg at her feet.

"Here," he said in a hushed voice. "You need this more than I do."

"There are many more who need this more than they do," the female corrected. He did not argue.

202

"What's your name?"

"Juniper," she said. "Come to the west, away from Jezebel's inner circle. There is someone who would like to speak with you."

"When? Why?"

"When the sky turns purple, but not dark blue. You'll see soon enough."

With that, she took the elk leg without a measure of shame and, vanished into the trees.

He wondered if he should follow her, but before he could decide, he heard a whisper behind him.

"Dante?"

He turned to see Saxton at the other side of the preserve fence, standing sheepishly between two messy holes, with Quill's weatherworn feather hanging from his neck.

Chapter Twenty-Nine

"Saxton!" Dante trotted to the fence, careful not to touch it. "What are you doing here?"

It saddened the fox to see him so surprised. "Silly wolf," he said, hoping for some levity. "Did you really think I would abandon you?"

Dante frowned and his lips formed a thin line. "I've feared it."

He lowered his ears unhappily. "I'm sorry. I'm so sorry. I didn't mean to be a poor friend."

For a second, Dante wondered what had become of Two-Step, but he quickly set that thought aside. "You're here now," he said at length. "That's what counts."

Saxton snorted. "Not quite. I've tried digging my way in under the fence, but it goes down so far I thought I'd wear my nails to the bone! I tried to think of another way in, but the only way I can think of is through that building, where the humans are."

Looking at the building in question, Dante nodded. "I don't remember how I got here, but I know I was in there before they let me out."

He turned back to Saxton, who was frowning at him.

"What?"

"What's that on your neck? It's bigger than a dog collar, and it has a blinking light on it."

"Oh, that. I don't know. The humans put it on me. We all have one."

"Hm ..." Saxton considered the device, but let it go. "Never mind. If I have to go through the building, I will. When do the doors open?"

Dante shrugged. "I haven't been here long, but I've seen the humans leave at sunset. Maybe you can sneak in when the last human leaves."

Saxton looked behind him, counting the cars in the parking lot. There were five. He looked at the sky. The sun would sink soon.

"All right. It will take some time, but I will get in before tonight. As to how we'll get out—"

"About that," the wolf interrupted, and Saxton promised himself to be understanding, "I'm not ready to leave just yet."

He was expecting an argument, but Saxton simply nodded and waited for him to explain.

"Things ... aren't right here. I can't just leave."

"What's happened?"

Saxton listened intently as Dante explained what he had seen festering within the pack. A few wolf names were dropped in his story here and there, but a name that kept reemerging with noticeable frequency was 'Juniper.' Though he hadn't seen her yet, Saxton could see very clearly that his friend was taken by the female and thought quite highly of her. Saxton quickly made a decision.

"Tell Juniper I am here to free you, and that she is more than welcome to join us on our journey east if she so chooses. In the meantime, I am at her service to assist her and those in her plight in whatever way she sees fit."

It was a generous declaration, and again Dante had to wonder what had happened to Two-Step. 'He gave her up,' the wolf thought, feeling quite the hypocrite. And now, here Saxton was, ready to aid strangers for his sake.

"It's dangerous in here, Saxton," Dante cautioned. "There are many wolves, and most of them are stronger than me. I promised I would safeguard your wellbeing. Coming in here—"

"Would be the least I can do," he finished stubbornly. "Come now, Dante. Have you ever known me to shy away from risk?"

Dante wanted to tell Saxton to go away, to go back to his vixen and stay safe. His mind and mouth may as well have been on different continents, for he heard his own voice say, "You? *Never.*"

Saxton napped outside the front doors of the preserve headquarters, waking every so often to check the number of cars still remaining in the parking lot. When only a single hatchback remained, the fox pressed himself against the building's brick wall, his feet ready to move at a moment's notice.

One of the doors opened, and a young woman with auburn hair bundled in a braid stepped out. While she searched the depths of her oversized bag for her keys, Saxton slipped inside just as the door began to close. He made it inside safely, his tail just missing the pinch of the door sliding snugly into its frame.

Inside, the building was dark, but glowed from certain corners with an unnatural light. Saxton searched for the back of the building, and tried not to flinch as his nails *tip-tap-tipped* over the slippery tile floors.

He found another pair of doors leading to the wolves' sanctuary, but they were locked, as he suspected they would be. Looking around, he found a set of windows that were similar to the windows in Two-Step's basement. He hopped onto a desk, and from the desk, onto the windowsill. He batted at the window's crank with his paws until the glass pane tilted outward and a soft breeze blew past his nose. Then he pushed against the glass with his forehead and squeezed outside. If Tootsie had seen him, he was certain she would have been proud.

When he landed on the ground, Dante was already there waiting for him.

"Good, you made it," said the wolf. "It's almost time to go."

They headed west as Juniper had advised, not sure of what they should be looking for. When it seemed as though they had been played for fools, Juniper stepped out of the shadows with two other wolves at her side.

"Juniper—"

"Shh ... Not so loud or Jezebel's followers will hear you." She did not move, but her eyes shifted to acknowledge the fox at Dante's side. "You must be Saxton. Dante has just told me many things about you."

He bowed his head. "Good things, I hope."

She grinned. "Only if you consider learning to read from a rat, showing kindness to an angry dog, saving a flock of dumb sheep, and befriending a lonely, but rabid raccoon good things."

Saxton looked at Dante, who shrugged. "What? They're all true."

Juniper glanced at her companions, two males, one nearly blue in color and another black with white undercoating, then gestured toward the foot of a mountainside with a lift of her chin. As they drew closer, they reached a narrow cavern carved along the sharp rock. The cavern's entryway was so narrow, it seemed invisible to the eye unless viewed from just the right place.

One by one, they wriggled inside. The rocky walls were lit with luminescent fungi and glowworms that hung from the cave ceiling. The sight made for a beautiful array of green and blue icicles and stars.

They reached the center of the cave. Dante and Saxton stepped back. There were more wolves sitting around in a circle.

"Ah," said a brown wolf crouched in the middle, "Dante, the wolf of everlasting honor, it is good to see you and your..." he paused at the sight of the *Lonely Thief*, but immediately regrouped, "... *friend* here."

Dante squinted at the wolf, trying to place his face. He had black markings beneath his eyes and around his ears, and he was older than most. He hadn't seen him often, but remembered he was usually alongside Sniper when the whole pack was gathered. "Buckeye?"

"Aye," the wolf said with a smile. "It's good to know you remember my name, especially with so many of us. Naturally, you know Juniper. The other wolves who escorted you here are Arrow and Fable." He motioned to the black-and-white wolf and the nearly blue wolf. "Welcome to the rebellion. Our membership is at eight, but still growing. Including you, we make nine, a good number."

Saxton looked around him, feeling eyes casting judgment on his presence already. "Excuse me, Buckeye," he began, "I know a little of what has been happening here, but would you be so kind as to enlighten me with respect to ... the history?"

Buckeye's brows crawled up his forehead. "Forgive my reservations, fox, but although I've been told Dante is your friend, this is not your fight."

"Perhaps not; at least, not in the sense it would be a fight for my kind. However, it would be a fight for justice, which I do believe in."

"*Lonely Thieves* don't believe in justice," Arrow mocked. "They believe in survival at any cost."

"*Arrow*." Buckeye warned, but Saxton let a fang peek from beneath his lips.

"The two are not mutually exclusive," he said. "But you see, I am not like most foxes. I am not *just* a lonely thief."

"Then what are you?" Fable challenged.

Saxton looked at Fable and boldly approached him until they were barely a nose apart.

"I'm afraid you've asked the wrong question, Mr. Wolf. It is not a matter of 'what,' but 'who.' I am Saxton. I have a name, just like the rest of you, and I will choose to define that name as I see fit." He sat on his haunches and raised his chin with pride. "At this moment, I am choosing to help my friend, and in turn help all of you. But the next question becomes, 'Will you trust me?' Most wolves, you see, would not. And so I must ask: are you like most wolves?"

When none of them spoke, Saxton turned back to Buckeye.

"No response? Very well then, tell me your pack's story. What do you have to lose?"

Impressed, Buckeye nodded. "All right, fox: let's see how long your interest holds. Four years ago, the head of our pack, Tough Shot, died of old age. At the time, there were two wolves vying for the position he left behind. Those wolves were Cassius, Jezebel's mate, and me.

"Cassius, for all his strength and stubbornness, was inclined to lean on Jezebel's judgment. Now understand, to Jezebel's credit she has a calm and capable mind. She led well her first two years as head. However, our territory being a wolf preserve, we have no natural enemies. The pack grew large. Perhaps *too* large.

"Our numbers became difficult to manage. She became strict in her ways, unbending in her belief of the ranking system: the Head, the Fangs, the Eyes, the Legs, and the Tail. The reality is that there are always more Legs and Tails in any pack than there are Heads or Fangs. Jezebel... seemed to turn a blind eye to that fact."

"Not completely," a gray, female wolf quietly interrupted.

"Larkspur, did you have something to add?"

"She's threatened by new litters," Larkspur said, "and she knows most of those litters come from the bottom rung simply because there are so many of us. If one of us births a wolf that may one day be Head, her leadership would be thrown into jeopardy."

The hairs on Dante's neck prickled with revulsion. "Is that why the Mongrel tried to kill those pups?"

"Yes," Buckeye said gravely. "The murders have been happening for some time now, though there's little we can do without risking getting killed ourselves."

"But I don't understand," Saxton said. "Why not allow you to form your own packs?"

Juniper laughed unkindly. The fox supposed he should have been offended, but the wolf regarded him with the kind of affection one might have for a small, naïve brother. "Oh, we've tried that. But the thing about having so many wolves bow down to you, Saxton, is that you eventually get used to it and you don't want to share."

"On our first attempt," Fable added, "Jezebel had both her Fangs, the Mongrel and Trigger, chase the defectors down in warning. On our second attempt, she had Pistol and Whiplash take whatever food we'd capture for ourselves and feed her highest ranking followers. When the murder of our young began, most of us were silenced by fear."

"We must take her down," Juniper growled passionately. "Nothing will change otherwise."

This time, Saxton snorted and Juniper scowled.

"I thought Dante was a good judge of character," she snarled. "You mock our cause?"

At that, Saxton chuckled. "No, not your cause, but your willingness to believe change can be that simple. I'm not sure Dante told you as it's rather personal, but I was raised by a crow. My brother and sister, on the other paw, matured under normal conditions. In the end, though I knew them for only a brief time, my brother and sister, *Lonely Thieves* to the letter, each had some measure of compassion, just as I still have some measure of selfishness."

"What's your point, fox?"

"My *point* is that it is difficult to control our basic natures. We are all selfish, are we not? We all have ideals, do we not? Well, if you truly want to keep the balance of power under control, a new leader is not the only answer."

Saxton waited as the other wolves murmured to one another. He could sense the way they were looking at him was changing.

"Saxton," Buckeye began, "like Dante, you have a rather appropriate name. Your mind, it seems, is as sharp as a blade."

"Thank you," Saxton answered, bowing. "But I must ask, for the benefit of my friend as well as your kind, how will you lead any differently than Jezebel?"

Chapter Thirty

To Saxton's relief, Buckeye and his followers did have a plan, however rudimentary, to prevent history from repeating itself. The rebellion members had unanimously chosen Buckeye as their head, while Buckeye had insisted that the pack be divided into smaller sub-packs consisting of family or close friendships. It was an effort, Buckeye said, to return the wolves to their normal way of living in the open wild.

At the same time, the head male and female of each sub-pack would report to Buckeye and apprise him of any disputes. Together, the heads and Buckeye would decide, as a group, how best to deal with a situation. The ranking system would still be in place, Juniper added, but with smaller packs, more Legs and Tails would be given the opportunity to climb up and prosper.

When Dante raised the issue of food, Arrow assured him sub-packs would help supplement one another's hunts if need be. The proposal vaguely reminded Saxton of Tootsie's colony, though it was not nearly as strict.

It was not a perfect plan. Power struggles among the heads would be unavoidable, Saxton thought, but it was certainly better than Jezebel's and Cassius' current leadership.

When the moon came out, the Mongrel and Trigger howled for everyone to gather for the night hunt. Saxton shadowed the wolves as they climbed up the mountain to meet. He hoped the night was dark enough to mask his movements, and that Buckeye's wolves provided ample shielding to hide behind and to mask his vulpine scent.

A beautiful, if reserved, white wolf stood at the cliff's edge. Saxton recognized her at once as Jezebel, and deduced that the male to her left was Cassius. A monstrous wolf, quite possibly a hellhound from one of Quill's scarier stories, stood to Jezebel's right. Saxton watched, transfixed, as Jezebel whispered into the Mongrel's ear. He stood straighter, and she rewarded him with a gentle nuzzle along his mangled cheek.

Jezebel called forth Sniper and Buckeye, commanding them to report which area in their territory was ripe for hunting tonight. Saxton barely listened, instead studying the body language of the three wolves next to Cassius. They spoke to one another quietly, glancing at the Mongrel and barely suppressing their laughter.

When the location of their night hunt was decided, Saxton bid Dante farewell and crawled beneath a thick shrub. He watched as a majority of the pack descended the other side of the mountain, while the Mongrel and Jezebel stayed behind.

"They should be gone until the stars shine their brightest," Jezebel said, her dark eyes never leaving his. "Go to the dens and destroy any litters you find. Kill them all."

"As you command."

He was about to leave, when Jezebel called out to him again. "Solomon."

Solomon looked at her, so eager to please. Saxton pitied him.

"You are a great wolf," she commended. "I am lucky to have you by my side."

He bowed his head. "No, I'm merely a half-wolf. It is I who am lucky."

Solomon took off toward the woods, heading for the lower ranking wolves' dens. Saxton slipped away and followed him at a safe distance.

It took equal parts restraint and common sense to not intervene when Solomon would dig-out the wolf pups, drag them to the surface, and break their necks with a thorough crunch of his teeth. The killing was quick and precise, but that did not stop the pups from crying one pathetic yip before their lives ended much too soon.

As he watched, Saxton thought he would be sick all over himself, but the compulsion to do so was stymied by a most curious thing.

From each litter, Solomon would kill all the young except the runt. At first Saxton thought the Mongrel wanted to destroy those young in a far more gruesome fashion, to scorn their sickliness, but instead he would carry them away by the scruff of their necks, impossibly gentle.

He took the frailest pups, male and female in equal numbers, and deposited them at the backdoor of the preserve's headquarters. By the time the pack should be returning from their hunt, there were six pups huddled together. Solomon waited by the door, silent and unmoving until a light from inside the building flicked on.

Solomon barked three times. He wagged his tail when a petite young woman with blonde hair stepped out.

"Hey, Sol," she greeted and gave him a winsome smile. "Looks like it's just you and me on the night shift again, huh? How're those cuts? They gettin' any better?"

Solomon made a low gurgling sound and touched his nose to one of the pups by the door. The woman crouched down.

"Oh, poor things. Barely the size of kittens."

In pairs, she lifted them against her chest and carried them inside. When she was done, she closed the door behind her and sat down next to Solomon.

"Don't worry, Sol. We'll transfer those little guys to the sanctuary in Massachusetts. They'll get better care there. What do you think?"

Sol panted happily and batted his tail. They shared one another's company in silence until a howl rose from the distance.

"Better go back to your friends," the woman said, rising to her feet and dusting the dirt off the back of her pants. Solomon got to his feet as well, but hesitated. The woman laughed. "Go on, handsome. I'll see you tomorrow night, okay?"

She waved at him and closed the door behind her. Saxton followed the Mongrel back to the mountain, wondering what was going through Solomon's head.

As soon as the pack split apart, Saxton chased Dante and Juniper down.

"What'd you find out?"

"Nothing you don't already know, except for one minor detail."

"What's that?" Juniper asked.

"As it happens, the Mongrel has a heart."

Dante nearly choked on air.

"He kills young!" Dante burst, his voice shaking. "Can you even think of anything so monstrous? I'll kill him myself as soon as I get the chance!"

212

"Dante, be careful," Saxton replied evenly. "If things were worse, don't you think you could have been the Mongrel?"

The wolf scoffed. "I'd never let myself turn into something that disgusting, that evil."

Saxton glanced at Juniper, who sighed.

"Look, I don't know what you saw, but he's a murderer, pure and simple. We kill to eat. We kill to survive. We kill to defend. The Mongrel ... he just kills, and I don't doubt he enjoys it."

"He doesn't just kill," Saxton argued. "He kills upon order."

"And the difference is?"

"He won't do it otherwise. Have you ever wondered why that is?" When the wolves said nothing, Saxton continued. "He is difficult to look at, yes, but I think that's where his weakness lies."

Juniper scowled. "What do you mean?"

"Look at how Jezebel treats him. She looks at him in the face and isn't disgusted. It's a kindness he returns with loyalty. However, he's not completely loyal. There is another he also seems to respect. A *human.*"

"You mean Gwen?" At the fox's nearly astonished look, Juniper rolled her eyes. "Don't get too cocky, fox. I've been here a long time. Gwen took care of the Mongrel when he got skinned three years ago. What's this got to do with anything?"

"Solomon spared the runts and took them to her."

Dante stopped in his tracks. "Why would he do that?"

"I don't know. Perhaps he saw the runts as no threat to Jezebel, and thought they would be safe with Gwen. As I've said, he is not without a soul."

They walked in silence until Saxton's thoughts circled back to what Juniper had said earlier. "Who skinned him?"

"Trigger and his brothers: Pistol and Whiplash."

After that, Saxton did not say anything for a long time. Dante watched him and could see the fox already forming a plan.

"What do you need, Saxton?"

"A means to get closer to Jezebel. But for the information I seek, I'm not so sure I can watch her in secret and hope she says something useful. I may need to speak to her myself."

"Whoa, you're out of your mind," Juniper breathed. "You'll get your throat slit so fast you'll wonder why you feel lightheaded. Besides, how's this supposed to help us?"

"The Mongrel is a symbol," Saxton answered. "He means different things to different members of the pack. To you and your friends, he's the corruption of your leadership. To his peers, he's an outcast and a scapegoat. To Jezebel, I believe he is merely a pawn she plays against both sides. Turn him to your side, and you will see her power crumble."

They settled inside Juniper's den. It was slightly cramped, but fortunately Saxton wasn't nearly as large as his companions.

"So what do you want to find out?" Dante inquired.

"The truth about the Mongrel and how he came to be. Tell the Mongrel the truth, and I am sure Solomon is yours."

"That's a great idea and all, but how on earth are you gonna get Jezebel to trust you? How are you gonna get the Mongrel to trust you?"

"I am counting on Jezebel to view me as a *Lonely Thief* merely passing by. I've learned many things from Quill and his stories, and the undoing of most gods and kings is their pride. After all, who doesn't like to hear themselves talk?

"As for the Mongrel ..." He took a breath and glanced at Dante, who cringed. "You should talk to him."

"Me? I fought him when I met him! No love lost there ..."

"Maybe, but I think he'd be more receptive to you than anyone else here."

"Why? Because of my face?"

The fox nodded. Dante groaned. Juniper giggled and licked his nose. The small gesture of affection seemed to placate Dante for the time being.

"It's a superficial thing, yes, I know," Saxton admitted. "But beneath that, it's clear you've both seen more than your fair share of battles."

Dante snorted derisively at the word 'battles.'

"I mean it, Dante. Maybe they were not battles you're proud of, but they were battles all the same. At the end, the both of you – you and Solomon – survived, though for different reasons. You must show Solomon the reasons you still stand. I think he needs the hope that he'll belong somewhere at the end of this."

Dante thought for a moment, peered at Juniper, then back at Saxton. "You sure he'll help us if he abandons Jezebel's side?"

Saxton shook his head. "I can't guarantee that, but he'll probably kill Jezebel."

Dante froze. "And you're amenable with that?"

The fox's jaw tightened.

"I have no stake in her murder save for your wellbeing, Dante. Still, I suppose I'd encourage mercy. Jezebel was a good leader once.

Mercy may help bring that goodness back out. That would be Solomon's choice, and if not his, then Buckeye's."

"What if she doesn't take it?" Juniper asked.

"Then she may as well be dead.

Chapter Thirty-One

While Saxton slept, Juniper beckoned Dante to come out of her den. They walked side-by-side beneath the stars, and Juniper had been so quiet, Dante found himself growing nervous.

"Did you want something?" He asked.

"No," she said, "Well, yes … you told me yesterday that Saxton had come here to free you. You don't want to stay?"

"It's not that I don't," he replied, "but I must see him to New Hampshire to repay a debt."

"Ah, is that how your friendship started?"

Dante grimaced. "Doesn't sound like a true friendship when you put it that way."

She merely shrugged in return. "Who cares? It doesn't matter how it began. I became friends with Buckeye the day he felt sorry for me. If you think I'm small now, you should've seen me when I was a juvenile. Buckeye said he'd seen jack rabbits two times bigger than my head. Would've given him a piece of my mind about that if he hadn't given me something to eat the next second." Juniper sighed. "Anyway, I was hoping you would stay. We could use more good pack leaders."

At that, he barked out a laugh. "Me? Ha! I've been my pack's Tail since I was born."

"So what? Anyone can grow strong with effort and time. Learning compassion, though, that only comes when you've been in the position of being weak." She looked at him, her eyes sparkling.

"Not all strong warriors make great leaders, Dante. It's too easy for them to become greedy for power and war."

He gazed at her with the admiration that had been budding since he first met her. This must have been what Saxton had felt when he found Quill, and later, Two-Step. "Wish Saxton was here to listen to that," he said. "He'd probably think it's something Quill would say."

Juniper grew confused. "Quill?"

"Don't worry," Dante smirked, "it's a compliment."

They stopped along a stream and drank the flowing water. The water was cool and crisp, a small luxury.

"What about you? Do you want to come with us?"

She raised one of her brows in doubt. "And where would we go once your debt's been paid?"

Dante fidgeted. He didn't think that far ahead.

"I don't know, probably north where it's safer. I have family waiting there. Not sure I want to go back."

Juniper looked around thoughtfully. "I suppose I've been here too long. Maybe it is time for a change."

He felt his heart pound. It was as if he had swallowed a live humming bird.

A twig snapped. They swung their heads around. They both sighed when it was only Fable.

"There you are," Fable groused. "I've been looking everywhere for you. We need to gather again."

It was common practice among those in the rebellion to avoid being too specific. Since the message came from Fable, the message was Buckeye's.

The wolves stopped by Juniper's den, but found it was already empty.

"Where'd your friend go?"

Dante raised his eye heavenward. "Knowing him, he's heard everything and is already there."

Sure enough, when then entered the cavern, Saxton was already sitting a moderate distance away from the gathered wolves. He nodded to Dante, Juniper, and Fable in greeting as they entered. The rebellion had grown larger once word of a plan had spread among the lower pack members by whisper. Their number had grown to fourteen strong in one day, which pleased Juniper to no end. With everyone present, Buckeye spoke.

"As some of you already know, we have reason to believe the Mongrel would be a useful ally for our cause. At the very least, if we

217

can persuade him to defect Jezebel's inner circle, she will lose one of her Fangs."

He looked to Saxton, permitting him to speak. The fox cleared his throat.

"As far as we know, Jezebel and her supporters are not aware of my presence. I plan on speaking to her directly ..." he paused at the abrupt murmurings that rose around him, "and hopefully will outfox her." Saxton directed everyone's attention to Dante. "Dante will have to convince Solomon to trust him. There is a high possibility that this will not work. If it doesn't ..." He exhaled noisily, "I think Buckeye will have to orchestrate the attack on the inner circle without removing one of its critical members."

"When will we begin?" one of the other wolves asked.

"In one full moon's time," answered Buckeye.

A few of the wolves balked. Saxton stared at Buckeye, annoyed that he hadn't been told the timeframe.

"You want to attack on Jezebel's and Cassius' Ascension Day?" Arrow asked, incredulous.

"They and their supporters will be too occupied preparing a ridiculously large feast to notice anything amiss."

"But most of us will be too busy hunting!" another wolf growled.

"Be that as it may," Buckeye replied calmly, "the attack will be at night when the actual feast begins. We will wait until Jezebel and her inner circle have eaten their fill. By then, they will be too tired and fat to fight us."

Buckeye looked around him until he found Juniper. "Juniper, I'd like to take you as my second."

Dante flinched, but did not move again.

"I'd be honored, Buckeye, but I'm not ready to take a mate," she replied as diplomatically as she could.

"Regardless, I need a second in command. Can you fill that role?"

Looking at her and seeing the ambivalence plain on her face, Dante knew whatever plans of what could have been were gone. From the corner of his eye, he could see that Saxton noticed as well.

"Good. As for the sub-packs, the heads have been selected unanimously as follows: Fable and Larkspur, Arrow and Snapdragon, Chief and Racket. If we are successful and more pack members join us, more heads may rise. Any questions?"

There were none.

"Good. Pack leaders, you have your instructions. Share them with your subordinates."

As the wolves separated into groups, Buckeye approached Dante, Juniper, and Saxton.

"Saxton, it's critical that the timing of everything is precise. If you meet with Jezebel and the Mongrel defects too soon, our plans will be ruined."

"How close to the attack do you need this to happen?"

"As close as possible. However, what if the Mongrel does not defect?"

"I doubt that," Saxton said with confidence. "There is something in his relationship with Jezebel that isn't genuine, and I do not think Solomon will react kindly to lies."

"That's putting it mildly," Juniper scoffed.

"What do you need me to do?" Dante asked.

"If we must do this during the feast, then you need to draw Solomon away before he eats too much. Keep him out of sight while I talk to Jezebel, but keep him close. I'm sure you'll think of something clever."

"And when will you meet Jezebel?" asked Buckeye.

"Tomorrow. It takes time to earn trust, and one moon's time should do it. "

They left the cave, and as soon as they were alone, Dante took Saxton aside. Juniper took one look at them and didn't ask.

"Summer is ending." Dante said. "What if we—"

"If I miss Fiddle, well … It's like you say: Quill's dead. You're alive. Quill matters, will always matter, but you're more important now." Saxton stroked the feather hanging from his neck. He wished Quill had seen everything it had seen. "It's all right, Dante. I'm sure we'll make it, and if not …" his shoulders shuddered with a breath. "Well, at least we would have had a most memorable adventure."

Dante swallowed. "No. Not finding Fiddle will cost you too much. You don't have to stay. You don't have to do this. We can think of another plan."

"We're friends, aren't we?" Saxton suddenly asked, and his mouth clamped shut. "Then let me do this for you."

Chapter Thirty-Two

Saxton emerged after the wolves had gone for their first hunt of the day. He picked out Jezebel's scent from a slew of others, recognizing hers as lavender and wet grass with a hint of oily musk. Saxton took a bone from one of Juniper's caches and carried it with him as he passed her territory, hoping it would draw her attention.

It did.

"Stealing from my brethren?" Jezebel asked silkily. "You are either lucky in your exploits or truly foolish, or perhaps you are both."

Saxton froze and turned to look at her. She approached him serenely, but her regal poise belied something far more menacing in her eyes.

"You're fortunate I found you, *Lonely Thief*. If the Mongrel had, you'd surely be dead. Where did you find that bone?"

The fox set it down, acting as though his plans were ruined.

"Found it in a cache in the west, Miss Wolf. It belonged to a female, I believe. She had tan and gold fur. Seeing as she was small and weak, I figured it wouldn't hurt. You want this back?"

Jezebel looked at the nearly naked bone in disgust. She set one paw forward and kicked it away.

"You are on my territory, and yet you are disrespectfully walking around without a care in the world." Her throat rumbled with a growl. "It would serve you right to feed you to the Legs and Tails. You are too filthy for my fellows to eat."

The fox cocked his head to the side curiously. "I might be filthy, but that only means I'm willing to get my paws dirty. Tell me, Miss Wolf, have you any unspeakable tasks you need taken care of?"

The white wolf showed her teeth and pulled back her ears. She was so ferocious, Saxton had to fight the urge to bolt. "How presumptuous! Why would I ever take a favor from a *Lonely Thief* like you?"

The best lies, Saxton knew, were those closest to the truth. "I've overheard some stirrings from your ... Legs and Tails ... I'm bargaining for my life! You think I'd lie to you?"

"Stirrings," Jezebel repeated, and by the tone of her voice, it sounded as though she had been anticipating this for some time.

"Yes," he went on. "Last night, I heard of plans to put a new head at the front of the pack."

Jezebel grew silent. Eventually, her stance became neutral and her frightening teeth hid behind her lips.

"Fox, what is that feather around your neck?"

"This?" he said, stalling for time as he frantically wove his lie. "A token from the first crow I captured. They are not easy for young kits to catch."

Her eyes narrowed, calculating. "Foxes are not sentimental creatures."

"No," Saxton agreed, perhaps too quickly. "But we are proud ones."

She moved closer to him, pushed him onto his side, and pressed her paw against his chest. Saxton coughed at the weight burdening his ribs and forcing air out of his lungs.

"Name me, *Lonely Thief*, five lessons your father taught you when you were young."

His heart raced, and he was certain Jezebel could feel it. He gasped a few times, and by some miracle finally managed to speak.

"Don't talk to strangers," Saxton choked. "Never stray too far from your territory. Answer to no one. Everyone lives and dies alone."

"And the fifth?"

"I ..." Panic seized him. He didn't know anything else. "I— I must do whatever it takes to survive."

She lifted her paw, and he heaved for air.

"Interesting. Where is your territory?"

"Lattice, Pennsylvania, in the basement of a human's house, and several yards all around it."

"So what are you doing all the way out here?"

"Looking for a mate."

"Why are you answering to me?"

"To *live!*"

Relenting, Jezebel smiled. "Come with me, you craven little creature. It seems I do have some use for you."

She took Saxton to her den, which was large enough for four wolves, yet curiously bore the scent of only one. He wondered if Jezebel and Cassius slept separately despite their union.

"Sit," she said, and he immediately obeyed. "How long have you been in the wolf preserve?"

"A day and a half."

"You said earlier that you heard plans to put a new head at the front of the pack," she went on. "Surely that means you know who that head would be."

The fox tried not to tremble. He didn't realize how much Jezebel might already know. Regrouping, Saxton said, "I didn't hear his name."

"Then what does he look like?"

Saxton thought quickly. She spoke as though she already knew who the rebellion's leader was. It was possible she was bluffing, but if she was not, it was too dangerous to lie outright.

"He's brown," he said hoarsely. "I can't recall much else."

He hoped he was vague enough that Jezebel might dismiss him, but instead she smiled. It wasn't pleasant. "I see. Here is what I want you to do, *Lonely Thief*. Find out which of the brown wolves is rallying the Legs and Tails, and bring him out into the open tomorrow. Do this and perhaps I will trust you."

"And … how am I to gain *their* trust?"

"Oh, you don't need their trust, *Thief*. Tell them if their leader doesn't step forward … I will have to … *eliminate* … any low ranking wolf with brown fur, male or female. Insubordination is unacceptable, after all."

"They will kill me when I deliver this message!" he protested, and gulped knowing it was probably the truth.

"They won't if you tell them I sent you and expect you back."

Saxton couldn't argue with that. Jezebel was set on doing this, and he was fighting a losing battle. He wanted to ask what she intended to do once Buckeye had been flushed out, but knew a fox desperate for his life would not be so bold. As if reading his thoughts, Jezebel added:

"If they listen to my orders instead of hiding their leader, we'll give my Legs and Tails a fair fight for leadership. If they're dissatisfied with the results, they cannot say I did not give them a chance." She paused, smirking. "Whoever their leader is, he will not win, of course."

This time, Saxton didn't stop himself.

"How do you know?"

"Cassius never loses. He was born to kill." She looked at him, her face revealing nothing. "Go."

He left.

When Saxton met with Buckeye and the others, he felt a coldness fill his stomach that he immediately recognized as dread.

"You underestimated her!" Fable snarled. "Who is fooling who here? She has you by the tail, and you've delivered our leader to her feet, ready for execution!"

"You were supposed to help us!"

"Now you've made things worse!"

The other wolves growled and jeered.

"I didn't give her a name!" Saxton protested.

"It doesn't matter! One of us will surely die!"

Saxton hunched close to the ground with his tail between his legs. He could not look at Dante for fear of seeing the disappointment there, but his friend simply stood in front him in the event one of the wolves dared to attack.

"Enough!" Buckeye barked. "We must make this situation work for us."

"I will fight in your stead," Racket, a brown wolf, offered. Whisky stepped forward as well.

"No, we need you to lead a sub-pack, Racket. I'm not as important. I will fight."

Two more male wolves with brown fur came forth. Saxton stared at them, in awe of their loyalty.

"Friends," Buckeye said, heartened by their courage. "A good leader fights for his followers. He does not hide behind them."

"Cassius will kill you!" Arrow snapped.

"He didn't kill me last time," Buckeye reasoned.

"That was years ago! What's to stop him from doing so now?" Juniper bit back. "Back then was an honest fight. Now he and Jezebel will do anything to stay pack leaders. If they can kill pups, they can kill you."

Everyone fell silent. After an awful moment, Buckeye replied, "Jezebel isn't just trying to smother the fire, she's making a point. If

I'm too cowardly to fight her mate, then what chance does this rebellion have?"

"And if you die?" Juniper said in a harsh whisper.

"Then another great leader will take my place. That is you, Juniper. I chose you as my second for a reason."

Her jaws snapped together, and she nodded stiffly.

"That's it, then," Buckeye said. "I'll face Jezebel and Cassius tomorrow."

He looked at Saxton, who bowed his head.

"Don't forget your mission, Saxton. The plan might have deviated, but we're still on course."

The fox looked away. He felt sick, sick to his bones.

"I'm so sorry. It wasn't supposed to be this way."

Buckeye shrugged. "You don't know that. Maybe it was."

Chapter Thirty-Three

When the meeting adjourned, Juniper followed Saxton out of the cavern. Her feet were shaking with rage.

"If he dies—" she sobbed, "if he dies, I will never forgive you, *Lonely Thief!*"

She ran off, not waiting for Dante.

Dante stood at Saxton's side. Saxton didn't sense any anger coming from him. Helplessly cross with himself, he looked at the wolf and snarled, "Well? Aren't you going to call me a coward, too? Because you *should.*"

As soon as his friend looked down on him, Saxton regretted his words. "You were only trying to help," the wolf said gently. "You can't help if you're not alive."

"I've taken two lives already, Dante!" He shouted, tears coming unbidden to his eyes. "I'm not much help alive either!"

"Don't you dare say that!"

"I killed Quill! I killed Tarlo!" The fox snorted, laughing harshly at himself. "Now I'm well on my way to killing Buckeye too!"

"Stop it! Stop it! None of that's true! I killed Quill. Tarlo fell. Buckeye is choosing this. Don't make his sacrifice less meaningful by blaming this on yourself!"

"You told me to own my mistakes! Don't make excuses for me now!"

"You *have* made mistakes!" Dante barked. "But you are not a murderer!"

They were both breathing fast, and blood was rushing to their faces in anger. Dante closed his eyes, forcing himself to calm down.

"You're impulsive. You're self-righteous. You're a know-it-all. These things get you and others in trouble. But you're brave, big-hearted, and moral, too. Don't forget all the good things you've done."

Saxton was trembling. He lowered his head and started to cry.

"What do I do? I can't let Buckeye die. I can't …"

"Buckeye's like the Mongrel. If he dies, it will mean something for the rebellion. I think he knows it too."

"What about Juniper?" the fox sniffed.

"I think she needs to be alone. She's … got a lot on her shoulders now."

Morning came too soon. Instead of meeting at the usual place off the cliffside for the first hunt, Pistol made rounds around the pack's territory, informing everyone to gather at the great stone in the clearing. When they arrived, Jezebel was already standing atop the stone, cool and collected as ever. She saw Saxton distancing himself from the pack members. When they made eye contact, she grinned at him with approval.

Saxton didn't want it.

"Good morning, my pack. It's been brought to my attention—" she eyed the fox meaningfully "—that some of you are not satisfied with the current leadership." She waited as the murmurs around her died down. "As pack leader, it is my duty to ensure fairness within our community. In truth, I'm disappointed I had to hear this news not from a fellow wolf, but from a fox who happened to hear whispers in passing. You should know that I am a leader open to hearing your dissatisfactions and that there are no repercussions for stating your mind. That said, I will allow a fight for dominance. The winner will claim or reclaim the position of head of the pack, and as the female head, I will dutifully step down if necessary. Cassius, please step forward for battle."

The pack murmured again. Cassius did as he was told and waited for further instructions. Jezebel returned her attention to her pack.

"Now, will the leader you have chosen face my mate? You know the consequences if you do not move."

Buckeye did not blink as he made his way to the front of Jezebel's stone. She controlled her grin, but Saxton could see the barely curled corner of her mouth. They watched as Buckeye faced

Cassius, and it was immediately apparent who had the advantage in size. The remainder of pack backed away from the two contenders, but formed a large circle around them to watch.

Jezebel lay on her stone, as if bored with the proceedings.

"On my count, you may begin. One, two, three … *Begin!*"

The two wolves launched from their positions, and met in the middle with a clash of teeth and nails. Buckeye bit Cassius hard on the ear and pulled, but Cassius backed into him and flipped Buckeye over with his shoulders. Buckeye landed on his back in a sprawl, but quickly rolled away before Cassius could leap on top of him and slash into his belly.

Buckeye bit his shoulder, his legs, and his tail, but no matter how far he sunk his teeth into Cassius' flesh, it seemed the wolf was immune to pain. Laughing, the other wolf swiped his claws across Buckeye's face, leaving four bright, red lines and a spray of blood over the forest floor. Arrow barked and nearly jumped into the fray, but the Mongrel blocked his path and bit him into submission.

Realizing he was at a desperate disadvantage, Buckeye did the only thing that made sense: take away Cassius' teeth.

He lowered his head, and burst forward, aiming for Cassius' jaws. He heard the distinct crack of bone and an unexpected yip. Buckeye backed away and lunged forward again, not sparing a second to see how many teeth had fallen to the ground.

By the third attempt, Cassius grew wise and dodged out of the way. Facing one another again, Buckeye nearly chuckled with glee at the sight of the big, black wolf looking irate and slightly bloodied around the mouth. Cassius spit. He lost one of his canines. Jezebel sat up straighter, and everyone took notice.

"Think you're smart, do you?" Cassius barked.

"A little, yes," Buckeye jibed.

Cassius leapt forward, enraged, and pushed Buckeye onto his side. He tore at Buckeye's fur, ripping his abdomen bald. Buckeye scrambled to get free, but Cassius held him down with his weight. Biting Buckeye's ear, Cassius lifted his head and slammed it into the dirt.

"You should have known better," Cassius growled. "With four less teeth, this will hurt so much more. I hope you enjoy it …"

Buckeye laughed, blood dribbling from his mouth. "Even if you kill me, I'll still live …"

Saxton watched in horror as Cassius held Buckeye down by his throat. He opened his jaws and aimed for his belly. The fox panicked when he realized just what Cassius was about to do.

"Don't kill him," Saxton whispered.

Jezebel turned to him, furious. "What did you say?"

"Don't kill him," he repeated. He thought quickly, as fast as he could. "If you kill him now, all the lower ranking wolves will descend upon you. Show him mercy, and you'll control them forever."

She thought about it, and seemed to agree. "Cassius, that's enough."

He looked at her in confusion. "Jezebel?"

"Finish your lesson. Break his leg. We're done here."

In one swift motion, Cassius bit into Buckeye's front leg. Bone shattered. Buckeye wailed and wailed. It was a pitiful sound, but at least he was alive. A profound silence filled the forest. Everyone's breath was snatched from their lungs— choked out of them.

Jezebel hopped off her stone and walked away. She didn't even bother to announce the winner. She stopped by Saxton, however, and said without looking at him, "Come with me."

Saxton reluctantly followed, glancing once behind him. Dante and Juniper stood by Buckeye, comforting him in his pain. Juniper fell to her chest and sobbed loudly. Her yowls – her *tears* – they reminded Saxton of a young fox who had lost his father and friend. They reminded him of a mother bear who had lost her only cub.

But Buckeye wasn't dead. He might not ever fight again, but he wasn't dead. It was a small victory, one that no one would celebrate.

As he trailed after Jezebel, Saxton tried not to think about the possibility that Buckeye would have preferred to die bravely and honorably, rather than to survive with only three good legs.

Nicely played, *Lonely Thief*. Nicely played," Jezebel said with genuine delight. "I've been leading this pack so exactingly I've forgotten that kindness can be a much worse punishment than death."

Saxton swallowed the bile that rose to his stomach. "Do you enjoy this game, Miss Wolf?"

"Enjoy it?" Her sneer wavered. "It's a matter of necessity, but I must say I've gotten rather good at it." She stretched herself over the dry leaves of her den. "A pack this size, it's difficult to manage. But if you eliminate the troublemakers, you can stay in control for a very long time.

"I've been wondering for a while now which of my wolves was setting up a rebellion. You confirmed my suspicions, and once they were confirmed, I was able to cut the weed before it took hold. The problem now is that new wolf, Dante. I welcomed him as a higher rank, but he seems to associate more closely with the Legs and Tails like Buckeye did. He might be a liability in the future."

The hairs on Saxton's neck rose.

"Pity," she went on. "He's a strong one."

"If he's new, he probably doesn't know of the rebellion," Saxton offered.

"Then why move down?"

He tried to act nonchalant. "Perhaps there's a female who caught his interest."

"Any idea who?"

"No," Saxton said, a bit too hastily. "I'm merely speculating. Besides, if he doesn't want power, he must be a fool, and fools are of no use to you."

"You are a fiendish little thing," Jezebel drawled. "Perhaps I was fated to cross paths with you. An unlikely friendship, isn't it?"

Observing Jezebel and seeing that she seemed to be floating on her latest victory, Saxton took a chance.

"Yes, it is. But Miss Wolf, I'm curious, when did you and your mate become pack leaders?"

"Ah, a coincidence you should ask. In a few weeks, fox, there will be a feast in our honor. You should come and sit by my side as my guest."

"Miss Wolf, that's too generous," Saxton replied coyly, but Jezebel met him with a severe look.

"You can guarantee loyalty in many ways, but I find two work best: fear and, as I was reminded today, *gratitude*. I already know you fear me, but now you must be grateful to me. What better way to achieve that than to fill your stomach?"

"I'm surprised Miss Wolf is so transparent."

"Unlike you, *Lonely Thief*, I am neither small nor weak. I have nothing to hide from you so long as you remember that I can end you." She yawned. "Now, go. I need my rest."

He climbed out of her den shaking filth from his coat, but no matter how fastidiously he attended to his fur and paws, Saxton simply felt unclean. For Dante's sake, he tried to convince himself that he would see this task to the end. And yet, the thought of being so close to a very possible, very real, violent death made him squirm.

'Foxes run for their lives. It is our way,' Father had said. Saxton certainly wanted to run now. He did not want his insides all over the forest floor, as Cassius had threatened to do with Buckeye. He did not want terrible pain to be his final memory before all went black.

Saxton's mind raced, and his memories brimmed with faces. He saw mothers and youngsters, mates and lovers, believers and survivors. He saw Two-Step and Boots, Goldie and Diamond Dust; Sputnik and Mars, Bandit and Clyde; the goat and the sheep, Tootsie and Scratch.

Clyde died. Tarlo was dead. Quill was dead. Someday, the rest of them would be gone too. Dante was no exception.

He ran to the site of the fight. There was so much blood, the earth was sopping with it. He looked all around for something that would be a reminder for Buckeye, a reminder that he did not lose and had everything to live for.

He found Cassius' four teeth.

One incisor.

Two molars.

One canine.

All victories Buckeye had won. Saxton gathered the teeth into his mouth. They rattled against his jaws as he went in search of Juniper.

He found her curled into a ball against the foot of a tree. Dante lay by her side with his head draped over her shoulders. The fox stopped before her, but she refused to look at him.

"What do you want?"

Saxton opened his mouth, and the teeth fell, *click-clack-click.*

Juniper stared at the teeth.

"Buckeye fought for these," Saxton whispered. "I thought he should have them."

"Buckeye's gone," she replied roughly, "The humans took him to the infirmary. I don't know how long they'll keep him."

"Then maybe you should hold onto them … until he comes back."

"He's alive, but he might *never* come back."

She pulled the teeth close to her chest with her paw.

"I'm not grateful."

"I know."

"You're a coward."

"I know."

Chapter Thirty-Four
AUTUMN

The leaves were falling. There was a nip in the air. Four weeks had passed. There was a lot of activity, but time had passed too slowly for Saxton, who continued to volley between Jezebel's pack and Juniper's. He watched her as she ordered such horrible things, and the Mongrel did her bidding. He saw more pups die, and more wolves collapse with hunger.

The world is so unkind. It is a cruel and dangerous place.

He wished he had never gotten involved. He wished Quill was still alive, that they had never left Lake Sakakawea. He wished Tarlo had grown up, and Napowsa could be proud. His wished Dante would be happy. He wished Two-Step and Boots would be happy. He wished and wished and wished, but the Silver Crane was just a crow's tale.

And the time had come. There was no turning back.

That night, Juniper led the rebellion gathering for the first time. She sat at the center of the wolves' circle, holding her head high and paying no mind to the fact that her peers were nearly twice her size. The fox, knowing his presence would not be accepted, hid away in the shadows, unnoticed.

"Buckeye fought for all of us," she said. "Now we must fight for him and what he stood for."

She dropped Cassius' teeth on the stone floor. The rattling echoed throughout the cave.

"He took four teeth from the jaws of Cassius. Together, we can take out the Fangs and leave the head of this pack bleeding and feeble. I— I know all of you—" she glanced at Dante and corrected herself, "—

most of you hate the fox for what he has done to our pack. But Buckeye believed in continuing the plan, and it would be dishonorable to ignore his wishes. We are wolves, and wolves always keep their promises."

Dante glanced behind him, and Saxton blinked in surprise when their gazes met. The wolf gave him a small nod, as if in reassurance, before shifting his view back to Juniper.

"Tomorrow night is the Ascension Feast. I will lead you to a new beginning in Buckeye's stead."

One by one, the wolves began to howl in anthem. Dante joined in as well, and his howl was the strongest of all.

Distantly, Saxton wished he could sing with them.

Dante was the last of the wolves to leave the cavern. He waited for Saxton to reveal himself, and the two of them went outside together.

"Saxton, this has gotten more dangerous than I ever thought it would. I can't protect you like this."

Rolling his eyes, Saxton breathed out, exasperated. "I know. It's fine. I don't want you to protect me."

"This isn't about the pledge. It's much simpler than that: I don't want you to die. I don't want you to get hurt."

"You can't protect me forever," Saxton said with a grin, trying for some humor. "Let me do this for you."

The wolf looked at the feather. It hung from the fox's neck, dirty, old, and strangely heavy. Dante knew how far guilt could take a creature, and it could certainly take one further than honor and love alone.

"You don't need to do anything to prove you're my friend … or Quill's. I know who you are, Saxton. You've made things right over and over again. I don't think you even realize it."

"It's not just about making things right. It's choosing goodness for the sake of it, no matter what fate throws at us, even if it's hard." He paused, thinking of Dante's own wisdom. "And you're right. Sometimes doing the right thing can hurt you. Sometimes doing the right thing isn't wise … But I think it's worth it this time around, don't you?"

Dante stood straighter and, after a moment, nodded. "All right. But make me a promise."

"Yes?"

"If things here get worse, if things go too far south, run."

Saxton smiled.

"I'm sorry. That's a promise I will not make."

Chapter Thirty-Five

The day of the feast, Saxton remained close by Jezebel's side. Though Jezebel trusted him, her inner circle was another story entirely, and he did not have to pretend to tremble before the company of wolves like Trigger. He was met with cool welcomes and doubtful looks, but none of the wolves questioned Jezebel's judgment in allowing him to celebrate alongside them.

As the sun set, the lower ranking wolves began dragging the carcasses of moose, deer, and geese to the clearing where Cassius lost teeth, and Buckeye, his leg. Jezebel sat before the high stone like a queen. Her mate sat to her right, silent in the proceedings, while Saxton sat to her left.

The Mongrel growled and snapped at the wolves bringing the food, and ordered them to move faster. Several feet away, Dante trailed behind Juniper and Fable as they hefted a sizable stag. He briefly made eye contact with Saxton before staring at the Mongrel himself. The Mongrel was about to reprimand a white and brown female, Snapdragon, when Dante intervened.

"That's enough!" Dante growled. "Barking and biting at her isn't going to make her move any faster!"

"Keep your nose out of it, Brother," the Mongrel snarled. "We all have jobs to do. I am only doing mine."

Dante stepped closer, and the Mongrel immediately reared, the hairs around his withers bristling. Yet instead of starting a fight, Dante lowered his voice and whispered something into Solomon's ear. As Solomon listened, his hackles lowered.

As soon as Solomon was calm, Dante led him into the thick forest, abandoning the feasting grounds.

"It seems Dante has a way with wild tempers," Jezebel commented offhandedly.

"The Mongrel's more feral than even the wild warrants. I didn't think that was possible."

She chuckled at that. "I've found that bad luck and tragedy do one of two things to the spirit: they either turn you into a coward or into a monster."

Silently, Saxton disagreed. He waited until the feast began before he said anything more.

When the last of the hunt was brought to the center of the clearing, Jezebel stepped forward and stood before the bounty. The offerings of food were an embarrassment of riches.

"My pack," Jezebel began, "today is the fifth year of Cassisus' and my leadership. Every year brings new challenges and harder decisions, and every year we must make sacrifices for our survival. But today, we celebrate. Today, we reward the strong and the fearless. May the feast begin!"

Saxton watched in dismay as the healthiest wolves gorged themselves as though they had not eaten in weeks, while the thinnest wolves watched without complaint.

"Come, come, my *Lonely Thief!*" Jezebel crooned. "If you don't eat, I'll take it as an insult!"

Saxton's stomach clenched at the sight of the moose carcass before him. Its sheer size would have been enough to feed at least five wolves. Instead it had been brought to feed only him.

He tore at the flesh reluctantly, but forced himself to smile with pleasure. He didn't know fresh meat could taste so vile.

They ate and ate and ate until it was painful. Jezebel and her followers laughed in delight, intoxicated from overfull bellies and pride.

"You must tell me some stories," Saxton said at last, relieved at the thought that talking would deny him of eating. "It's a special night, after all. How did you and Cassisus take leadership?"

Jezebel laughed and eagerly told the tale. She bragged about how strong Cassius was against Buckeye— how Buckeye had no chance from the start and was unfit to be leader. Yesterday had proven her right. "The ferocious are rewarded in life," she preached, "and there is no room for compassion. One must harden their heart to lead and control. Feed everyone equally, and no one will be strong. Let the weak and lowly lie in the beds they have made for themselves, so that the powerful may prosper."

Saxton knew it all already, but he patiently bided his time until he saw a shadow of movement not too far from where he was sitting. He sniffed the air and found Dante's scent. It was accompanied by another smell that was sour like vinegar and salty like brine. Dante had done his part; it was nearly time for him to do his. He continued to ask questions in all the right places and offer praise at others, and when he felt the timing was right, Saxton asked, "The Mongrel, he's so violent, how do you manage to control him?"

"He was damaged from the start, fox," Jezebel began. "He's insecure of himself— resentful and full of hate. Destroy his hope, and you can control him with just an ounce of kindness. The Mongrel is hopelessly loyal to me, and viciously so, for these very reasons."

"What did you do?"

She smiled and showed the tip of her canine. "I sent Trigger to take his face. I sent Pistol to take his skin. I sent Whiplash to take his dignity. He was already born a half-wolf, but now he's a half-wolf that's as naked and ugly as a human baby. Who would talk to him? No one, of course. No one, but me." She lowered her head and leveled her eyes with Saxton's. Her voice came out in a venomous hiss. "While misfits are born, monsters are made. *I* am the master of my monster."

What happened next occurred in a blur. A ghostly howl filled the wind. It was followed by growling and the sound of feet tearing across the grass. Saxton didn't see it happen, but Jezebel had been knocked onto her back. Solomon stood atop her, holding her throat down with his paws.

"I've *killed* for you!" Solomon roared. "The old, the infirm … the prime and the young! I killed them all, and you *destroyed* me! If I am a monster, what are you?"

The lower-ranking wolves descended upon Jezebel's inner circle like a swarm of hornets freed from its nest. Arrow and Fable blocked Cassius' path to Jezebel, and wolves on both sides came together like two violent tides. Juniper jumped upon Jezebel's great stone.

"Tonight!" she yelled. "Tonight it all ends!"

Solomon pressed more weight against Jezebel's neck, slowly choking her. She struggled for air and kicked against the ground. Trigger leapt at Solomon and pulled him back with his teeth.

236

Saxton slinked away from the chaos, careful to avoid any of the wolves. Once a safe distance away, he snapped a branch off a tree limb.

"What are you doing?"

"If we are to get out of here, tonight is the night to do it. Go help your friends. I'll be back."

The wolf nodded and returned to the melee, knocking Sniper on his side before he could maul Chief from behind. With the branch between his teeth, Saxton sprinted for the reserve headquarters. There, he searched for the electrical cable he had tried to gnaw through. He found it, and carefully held the branch against the exposed wires. He lurched back as the branch sparked before bursting into flames. He ran along the fence, bringing the flames to the large wooden poles holding the electrical cables up. One by one, the poles lit up with a roar.

Saxton turned to return to the fight, when another roar, one he had heard before and feared he would again, reverberated around him.

Napowsa stood at the other side of the fence, her face surrounded by flames. She tore through the cables and ran through the fire like an angry bull that had been penned. Flames patched her fur. They blew out as she barreled full speed after him.

He dropped the burning branch and broke into a run. He didn't look back as death and fire chased after him.

"You thought you could get away from me, fox?" Napowsa yelled. "You thought you could get away?"

Saxton lead Napowsa through the thicket and toward the rebellion. Napowsa destroyed everything in her path: overhanging branches, fallen trunks, and even full trees. He ran and ran and stopped in front of Cassius. The black wolf snarled at the sight of him.

"Traitor!" he barked.

Napowsa swung her arm. Saxton jumped out of the way. The bear's mighty paw with its nail-sized claws knocked Cassius off his feet and threw him onto a sharp stone.

His head split open and he stopped moving.

Saxton darted about the battleground, weaving Napowsa around the wolves and the fire, tricking her into immobilizing or killing Jezebel's followers with every dodge. He looked quickly around him, searching for those who needed help. Fire was rapidly spreading everywhere. The air smelt of ember, bright and bitter. Dante and Solomon squared off with Trigger, while Juniper and Jezebel stood on their hind legs, pummeling each other on the chest with their claws.

Three feet away, Whiplash knocked Snapdragon unconscious and turned his attention to Juniper.

"Juniper!"

Saxton sprinted as fast as he could and leapt onto Whiplash's back. Whiplash bucked and spun and rolled over, but Saxton kept his jaws firmly clenched around the wolf's pelt.

"Get off me!" Whiplash growled. "Get off me, *Lonely Thief!*"

Whiplash rolled over again. Saxton exhaled and held his breath as the wolf's weight barreled over him. He tightened his grip and hoped he could keep Whiplash in one place long enough for—

They went flying.

Whiplash hit a tree – shaking the leaves out – and slid down to the ground with a whimper. Saxton tumbled across the fallen leaves. The world was flipped over and over again until he came to a stop.

Dizzy, he tried to stand, but something sharp caught him by the foot and lifted him into the air again.

His right foot was ankle deep in Napowsa's jaws. Her teeth sank into his flesh, tearing it open and hitting bone.

Saxton screamed.

He hung upside-down, swinging and pulling in a vain effort to free his foot. Napowsa shook her head violently from side to side. Something cracked and Saxton yowled.

Painful stars filled his vision. Saxton couldn't see a thing, everything was too blurry—too gray, but he heard Dante's howl.

"Let him go, you *Terrible Beast!*"

He felt more than saw the weight of a wolf jumping upon Napowsa's back. The bear bellowed, twisting around to get Dante off her shoulders. She released Saxton, and he hit the soil once more.

The fox laid there, dazed. He looked down on his hind leg.

His foot was missing.

Dante fought Napowsa with all his strength, pulling at her fur and drawing thin lines of blood with every desperate scrape of his paws.

But he couldn't take her down, not alone.

Juniper abandoned Jezebel, leaving her free to run off. She raced for Dante, slid beneath the bear's vulnerable belly, and bit there as hard she could. Napowsa cried out and the forest shook. She threw Dante off her, and Juniper let go. Napowsa clutched her bleeding stomach with one arm, limping away and disappearing into woods.

Dante was shaken, but uninjured. Juniper licked his nose to snap him out of his stupor. His eyes widened, and he ran to Saxton's side.

"Saxton!"

The fox was frantically licking at the stump of his leg, slowing the flow of blood. "I'm fine! I'm fine!" he snarled through gritted teeth. "Get Jezebel before she escapes!"

Dante glanced behind him. Juniper nodded, waiting for him, while Solomon and the rest of the rebellion were already running after their fallen leader. He looked back at Saxton, who, in all his pain, did his best to smile ruefully.

"Don't worry about me," he said, ignoring the throbbing agony crawling up his spine and the urge to be sick all over himself. "Let's finish what we started. I'll be behind."

Dante hesitated for a moment, but took Saxton's word for it. He followed the others, twisting around burning trees, jumping over large boulders, and splashing through the creek. When he found a ring of wolves pressing against the foot of a mountain, he squeezed through.

Jezebel was cornered against mountain rock, her normally pristine white fur sullied by mud. Her eyes darted about, desperate, hysterical and paranoid.

The Mongrel, as always, was the closest to her.

"I will never kill again," he said. "But tonight I will kill for the last time."

"Solomon," Dante implored. "Don't do it."

"Why?"

"Because you're a better wolf than she is. You're more of a wolf than she is."

Saxton limped forward on his three legs, standing next to Juniper who was covered in soot and blood.

"And you have a new leader now: a kinder, fairer one." The fox nodded to the female wolf beside him. "What do you think, Juniper?"

She flinched, and though it was hard, she forced herself to say it: "Show her mercy."

Solomon turned back to Jezebel, his face twisted and raw. "What's your choice, Jezebel? Do you yield? To *her?*"

Jezebel took one look at Juniper and spat.

"I will *never* serve one so weak and small."

She kicked dirt in the air, momentarily blinding the wolves closest to her, and escaped.

Solomon went after her. Despite his shorter legs, he had more strength and tenaciousness than any full-blooded wolf could hope for. He grabbed Jezebel by her flanks and dragged her down. She collapsed face-first on the dirt, and before she could get away again, Solomon grabbed her by the scruff – as though she were nothing more than a wayward pup – and pulled her to a blazing tree.

"Sol!" Saxton cried out. He knew what the half-wolf intended to do.

Solomon didn't listen. Instead he reached above him to break off a branch and set the leaves around them ablaze.

For the first time, Jezebel's eyes filled with true emotion: abject horror. "What are you doing? You'll kill us both!"

As the circle of fire crept closer and closer, and the pocket of land they sat upon grew smaller and smaller, Solomon said, in a calm voice:

"That's the idea, Jezebel."

When the flames engulfed them, the pack heard Jezebel's pitiful howls and screams. Then they disappeared, and all was silent save for the crackling of burning leaves, and the roar of fire in the cold night wind.

Chapter Thirty-Six

Sirens blared in the distance. Bright lights flashed in red. The humans were coming, and it was time to run.

Four loud trucks came to the scene, and men wearing strange jackets and hats ran out of the vehicles carrying long, snake-like objects that spat water instead of venom into the fires.

Several cars pulled into the headquarters' parking lot. Gwen and the other humans who worked at the reserve hurriedly set about tracking the wolves and corralling them into a safe zone while the fires were dealt with. Saxton, Dante, and Juniper fled and observed the humans handling the mess they had left for them from a distance. They watched as Gwen cried over Sol's charred, unrecognizable body. She knew it was him all the same.

They rested for a time, Saxton tending to his damaged leg. He licked it often enough that the bleeding slowed and then stopped altogether. He left a trail of red dots on the ground if he moved too suddenly or put too much weight on his leg. He took care in walking slowly.

Once the fires were in some state of control, Saxton and Dante walked over the destroyed electrical fence. Juniper followed them, saying, "I'll help you get back on track. It's the least I can do."

She led them to the nearest road leading north, telling them that if they followed it all the way up, it should eventually reach the highway Saxton needed to get to New Hampshire.

Juniper and Dante exchanged meaningful looks the whole way. Saxton tried to be discreet observing them, but he could tell quite easily how sad they were. When they at last reached the road, Saxton repeated, "I said before, you could come with us. I meant it."

Smiling, she shook her head. "I have a pack to lead," she said. Then, gesturing the device around her neck, she added, "Besides, this tracker will get the humans on us soon. If you don't want them to find you, I can lead them away."

"What about mine?" Dante asked.

"I can gnaw it off," Saxton said. He looked at the street as a car drove past. "And I can break it."

Lowering his neck, Dante allowed Saxton to saw the collar off with his teeth. When it fell to the ground, he picked it up and threw it across the road, where it was immediately crushed to pieces by a large truck.

Juniper laughed. "I don't know where you get your ideas, but they're always crazy enough to work."

Saxton grimaced. "One of my crazy ideas almost lit your whole home on fire."

"Almost," Juniper agreed. She studied the way he limped, and her face softened. "I'm sorry you lost your foot to the bear, but I'm glad she didn't take anything else. Thank you, by the way, for fighting for us when you had nothing at stake."

Saxton adjusted his balance, holding his bad leg off the ground. He peered at Dante. "Ah, but I did."

Juniper nipped him gently in the ear. The fox hoped it was a sign that she had begun to forgive him for putting Buckeye in danger.

She turned to Dante and rubbed her cheek along his.

"You're always welcome to come back." She stepped back. "I hope you do, at least to visit."

Dante licked her on the nose, and she licked him back. She gave him one last fond look before turning to leave.

They didn't say goodbye.

The fox and wolf continued to walk for several hours before Saxton succumbed to pain and the exhaustion of limping on three feet. Dante looked worriedly at him.

"Saxton—"

"I'm fine," he lied.

"You lost a foot. You are *not* fine. You are the opposite of 'fine.' Do you need me to carry you?"

Saxton gave him a nasty scowl. "No, I can walk. I just need rest." He screwed his eyes shut and sighed. "I'm sorry. I didn't mean to snap at you. I'm just—"

He wasn't the same anymore. He looked strange, felt strange, and wished the pain would stop. But there was nothing he could do except keep surviving, and that would prove to be more difficult in this state. He suddenly hated Napowsa, but he kept that hatred at bay by reminding himself that he deserved this.

Dante sat on the grass, a silent invitation for Saxton to do the same. He waited for Saxton to regroup before saying, "You think the pain will never go away, but it will, eventually. What's gonna take longer is … accepting that this is going to be the new normal."

He gazed at the scabbing leg, and swallowed thickly. Saxton looked up at him, and must have seen the mixture of emotions he felt, coming one after another in rapid succession.

The last thing he felt was grief.

"Don't say it," Saxton said almost angry again. "I won't forgive you if you say it."

"You hardly knew her." He didn't recognize his own voice. It came out in a rasp.

"I knew you cared about her. What else did I need to know? And before you go into it, you did not fail to protect me, understand?"

Dante gave a curt nod, not quite believing it, but not wanting to tire Saxton any further. Yet the fox spoke again, calmer this time.

"I came out with my life," he said. "It's a minor loss, and a small punishment."

The wolf shook his head. "She was going to kill you."

"And you stopped her. You see? You did not fail to protect me."

"Actually, *Juniper* stopped her." He smiled in spite himself. "And you're ever the optimist."

"I'm trying to be," Saxton replied. "Now I'd rather sleep, if you don't mind. There's a lot of walking to be done, and the air's getting cold."

"All right, wake me if you need me."

They lowered their heads onto the soft grass. Saxton thought about what Dante had said. If anyone knew what it was like to feel so vulnerable and robbed, it was him; and if Dante could move past something like this, then surely he could as well.

Saxton curled into a ball and fell asleep, keeping this thought close to his heart. In the back of his mind, he prayed that the ants would be kind enough to leave his injury well alone.

Chapter Thirty-Seven

Their walk east was slow going, Saxton needing to stop every so often to rest his legs. As the days went by, the ache that bothered him incessantly faded little by little, and he managed to walk at a pace that was as close to normal as he could hope for.

They soon came upon a fork in the dirt path. One way continued north, and the other pointed east with a sign for the ninety highway. They stood in the middle of the fork for a long time. Strangely, despite all the hunger, fear, and blood they had seen, neither of them felt compelled to take their journey to its conclusion. At length, when the silence stretched far too long and neither of them deigned to look at the other, Saxton spoke.

"You should go back to your family, Dante."

"I knew you eavesdropped."

Saxton cringed guiltily. "Yes, well … I am still a fox, after all." He looked Dante firmly in the eye. "You will regret not seeing them again. You know I was separated from my family when I just a kit. If I had not found them, I would have wondered for the rest of my life what had become of them."

"You didn't stay." It wasn't a question.

"No, but that was my choice, and an informed one at that."

Dante glanced at Saxton's three legs. With the way he stood, head high and proud, it would be difficult at first to notice the fox was permanently lame.

"What about Napowsa?"

"She's my problem, not yours." Dante gave him a withering look. "I won't die. That, I promise."

"You're barely in one piece."

"I know. Two-Step is going to have a fit about that." He tried to be funny, but Dante wasn't laughing. He didn't think he would. "Your future shouldn't be shackled to mine."

"But we're still a few states away from Exeter and you're still healing, Napowsa will—"

"Your *future*," Saxton repeated, "shouldn't be shackled to *mine*."

The wolf stood, unmoving. "You've forgiven me."

"A long time ago," he replied. "I honestly don't know when."

Dante moved close and bumped shoulders with him. Saxton sat on his haunches and laid his chin across Dante's shoulder, taking him into a warm embrace.

"You're my friend," he said, thinking of Quill. "You're my family. You're my brother. But there are some things we must do on our own ..."

"Where will you go," Dante asked as they pulled apart, "when you've finished what you've set out to do?"

Saxton looked away. "I don't know. Find a place to rest my head, I suppose."

Another pregnant silence fell between them. It was as if the lack of any speech would keep the farewells at bay.

"Saxton."

He said nothing else. There was too much to say, and yet not enough.

The fox grinned at the wolf. Sometimes silence was better. He took the path east without looking back, for fear he would never take another step forward.

PART III

Chapter Thirty-Eight
WINTER

Saxton crossed New York and Massachusetts in eight weeks. It was cold, but it was not yet snowing. A bit of frost would dust the windows of houses and cars, yet it never stayed for long. The sight of it made him nervous. He had walked as fast as he could, and ran when he could manage it. His limp had slowed him down, but the awkwardness of running on three feet gradually disappeared. Soon he grew accustomed to relying on his front legs for balance and speed. Humans had to look twice before noticing the missing foot.

In Boston, he asked a murder of crows sitting on a power line which direction to take to Exeter. One of them kindly directed him, asking why he was in such a hurry. When Saxton replied, one of the other crows cawed.

"Don't waste your time dawdling around here!" she said urgently. "The trees in Fiddle's territory will be cut down next spring!"

"*What?*" Saxton balked.

"It's true! The humans are going to build more houses."

"What do I do? If I'm going to find Fiddle, this is my only chance! At this rate, I'll never make it!"

"Use the commuter rail," another crow advised. "One of the rails goes as far north as Newburyport, and that's not too far from Exeter. You can hop off there and follow the ninety-five freeway north. When ninety-five meets one-oh-one, take one-oh-one east."

"Thank you! Thank you!" Saxton said in a rush. "Which rail do I take?"

The crows looked at one another, shrugging their shoulders.

"Ask a stray in the city," a different crow replied. "They'd know better."

There was a stray dog, a Jack Russell terrier, who knew his streets almost as well as Tootsie knew hers. He was a dirty, skinny dog, but friendly all the same.

"You need to get on the Newburyport/Rockport line, but you're gonna have to take another line before you get to that one," he said. "Downtown Crossing is the closest stop to us, so that's the platform you should board on. Take the Orange Line from there and ride it to North Station. Get off at North Station, then take the Newburyport/Rockport line to Newburyport. Ride it up, all the way to the end. Don't get off before then."

As Saxton listened, his head spun.

"How am I supposed to remember all that?"

"You really wanna get to Exeter?"

"Yes."

"Then you'll remember 'all that.' Don't worry, it's not as bad as it sounds," the dog smirked. "When you get on the train, hide under the chairs where no one can see ya, and keep an ear out for all your stops."

"And how do I find the ninety-five freeway from Newburyport?"

"Just head east. You'll run into it pretty quick."

Saxton followed his advice, doing his best to go unnoticed, but every so often he'd hear a human whisper 'fox' to one of their companions. A second later there would be a click and a brilliant flash of light. He didn't know what they had done. It left him blinking and slightly confused, but it didn't hurt him. Whatever device they had pointed at him, it was certainly better than a gun.

He knew his welcome on the commuter rails would eventually expire, but he was grateful he made it to Newburyport before he caught sight of the train conductor with a pole and snare. He immediately fled the premises before getting captured.

After much running, he found the ninety-five north and followed it until he was finally on one-oh-one east. He felt a quiver of excitement and a hint of dread settle into his bones. He followed the highway, and in a week and a half he was in Exeter, New Hampshire.

Exeter was a lovely town that reminded Saxton of Lattice, although it was bigger, more populated, and had, in his opinion, more aggressive drivers.

He discovered a tavern called 'The Loaf and Ladle,' and helped himself to bread and chicken soup that had been discarded in the back. He then crossed a wooden bridge near town, and climbed down the embankment for fresh water from what was called the 'Squamscott River.' With his stomach full and his thirst quenched, he knew it was time to see Quill's sister.

But for whatever reason the initial excitement he felt upon arriving drained away.

After three days of meandering about the town, with the clouds above threatening to snow at any moment, Saxton realized he was procrastinating. 'What if Fiddle won't listen to me?' he thought in a panic. 'What if Fiddle doesn't *trust* me? What if she turns me away?' Even the threat of this being his one and only chance of seeing her didn't quell his fears.

He wished Dante were there to bolster his courage, but Dante *wasn't* there. He had to do this on his own, and even after everything he had been though, he was terribly frightened.

Grabbing the nerve before it got away from him, Saxton glanced around for the nearest crow or raven and walked straight up to him before he could change his mind.

"Excuse, Mr. Crow—"

"Raven," the large black bird corrected.

"Mr. Raven," Saxton amended. "Do you know of a Miss Fiddle? Quill's her brother … well, late brother."

The raven eyed the feather hanging around his neck.

"I take it you knew Quill personally?"

"Yes."

He snorted, but it seemed to be in good humor. "Ah, of course you did. Quill had a way of making the strangest friends."

"So you know her?"

"Of course, I know her. Corvids have amazing memory, and a crow like Quill is hardly one to forget."

Saxton smiled at that. "That's true."

"She's in a tree on the corner of Green and Cass. Do you know what numbers look like?"

"Yes, in fact, I do. A rat taught me."

The raven chuckled. "Well, that certainly sounds like the kind of escapade Quill would fall into. Go north on or along eighty-five" – he scratched the numbers on the ground – "then head west. You can't miss it. Just give a little call, and Fiddle will come right down. You better hurry, though. It's going to snow soon and the crows will be off."

"Thank you," Saxton said, bowing slightly.

"No trouble at all. Please give Fiddle my regards. I'm sure she'll take the tragic news better when you tell her what Quill's been up to all these years."

Saxton followed the Raven's directions. It was getting nippier and nippier by the moment, and without warning, a tiny white flake descended from above and landed lightly on Saxton's nose.

"Oh, no!"

He sprinted down Green Street until his front paws throbbed. When at last he came to the corner and found Fiddle's elm tree, a billow of black birds took to the air, cawing as they went.

"Stop!" He shouted at the top of his lungs. "Stop! Wait! I need to speak with Fiddle! *Fiddle!*"

The elm's trunk was slanted to one side, and was at such an angle that Saxton could actually climb it. He jumped upon the trunk and climbed up, careful to duck his head beneath the overhanging branches which were sharp and barren of leaves.

He poked his head out from the top of the tree. The murder of crows had become nothing more than specks in the distance.

Saxton lowered his eyes, then his head, and silently began to cry.

He chided himself for being a coward yet again. He could have spoken to her days ago if he hadn't overthought all the things that could have gone wrong. Now the worst possible thing that could happen had come to pass. Fiddle was gone. He would never see her, and Quill would never be home.

"Are you all right?" a sweet voice asked, "You seem lost."

Saxton sniffed, but frowned at the words he had heard. Suddenly, he was a kit lying helpless along the sandy embankment of a lake in Montana. He had lost his family. His right hind leg was sprained and useless to him. He didn't know what to do, but a crow came to him, speaking to him in the same kind tone and asking the very same thing.

"Fiddle?" Saxton tentatively asked.

There was a long pause, which made his heart sink. But the owner of the voice spoke again. "How do you know my name?"

He looked up and saw a crow, who looked very much like Quill, peering over the edge of her nest. She studied him a little warily.

"Who are you?"

252

"I—" He frowned as his tongue went into knots. "I'm Saxton. Quill's my friend."

She cocked her head to the side. He noticed the way her eyes immediately traveled to the feather he had. "I take it you don't have good news."

"No," Saxton answered quietly, "but I do have a lot of good things to say ... about your brother."

Fiddle nodded, her face carefully blank. "Come on up, then. My mate won't be back for a while. Quickly, though. In a few hours our murder will be flying off."

He scaled the rest of the way up and was surprised to see how large a crow's nest was. It was easily two feet across.

"I thought all of you would be gone," Saxton said, relief seeping into his voice. "I saw so many of you leave already ..."

"No, we stagger our departure so no one gets left behind. Quill would have wanted it that way. It's a practice we've put into place ever since he left," Fiddle swallowed. "I haven't seen my brother in years. You can imagine him not ever visiting has left me a little bitter, but I don't blame him for what happened. I don't blame him for leaving."

"What happened?"

"Stories like these are earned, Saxton. I won't just give them away to anyone. Besides, I think you have your own story to tell."

It was an invitation to begin talking, and Saxton gratefully took it. He told Fiddle how he was separated from his family and how her brother had helped him to survive. He told her that he had a chance to live with his parents and siblings again, but chose to stay with Quill instead. Then, choking around the words, he told her how Quill died and how he had wanted to return home. Now he was here, carrying what was left of his friend around his neck.

Fiddle's eyes brimmed with tears, but she didn't let a single one go. "It's just like him," she said, "to help someone when they needed it most ... You know, he left Exeter because his generosity wounded him."

"I've heard. I don't know what happened, but I heard."

She shook her head; then brushed her wings with her beak as if needing something to do as she spoke. "Years ago, there was a terrible storm. My skies, it was ugly! Branches were ripped from their trees and houses everywhere lost their windows and roof tiles. Members of our murder quickly spread the word to evacuate our homes before dusk. Quill being Quill, of course, took it a step further. He didn't just tell the other crows, he told every living creature in the vicinity that he could find.

"By the time he returned to his roost to gather his family, his tree had been struck down by lightning. His chicks, all three of them, two boys and a girl, were crushed. The tree pinched his mate's wing against the mud and she drowned. Once the storm passed, he spent days trying to retrieve their bodies. We convinced him it was no use – that he was only hurting himself – and he became a shell of a bird. He wouldn't eat. He wouldn't speak. Then, one day, he was gone. Some of the crows thought he had died quietly. But those close to him, we knew his heart was too big to give out, but also too big to have the strength to stay here."

"I'm sorry." It was such a poor thing to say; nonetheless it came out of Saxton's mouth because he meant it all the same.

"It was who he was," she looked at Saxton fully this time, memorizing every detail of his face. "And by the sound of it, that naiveté didn't change despite what happened to him. This time, it looks like his generosity was rewarded." Fiddle's voice warmed, and as it did, Saxton could hear more and more of Quill in her. It was a comforting thing. "I've often thought of him and how sad it would be if he lived out his life alone. Life's already hard, but going through it without someone by your side, I can't imagine it. Thank you for being there for him."

The fox shook his head. "You don't need to thank me. Really, I should thank you for letting me tell the end of his story— and for you sharing with me the beginning. This journey … it was for the both of us."

She looked at him, still tenderly, but with a touch of concern.

"A little bit of selfishness is a good thing, Saxton. Now that you've ended my brother's tale, it's time for you to embark on your own, with no strings attached."

Saxton glanced at Quill's feather. It had been through so much, and he felt a sudden pang of grief at the thought of parting with it. But remembering this was the home Quill had wanted to return to, that this was the home in which Quill wanted to rest, Saxton knew that he couldn't carry this feather – both a remembrance and a burden – with him any longer.

He gently lifted the string holding the feather over his head and nudged it toward Fiddle with his nose.

She picked the feather up with her beak, and carefully laced it into the weavings of her nest.

"Welcome home, Quill. It's good to see you again."

Chapter Thirty-Nine

Dante traveled for two and a half months before he reached Canada. When he found his family's scent, he followed it until the bouquet grew stronger and warmer. He had forgotten what home smelled like. It was a mixture of mint and pine, wood and river water, snow and leaves. He paused in mid-step when he finally saw them mere yards away, lying on the ground with their heads up watchfully surveying the area. He wondered if they were always waiting for him like this. The thought was comforting and disquieting at the same time.

He saw the moment his father's nose and ears twitched in his direction. Father jumped to his feet. His mouth spread into a large, welcoming grin while his tail wagged in unabashed excitement.

"Dante!" his father shouted. "Dante, you're home!"

His father ran toward him, kicking up snow in his wake. Mother, Grandmother, and his siblings were not far behind, and before he could say 'hello' in return, he was accosted by rambunctious hugs, nudges, and licks from his family.

"Look at you," his father said, circling him and eying him up and down with pride. "Just ... look at you!"

Dante didn't know what he saw, for he felt no different, but before he could ask, Father went on.

"I've never seen you stand so straight. You look so confident! And what's this? Battle scars?"

"I ran into another pack. I'm fine, really."

Mother rubbed her shoulder against his and sniffed.

"A female?" she asked with excitement. "Where is she? Did you bring her home?"

Dante felt his face heat. "No, she ... had other things to worry about. I guess the timing wasn't right. I hope to see her again, though."

Mother was about to ask more questions when Rush stepped forward. He looked as foul-tempered and cocky as Dante remembered, but this time he seemed ... shorter. It was then Dante realized that Rush only loomed over him when his back was hunched.

"You look about the same to me."

Their father shot Rush a warning look, and Rush said nothing more. Timber, however, chimed in.

"No, you're quite different," like Father she said this with quiet pride. "You've changed, but you're still the same ... in some ways."

"This is so silly," Mother said. "We should be celebrating. Let's begin a hunt!"

At that, Rush grimaced. "You sure we won't be held back again?"

Father was about to bark, but Dante stepped forward and looked down his nose at his brother.

"It's all right, Rush," Dante said calmly. "I won't trip over my feet this time."

Indeed, he never tripped over his feet. Not once.

They had followed a herd of deer into the plains and Mother encouraged Dante to pick whichever stag or doe he desired. Feeling he had something to prove, he had wanted to go after the biggest buck of the herd, but after more consideration, decided against it. Instead he chose a modest stag that seemed to have lost too much fat and was all the weaker for it. Rush and Oakley, his other brother, rolled their eyes, claiming they both would have taken down something larger and more grand. Dante ignored them.

The three brothers flushed the stag out and separated him from his herd. Father caught the stag by the hindquarter, while Mother and Timber attacked from the sides. The stag put up a great fight, and managed to throw the wolves off his massive body.

Badly wounded, the stag bounded away, only to be brought up short by Dante, who leapt at his throat and tore. The stag collapsed, and Dante held his capture down with his weight. His family gathered around him, impressed and bewildered and shocked all at once.

He noticed, with pleasure, that neither of his brothers said another word.

By the seventh day with his family, Dante found he was growing restless and dissatisfied. He didn't let what troubled him affect his mood, and so he did his best at reconnecting with his family and falling into the motions of being a pack member with a cheerful grin.

It was no surprise Rush noticed he was out of sorts. When the pack returned from a hunt and was ready for a mid-day nap, Rush cornered Dante and moved him away from unwanted ears.

"You don't belong here."

Surprised by those words, Dante ignored the hurt he felt and immediately went into outrage. "What are you talking about? This is my family too! I have every right to be here!"

"Yeah, of course," Rush said, impervious to his outburst. "I mean you don't belong here because you shouldn't be here."

"What is that supposed to mean?"

"It *means*," he growled bitterly, "that you're not a Tail anymore. I am."

Still confused, Dante said, "I won't treat you poorly if that's what you're worried about—"

"Oh, shut up, will you? I'm trying to talk, so let me talk. This pack? It's too small for you. So leave."

"That's not true."

"It *is* true. When you left, I had a chance of taking on Timber when Mother and Father are gone. Maybe I would've lost. Maybe I would've just moved up to being an Eye or a Fang. But now that you're here, you've shoved me down the pecking order! Now I don't have a chance at all!"

"Rush … that's not my fault" Dante said patiently.

"Just let me finish!" he huffed. "If you stay, you're not gonna lead the pack; Timber will, and she will 'cause you'll let her. Then you'll never be mates with that— that female you met 'cause you're stuck here. And you're just gonna … be okay with it, like you always are."

"Why are you telling me this? Why do you care?"

"I don't! I want to move up, but I can't do that with you in my way!" he said a little too vehemently. Then he stomped off, fuming so hotly there may as well have been steam coming from his ears. Dante watched him go, thinking over what he had said.

Later that evening, Dante barely touched his food. Rush ragged on him as usual, though this time he was surprised to find he appreciated it.

He loved his family, but he realized he wanted something of his own. More than once he tried saying something about it, but each time he changed his mind.

Oakley filched his untouched food, and Mother scolded him, but Dante said he could have it. Timber lectured him on standing up for himself, and Dante replied he could, but simply wasn't hungry. That, of course, caught Mother's and Grandmother's attention, and he spent most of the meal convincing them that he was not feeling ill.

His father studied him, not with concern, but with a look of tranquil knowing. "What's on your mind, Dante?"

And then there was no escape.

"Nothing. Well, nothing that's wrong."

"But?"

Dante braced himself and sighed.

"I feel … like it's time for me to move on." He looked at all of them, then added quickly, "It's not that I don't love all of you, but …" He struggled to find the right words, and then thought of Saxton. "But the world is so big, and I want to see more."

His family fell silent, and everyone but Rush, who rolled his eyes, stared at Father, waiting with bated breath for his response.

Father spoke slowly, measuring his words.

"When you left, we were worried about you. We wondered if you were hurt or hungry, if you were lost, or worse, dead." Dante looked away, embarrassed and guilty, but Father never stopped looking at him in the eye. "We spent days looking for you, and those days turned into weeks, then months, and eventually four full seasons. We never gave up. I didn't care how far we had to walk. I didn't care about leaving the home we had made. Your Mother and I would move mountains if it meant having you with us again. It's the burden and the joy of being a parent, you see. But now you're here, and it's clear we've worried over nothing."

Dante felt blood rush to his cheeks. "I'm sorry I put you, all of you, through that."

"Actually, it's a point of pride that we *didn't* have to worry." Father looked heavenward and closed his eyes. "We didn't want to fail you as your mother and your father, Dante. We thought we had. We had nightmares, nightmares of men trying to shoot you dead or bears trying to tear you to pieces. We swore that if you were gone, we'd hunt down whoever had taken you away from us. Some days, all this nearly … very nearly tore us apart."

"I— I can stay," Dante said. "If that's what you want."

"No," Father replied firmly. "That is not what we want. What we want is to see you grown, self-sufficient, and happy. It's what every good parent wants of their young, and if leaving the pack means those things, then we should not hold you back."

"But I'm happy here too." Rush groaned at that, and he pointedly ignored him.

The corner of his mother's mouth curled into a small smile. Her eyes were just shy of being watery, but she said gently: "Then perhaps, you need something that's yours?"

His good eye stinging in return, Dante rasped, "Yeah. Something that's mine."

Timber snorted. "Really? We must draw this out like we always do over dinner? Enough of that. Whatever it is you want, go get it. You can always come back, after all."

They finished their evening meal together, and Dante set about saying how he would miss everyone, but was glad to have seen them again. Rush threatened him to leave now or he'd bite his tail, and in return Dante nipped his ear playfully.

In the end, he stayed one last night, but as dawn approached, Dante was seized with the very real fear that if he didn't leave now, he would never leave. And so, he quietly departed his family's territory while the sun's light was still soft. The scent of his family faded with every step forward, and when he reached the point where the scent would vanish, he froze with uncertainty.

He could hear footsteps coming up behind him, and the scent he detected told him right away that it was Father. Father stood next to him, surveying the great expanse of land before them. Canada was most beautiful at sunrise.

"Don't feel that you are abandoning us, Dante."

"Then what am I doing?"

"Making your own way." He glanced at his father, who smiled and looked so much older than he should be. "Go. The world waits for no one."

Chapter Forty

Saxton stayed with Fiddle until it was time for her and the remainder of her murder to depart. "Where will you go," he asked, "if this tree will no longer be here when you return?"

"Somewhere new," she said, "somewhere different. It's fitting, really, that this nest and Quill will be buried come spring."

When he inquired about the nearest train yard, Fiddle happily gave him directions and told him he would always be welcome in Exeter, though she would not return until next spring. Saxton politely thanked her for such kind remarks, but Fiddle meant every word.

She introduced him to the other crows as they gathered atop the elm, and they all vowed to pass down the story of the fox that was raised by a crow and befriended by a wolf, for generations to come. It was, after all, a fairly unbelievable story, and the young tend to love the unbelievable, as it so often holds more truth than the ordinary.

As he set foot at the bottom of the tree, he turned to watch the murder swarm into the sky. The snow came down more heavily then, and he touched the trunk of the elm to silently say 'Farewell.'

Chapter Forty-One

He knew she would find him.

It was only a matter of time, really, so when he caught her scent in the wind, he didn't bother to run.

He had been walking through the woods, his feet sinking into the snow that had quickly blanketed the grass and the dirt for miles beyond what the eye could see. A great shadow fell over him, dulling the brightness of the white

"Napowsa."

Saxton said her name not with fear, but with greeting. He looked over his shoulder to look at her, and saw not a *Terrible Beast*, but a mother still in mourning. He blamed himself still, but found that with time, he blamed himself a little less.

"You're not running," she sneered. "Why aren't you running? Aren't you afraid?"

'Dante fought for my life,' he thought. 'It's time I do the same.' To her he said, "No, only ... very sorry for your loss."

She raised her arm over her head and swiped at him. He jumped out of the way, and she saw her paw shovel nothing but snow into the air.

"How dare you mock me!" Napowsa roared. "You have no idea— no idea what I've been through!"

She swung at him again and missed, this time hitting a tree. The tree creaked loudly and tilted to one side, icicles breaking off and hitting the ground like spears.

Saxton eyed the damaged she had done, and thought quickly.

"I'll never understand," he agreed. "Not ever. I don't have young, but one day I will, and maybe then I'll know a little of how much you suffer ..."

He leapt to and fro, left and right, forcing Napowsa to chase him in circles and hit the same tree over and over again until the middle of trunk began to crack.

"You will never have young!" she cried.

"Please," he pleaded. "Please forgive me. I meant no harm. I wanted to help—"

"I would've found him!" Napowsa sniffed, tears running down the corners of her eyes. "If you had stayed out of it, I would've found him, and Tarlo would be here! He'd be here with *me!*"

Her painful words brought him up short, and he froze.

'Let it go, Saxton,' he heard Dante say in his thoughts, 'You're worth protecting, so stay alive, you crazy fox.'

But he dodged too late, and was thrown across the field, leaving a perfectly straight trail in the snow. Dazed, he shook his head and found Napowsa charging at him with snapping jaws.

Saxton got to his feet, forgetting for a moment he had already lost one to her. He scampered for the tree he had tricked her into hitting repeatedly, and jumped as high as he could. He latched onto the bark and climbed through the juncture between the branches and trunk.

"What can I do?" he shouted down at her, "What can I do to make things right?"

He already knew her answer, but hoped she would prove him wrong. Instead, she rammed the side of her body against the tree, shaking it and the ground all around. The tree trunk split in two, and the upper half with all its branches tilted forward. It hovered over Napowsa and threatened to fall.

"Come down here and let me destroy you like you've destroyed me!"

Saxton clutched onto the branches for dear life. "But I ... I don't want to die. I want to *live.*"

"Then there's nothing you can do for me. Nothing!"

She rammed the trunk again, and just as her body made contact, Saxton jumped to the ground. Half the tree came crashing down, pinning Napwosa to the snow by her neck. She let out a mighty roar, but could do nothing else. He came around to see her, but stood a safe distance away.

"Please don't make me leave you here," he said gravely. "Don't make me let you die."

Napowsa stared him down from the corner of her eye. She was panting, slobbering, crying and clawing. He had never seen a creature driven so mad. Saxton lowered his eyes, remembering a time when he wanted nothing but misfortune for Dante, once upon a time.

"I lost someone too," he whispered. "He was also taken from me. But I can't bring him back, and I can't bring Tarlo back either. The only thing I can do is ask for your forgiveness and help you out of this tree."

"I'll never forgive you! Never!" She swatted both paws back and forth, breaking branches, but doing little to free herself or injure the fox. Saxton stepped back, watching her struggle and cry and roar. When she finally tired herself out, he moved close again.

"Don't do this," Saxton begged. "Please ... let me help you."

She stared at him, eyes wide and fiery.

"I'd rather ie."

The fox stared back at her, defeated.

"Then, I'm sorry. I'm so sorry, but there's nothing more I can do."

Saxton turned and reluctantly began walking away when his feet knocked into a dried-out honeycomb. He looked at the collapsed tree, and realized it must have fallen out of it. He picked up the honeycomb with his teeth, returned to Napowsa, and gently kicked it to her.

Her eyes watered when it rolled close to her face.

"My little honeycomb," she whispered. She pulled the empty husk to her, a small comfort, and began to sing with all her heart and all her sorrow.

"Little cub, little cub, who loves you most?
No one, but Mama Bear with her grizzly coat

"She'll clean your ears and feed you honey
And when you cry she'll make it sunny

"She'll cover you from rain and hold monsters at bay
She'll never, ever go running away

"And when you're grown up and ready to leave
She'll shed a single tear, but will never grieve

"Because Mama Bear, Mama Bear loves you most
As long as you're happy, she'll always boast

"Little cub, little cub, who loves you most?
No one, but Mama Bear with her grizzly coat"

Saxton left her there, resisting the urge to look back. He screwed his eyes shut and lowered his ears, hoping to drown her out.

Freeing her would have been the right thing to do, regardless of what she promised to do to him. Yet selfishly, he preferred to live.

Quill and his father weren't completely wrong about the world, but neither was completely right about it either.

It was strange to want to be good, yet be forced to make terrible choices. He wasn't sure what kind of creature this made him.

He supposed all he could do – in this unkind and unjust world, in this beautiful and *exciting* world – was to live and be true.

EPILOGUE

WINTER

Saxton stood in the train yard, studying the transit schedule posted on a corkboard mounted outside the engineers' office. As he debated which train line would get him to Two-Step the fastest, a familiar shadow cast itself against the wall.

He felt the corner of his lip quirk up.

"Dante."

The wolf stepped beside him, staring at the chart as if it were just another day. But when Dante looked down on him, and he saw that familiar face riddled with scars and sad memories, it dawned on Saxton just how much he missed him.

"What happened to the bear?" Dante asked quietly. "Did she follow you?"

"Yes, but she won't anymore." His eyes darkened. "I trapped her beneath a fallen tree. She's ... chosen to stay there." Neither of them said anything for a while. The pause was grave with regret and death, guilt and sorrow.

Saxton cut through that silence, believing in the future instead.

"What are you doing here?"

Dante tried to smile. It was genuine, but a little sad, too. "Same thing as you: moving on." He looked at the corkboard, and said more lightly, "So ... Where to next?

Saxton grinned, bittersweet.

"Well, there is a vixen I have to see about."

"Ah. You know, that's quite a coincidence. I've got a she-wolf in waiting as well."

Saxton laughed. He felt a little less heavy, a little less lost.

"I suppose a brief return is in order then." But then his easy smile turned rye. "Although, we shouldn't get our hopes up. After what we've put them through, they might turn us around and throw us out on our tails."

"I hope they're not too cross with us," Dante said, and his eye sparkled with mischief. "Should be fun, though, shouldn't it? Raising pups with our mates. Paying each other neighborly visits ... But what if you're right? What if they don't want us back?"

Saxton shrugged. He hadn't thought that far ahead. "Then we'll respect their wishes. Let them move on like we are now."

He recalled what Quill had said, one year ago on a day like this, before they began their journey to Exeter. "We can find new family anywhere, Dante. I had Quill for my father, and now I have you for my brother. If we don't find family there, then we just need to look—"

"Elsewhere?"

And though it was spoken like a question, the world held so much promise.

Thank You for Reading.
Your review on Amazon or Barnes & Noble
would be greatly appreciated.

About the Author

Beatrice Vine is the penname of Bettina Selsor. She is a University of Southern California graduate with a bachelor's degree from the School of Cinematic Arts: Writing for Screen and Television. She now lives in Los Angeles with her husband, best friend, and fellow writer, Andy Selsor, and their beloved cat, Cici.

For more about the author and her upcoming books, please visit:
http://www.beatricevine.com

Made in the
USA
Columbia, SC

79662902R00162